CW00972677

31.

Benchmark

Benchmark

Hugh McLeave

ROBERT HALE · LONDON

© Hugh McLeave 2006
First published in Great Britain 2006

ISBN-10: 0-7090-8172-3
ISBN-13: 978-0-7090-8172-2

Robert Hale Limited
Clerkenwell House
Clerkenwell Green
London EC1R 0HT

Typeset in 11½/14pt Dante Regular
by Derek Doyle & Associates, Shaw Heath
Printed and bound in Great Britain
by Biddles Limited, King's Lynn

BOOK I

The Quest

I

In the still, sultry atmosphere, through the muted, droning dialogue between counsel and witnesses, the judge felt his mind jump involuntarily into a lower gear and his attention flicker elsewhere despite the fact that he was conducting a murder trial involving two lives. That clue, now. It had stumped him in *The Times* crossword over breakfast: Casual solicitation to fine-feathered, foppish fellow of dubious character. All he had were an unhelpful I and A. Normally, he blocked in the whole puzzle between the shredded wheat and toast and marmalade.

Was he slipping? Or just weary on the final leg of a trying court session before his long holiday?

Holiday? That threw up a fresh sequence of mental images. Converging rows of silver-blue lavender against a dazzling background of limestone crags stippled with ilex groves. And beyond, the plough-blade profile of Sainte-Victoire, Cézanne's sacred mountain. Inside a week, he'd be tramping through the Provençal *garrigue*, redolent of pine resin, rosemary, thyme.

Every year he spent at least half his thirteen-week vacation on a long hike coupled with some cultural quest. This year, he meant to trace on the ground the development of the friendship between Cézanne and Émile Zola, in his view one of the most intriguing in nineteenth-century art and literature. Months before, he had meticulously charted his holiday, booking hotels between Avignon and Aix-en-Provence. He invariably chose France because he spoke the language and there he could be himself; no one would recognize him and he did not experience that 'hunted' feeling that often gripped him outside his court in England.

'You affirm you saw the accused man hand a small packet to the young man you have already identified as the dead person?'

That question abruptly ended the judge's reverie and swung his mind back to the trial and the vital link between the drug-pusher and the victim who had died from an overdose.

'Yes, I saw him.'

'Did you also see what sort of packet it was and what it contained?'

'It was a small, paper packet filled with a white powder.'

'A white substance like powdered chalk or bicarbonate of soda?'

'Objection,' defence counsel interrupted.

'Sustained,' the judge murmured. 'You mustn't try to lead the witness, Sir Geoffrey.' He had no time for Sir Geoffrey Boult, the Treasury counsel, who was prosecuting.

For several minutes, Judge Knox listened to the identification evidence and the defence attempts to refute this. It all sounded drearily familiar since he had already absorbed so much of it through the depositions.

How many hundreds of similar cases had he judged in this same Number One Court at the Old Bailey? Although the most famous of all British courts, it might have been any criminal court from its furniture, he reflected as he glanced round.

Oak benches with green-leather seats for the lawyers and public, oak boxes for the accused and witnesses, all covered with a yellow patina under the aqueous light from the cupola above. Everything neutral. Impersonal. As if to focus eyes and minds on the bench with its judicial symbols, its DOMINE DIRIGE NOS emblem, its scarlet-robed, wigged judge. And cold. Even on a hot, sultry day like this, the air seemed frigid, leaden.

Nothing to hint at the dramas played out here over the centuries, many of them in his five years as a High Court judge. Life and death dramas with the script pencilled in roughly for the beginning and middle of each story. Never the end. That he and the jury wrote.

Earlier in the day, he had passed sentence on a woman of eighteen who had killed her seven-week-old baby and tried to burn the body. She had pleaded guilty to infanticide, though her counsel had made an eloquent and moving plea for leniency because she was unmarried, had neither money nor a roof over her head and all this had turned her mind.

Judge Knox had sentenced her to five years, which caused uproar in the public gallery and protests from the young Queen's Counsel who had defended her. Why, he thought, when he could have given her ten years!

Now he was trying to listen with more than half an ear to this murder case which he hoped would end that afternoon, leaving him with a clear mind to prepare his holiday.

A young addict had been found dying in a doorway a few steps from Piccadilly Circus. Blood analysis had revealed not only heroin but traces of bicarbonate and tartaric acid salts. It was these and other impurities in the heroin that had killed the youth and compelled the police to charge the drug-pusher with murder and manslaughter.

Judge Knox had heard so many such cases and the legal wrangling they provoked, Now, Charles Manson, the QC defending Russell Lannagan, the West Indian accused of selling the adulterated heroin, was knocking holes in the Crown case by refuting evidence identifying his client as the drug-pusher.

However, Boult had retaliated by springing an eleventh-hour witness for the prosecution, claiming he had been out of the country during the preliminary hearings. Judge Knox did not credit a word of this from the arrogant, flamboyant and loud-mouthed Treasury counsel. He was examining his witness, a friend of the dead boy.

'You say you overheard Grimes, the dead man, tell a friend about buying some dud stuff,' Boult asked, raising the judge's hackles by putting words into his witness's mouth.

'Sir Geoffrey. . . .'

'Apologies, m'lud.' He addressed the unkempt, ashen-faced youth. 'What did you overhear?'

'Ted . . . that's Grimes . . . he said Zooty had palmed a load of sludge on him.'

'Sludge?'

'His word for cut stuff . . . stuff as 'as been doctored . . . mixed wiv bakin' soda and stuff to look like the real thing.'

'Who is Zooty?' Sir Geoffrey asked.

'Him in the box . . . Lannagan. Ted and a few others got their stuff from 'im.'

'Did Grimes say anything about the "sludge" he had bought?'

'Didn't 'alf, he did. Said it nearly done 'in in. Zooty swore he didn't know, but I reckon—'

'Objection. . . .'

'Sustained.' Judge Knox turned that icy gaze of his on the witness. 'You will confine your remarks to answering questions put by counsel and keeping your opinions to yourself.'

When he had established when and where the dead youth had received the impure heroin, Boult passed his witness to Manson, who could not shake him or his evidence. Within quarter of an hour, the defence counsel asked for a short recess. Judge Knox guessed what was coming. At their request, he received them in his chambers.

'My client wishes to change his plea, m'lud,' Manson said. 'He wishes to plead guilty to the charge of manslaughter. . . .'

'Provided the prosecution drops the charge of murder, is that it?' Judge Knox turned to Boult. 'What do you say to that, Sir Geoffrey?'

'In this case, we are prepared to drop the murder charge and accept the guilty plea for manslaughter, m'lud . . . if, of course, you see no objection.'

That *if you see no objection* riled him, for Boult knew his aversion to this form of plea-bargaining and his incapacity to object to the request.

Why waste the court's time and the country's money, then finally plead guilty? Judge Knox only judged cases which entailed swearing-in juries, summoning witnesses, taking forensic evidence; he hated the sort of backstairs horse-trading that truncated the judicial process.

What passed for truth in a criminal case should be gradually but implacably revealed through courtroom dialectic.

'No objection,' he said through his teeth.

He draped his scarlet robes over his shoulders, clapped his bench wig on his head and marched back into the court where he made short work of the proceedings; his stern admonition to drug-pushers like Lannagan set the press scribbling and clenched Manson's jaw.

'I sentence you to twelve years in prison,' he said, ignoring the cries and gasps from the public gallery.

In his chambers, Judge Knox disrobed, handing his scarlet gown and horsehair bench wig to his clerk, Michael Gresham, a former warrant officer who had been with him for his five years at the Old Bailey. He would not need them until the autumn.

Gresham helped him tidy his desk and he spent quarter of an hour scanning two appeal cases of robbery with violence which would be heard after his holiday. He glanced at his watch. Four o'clock. Time for nine holes at Hampstead. Ranald Birley, an appeal court judge, would probably be there and they might have supper in the club afterwards.

A taxi waited for him in the back court. Settled in the rear seat, he flipped through the *Evening Standard* his clerk had handed him, grimacing at the headline over the infanticide case and curling his lip at the editorial criticizing his severity. They'd doubtless do the same about the drug-pedlar.

He stuffed the paper into his briefcase, closed his eyes and tried to relax by fixing his mind on Provence. Next year he would revisit the Camargue with its pink flamingos, its herds of fighting bulls and white horses roaming the salt-marshes, its silver-blue light and infinite horizons.

But the jolting and jinking of his cab pulled him back into the moment. All that traffic in a mindless scramble that was suffocating the city. Thank God he had put up his car. Of course, he had other more important reasons for that. No one with even a hundredth part of his knowledge of the mass of traffic legislation could drive without apprehension. And no judge could compromise his position on the bench with a drunken or reckless driving conviction on his sheet. So, when Joan, his dead wife, was no longer there to act as chauffeur, he took taxis.

When he entered the clubhouse, his heart sank. Neither Birley nor Tony Mansfield, a crown court judge he sometimes partnered, were there. But at the end of the locker-room in cap, pullover and plus-fours and admiring himself in the full-length mirror swinging his new carbon-fibre driver, was the Rt. Hon John Spencer-Smith, the Attorney-General.

How he disliked the country's principal law officer! From the tip of his oily head to the spurious hyphen in his name. They had been young barristers together, but Judge Knox had beaten Smith by taking silk three years earlier, then beating him to the bench.

Anyway, Smith would have made a worthless judge, perpetually swayed by his political beliefs or the empty eloquence or legal jabber-wocky he himself practised. As a recorder or part-time judge in Nottingham, the local bar knew him as Judge Right, because he was, politically, on the right of Attila the Hun. 'Whether you're right or wrong, if you're on the right you'll be all right with Judge Right,' they quipped. So, Spencer-Smith went into politics, finding a tame Tory constituency in Hereford. By string-pulling he had weaseled into the office of Attorney-General and used his power to prosecute – or not – partially and arbitrarily in Judge Knox's view.

But the man also cheated at golf! In the roughest rough, the thickest thicket he would invariably find his ball and deem it playable. He was the sort of man who would sidle up when you were addressing a three-foot putt and whisper, 'Summing up a bit askew, Laurence. Grounds for appeal there, y'know.' As a barrister he would pull any trick to win his case.

Looking at him waggling his carbon-fibre club, a word flashed into the judge's mind.

'Popinjay,' he blurted out before he could censor his tongue.

'What's that . . . what did you say, Laurence?'

'*Times* crossword . . . a word of eight letters. It stumped me this morning.'

'Oh, that! I kissed that off in ten minutes at breakfast.'

You would, wouldn't you! But wasn't this the man who had everything? Joan had come home laughing with the story. She and S-S's wife had gone Christmas shopping, and Iris didn't know what to buy S-S, as she called him. He had everything. Then she spied it in a Regent's Street jewellers. A tiny gold stick with a spatulate end, smaller than a toothpick. FOR THE MAN WHO HAS EVERYTHING, ran the ticket on the black-velvet box. Discreetly, the jeweller explained it was a navel pick for removing foreign material lodged in the umbilicus. He'd often wanted to ask a nombrilist like S-S how his navel-pick was functioning.

'Well, Laurence, how about nine holes? What'll it be – a tenner or the loser stands dinner here?'

'Sorry, but I merely came to collect my waterproof clothing and golf umbrella for my walking tour. I'm off in the middle of next week.' At least a partial truth, he thought.

'But you've let your cab go,' Spencer-Smith came back in his best court-room style.

'Well, I fancied a glass of beer at the bar when I'd collected my equipment,' Knox said, thinking one lie borrowed another.

'Good, in that case I'll join you. I'll have them set up.'

Reluctantly, the judge nodded and when he had packed his hold-all followed the Attorney-General through to the bar where S-S had put up a lager and his own gin and bitters. 'I shouldn't really in case Birley and Smithson turn up and tee-off sober – well, here's to your foot-slogging and another couple of strokes on my score.'

Judge Knox sipped his beer, reflecting that Spencer-Smith, with that cunning foot of his and a few spare golf balls all numbered alike, was a match for anybody, gin or no gin.

'Saw you shared a chop and cheese with the Lord Chancellor the other week,' Spencer-Smith said, working his tongue and yellow teeth over half a dozen cashew nuts from the bar counter. 'Say anything of tremendous moment?'

'Not that I can recall offhand,' the judge replied, this time lying by omission. In fact the country's foremost judicial officer and the man who appointed all but the most eminent judges, had asked his opinion about several Queen's Counsel who might make crown court or even high court judges.

'We talked about Cézanne,' he said

'Cézanne, eh! Didn't know he was in the running for the court of appeal.'

'The painter, the post-impressionist, I meant.'

'I know what you mean and you know I know what you meant,' Spencer-Smith said, irritably. 'Didn't the Lord Chancellor just happen to mention that Lord Manners was giving up his seat on the appeal court at the end of the year?'

'I believe he did.'

'You believe he did!'

Spencer-Smith's jowls vibrated with derisive amusement. He flicked a finger at the barman to refuel their glasses, but Judge Knox put a hand over his beer-glass and shook his head, wondering how he could avoid admitting that the Lord Chancellor had hinted broadly that he would take Lord Manners' place after the recess. Flight was the answer.

But as he was poised to flee, Birley walked through the door. Judge Knox breathed again. Spencer-Smith would never dare discuss gossip in front of a senior appeal court judge, who might just become the next Lord Chief Justice of England.

Birley he liked. Though looking at him, he could never help thinking that, divested of the trappings of his office, this eminent jurist might have passed for any of the dozen men he had sentenced that week. Squat, stumpy figure, prognathous chin. That fierce clench of both upper and lower racks of his porcelain teeth and those close-set eyes. Yet, his mellifluous voice and subtle legal argument made up for all that.

'Good to see you, Laurence. Care for nine at the gallop?'

'Sorry, Ranald, I can't.'

'I'll do nine with you,' Spencer-Smith said.

As Birley hesitated, Judge Knox excused himself. When he was collecting his equipment in the locker-room, Birley caught up with him.

'Laurence, you've probably heard this, but if the Lord Chancellor hasn't told you in so many words, he means to offer you Lord Manners' vacancy on the appeal court – that is, unless you want to stay in the Bailey.'

'Hmm, no. Five years of that and the cases and faces are beginning to look alike.'

'Fine, I'm glad.' Clapping Knox on the shoulder, he whispered, 'You're a bit young to sit in with geriatric cases like us, but we need your kind. You've got what it takes to make LCJ in ten years from now.' His voice dropped. 'Spencer-Smith was pushing his friend, Goodman, but he didn't have a hope. Where are you off to this year?'

'Provence . . . Avignon, Nimes, Aix . . . Cézanne and Zola country.'

'Ah, Provence!' And in his best declamatory style, he intoned:

O for a draught of vintage that hath been
Cool'd a long time in the deep-delvèd earth
Tasting of Flora and the country-green,
Dance, and Provençal song, and sunburnt mirth!

He grinned at Judge Knox, then dug him in the ribs. 'Well, have a good time, don't drink too much of Provence, don't get lost, and keep thinking of me sitting in a Scotch mist in that damned holiday house Chrissie bought us in the frozen north.'

His cab dropped him in Piccadilly where he bought some stationery before walking down Haymarket to his club in Pall Mall. Although the evening streets of central London were thick with people, not one of them gave him a passing glance.

In his younger days as a successful Queen's Counsel he would notice people staring at him in the street or shops; a few would even accost him to ask if he was Laurence Knox, who had defended such and such a criminal. Yet, now as a judge in the most famous court in the land, with his picture in the paper every other week, he still seemed anonymous.

It had puzzled him before he realized it was the full-bottomed horsehair wig. That symbol of justice disguised him, rendered him as abstract as many of the judicial precepts he administered. Only those photographs of him in that wig were issued to the media.

At his club he read the papers and sipped a glass of Perrier water, suppressing the impulse to order champagne and toast Birley's news. In the library where he sat, Vallance, a Lord Justice of Appeal, was playing chess with an Anglican bishop and he might spot the champagne and put two and two together.

Later editions of the *Evening Standard* were castigating him for handing down that day's swingeing sentences; they hinted at his sadism and even compared him with the notorious Judge Jeffreys. 'In former days,' he read, 'Mr Justice Knox would have been one of those chop-or-stake judges sending people into eternity in droves.'

Was that what they really thought of him?

He could not face going home to cook his own supper, even though Mrs Evans, his daily woman, would chide him for not eating what she had left in the fridge. In the dining-room, he ordered smoked salmon with scrambled eggs, one of his favorite meals, then cheese, a morsel of Chaource; he washed the meal down with a half-bottle of Pouilly.

Just after nine o'clock a cab dropped him in Fleet Street, a few steps from his flat in the Middle Temple directly opposite the Law Courts. He climbed the fifty-two steps to his third-floor flat, relieved that he could still arrive there without feeling winded.

What a day it had been! As he undressed he glanced at one of the TV bulletins where they referred to the infanticide case, though without commenting. He could guess the sort of scurrilous headlines they would put up when he was given a seat in the Court of Appeal at £10,000 a year more.

In bed, he lay in that twilight phase between waking and sleeping, his mind reviewing the thoughts and images of that day. As he was falling asleep he imagined he was sitting by that brook tumbling through the wild gorge below the Zola Dam between Aix and the Sainte-Victoire mountain. Joan was with him, though much younger, laughing under her sun-hat. They were wrenching fistfuls of bread off a stick loaf and devouring it with goat-cheese, olives and black grapes. Joan poured them glasses of that strong, local wine, reddish-purple, full-bodied and heady. He heard the echo of his own voice declaiming:

O, for a beaker full of the warm South,
Full of the true, the blushful Hippocrene,
With beaded bubbles winking at the brim,
And purple-stainèd mouth. . . .

'Surely Keats got that round his neck,' Joan broke in. 'They don't drink fizzy wine in Provence.'

'Poetic licence, darling, poetic licence.'

He never heard her reply, for sleep enveloped him.

II

He had showered, was shaving and listening to a tape of himself reading Provençal phrases out of a language primer when he realized that he had gone to bed without checking the messages on his answering machine. Present or absent, he left his machine on.

Although his number had always been unlisted, even as a barrister, on various occasions people he had prosecuted or sentenced had discovered it somehow and had rung to insult or threaten him. They still did, so he had to change his number from time to time; his machine took the sting out of their threats and made them more careful about having their voices identified.

When he had cleaned then whetted his open razor (he liked its 'bite' on his skin) he listened to the messages. There were four, three from Judge Dawson at various times of the evening, and a fourth from Gresham, his clerk, with the answer to a query he had raised before leaving the Old Bailey.

What could Geoffrey Dawson want so urgently that he had left three messages and his home number in Oxford for him to call back? Dawson he had used as a junior when he was a QC and defending in two murder cases in Oxford; he had since become a crown court judge in that university town.

Dawson answered his ring, relief in his voice. He apologized for not leaving a more specific message on the recorder, but the matter was delicate.

'Laurence, you have a stepdaughter at Oxford, I believe.'

'Yes.' Despite his calm voice, the judge felt ants with icicle feet were parading up and down his spine. Had something happened to Julie? An assault? A car accident?

'Julie Armitage, isn't it?' Through the judge's confusion, Dawson's voice sounded light-years away. 'Aged twenty-two, from an address in Cedar Grove, is that her?'

'Yes, yes.' In heaven's name, why didn't the man drop his official manner. 'What has happened to Julie?'

'Well . . . well, the fact is, Laurence, she's been arrested.'

'On what grounds? What's the charge?'

'Being in possession of a stolen car.' Dawson harrumped several times to clear his throat. 'She was stopped early on Friday morning by a patrol car on suspicion of driving dangerously. She appeared before me on Friday afternoon and I remembered her name . . . and she does look like Joan.'

'What did you do?' Judge Knox had recovered his poise and now felt on familiar ground: the law and justice.

'I remanded her for a psychiatrist's report,' Dawson said, going into his throat-clearing routine. 'I must tell you, Laurence, she was acting oddly.'

'In what way, oddly?'

'She couldn't remember much about the incident, where she'd been and how she picked up the car. The police said . . . well, they thought she was drunk.'

'Where is she now?'

'I've arranged for her to be put into the prison hospital . . . ahem . . . ahem . . . it was all I could do until I had spoken to you.'

'All right, but what do you expect me to do about it?'

'I . . . er . . . I thought you might have some suggestion as to what I should do.'

'I don't see how. My only suggestion is that you apply the law in her case as you interpret it. That's all I can say.'

'Wouldn't you like to see her?'

'Did Julie mention my name, or ask you to contact me?'

'No, but—'

'But what?'

'Perhaps you should come down and have a word with her to see if she needs help.' Dawson sounded embarrassed, as though he was holding something back.

'Oh, very well. I shall come down this morning if you can make arrangements for me to see her in a room at the prison hospital.'

'I'll meet you at the station and drive you to the prison,' Dawson said, now more relaxed. 'The 10.50 gets in at 11.45 if you can catch it.'

Judge Knox said he would, replacing the phone and cursing the incident for interfering with his weekend. However, it need not take up too much time, a car-theft charge. He'd hire a good barrister to defend Julie. After all, they had to prove she had stolen the car, that she meant to deprive its owner permanently of the vehicle. No, a reasoned defence could secure an acquittal or, at worst, a small fine or suspended sentence.

That problem relegated, he breakfasted, blocked in *The Times* crossword, then immersed himself in the new Provençal textbook he had bought.

Judge Dawson was waiting at Oxford Station. In the five years since they had met he had lost some hair and gained nearly a stone in weight. But then, Oxford Crown Court was a much more comfortable bench than the Old Bailey, the judge reflected. He wondered why Dawson eyed him so nervously.

As they headed for the Randolph Hotel, Dawson apologized for bringing him down from London after his busy session at the Central Criminal Court. 'The pity is I didn't know it was your stepdaughter until I saw her . . . the name fooled me or I'd have intervened with the police to quash the case.'

'Then you would have been exceeding your judicial powers and legal right,' the judge said. 'You would have compounded the offence and committed one yourself, that of obstructing the due process of the law.'

Dawson bit back an angry retort, saying instead, 'Well, at least I could have seen she had a good barrister before she. . . .'

As he hesitated, the judge put in, 'Before she admitted the offence to the police, is that it?'

'Unfortunately, yes. That was why I sent her for a psychiatrist's report before she pleaded guilty in my court . . . the only thing I could do.' He took his eye off the road to flick a glance at Judge Knox, who was staring impassively ahead. 'You don't object to that, do you?'

'No, if that was the way you saw it. You know it is up to you to apply the law as it should be interpreted, not as you see fit.'

'I was thinking of you as well.'

'I'm grateful, but just remember that if it was your daughter, I would have to apply the law regardless of any personal sentiments I might have about her or you.' Suddenly, he raised a finger and pointed ahead. 'Look out, a red light.'

Dawson braked, jolting both of them. After that he kept his mouth shut and his eye on the road, though he was still wondering what made his companion function like a software program and where he kept his feelings. However, they did say Sir Laurence Knox would one day make Lord Chief Justice. And they were probably right.

At the Randolph they had coffee while Dawson explained the circumstances that had brought Julie before him. He was detailing the police case when the judge stopped him. 'Leave all that, Geoffrey. I would like to question Julie myself so that I get her story and not an amalgam of the police version and hers. He pulled a notebook out of his pocket.

'Tell me about the car. To whom did that belong?'

'A certain Henry Redhead who's a bookseller in town.'

'When did he report it missing?'

'Just over two weeks ago.'

'And it has since been restored to him, I suppose?'

'No, the police still have it.'

Dawson shot him that troubled look again. He might be a good judge, but he made a bad witness, Judge Knox thought.

'Why are they not releasing it?'

'They're running tests on it.'

'Tests? What for?'

'Oh, you know what the police are these days – they have a phobia or a mania about explosives and drugs.' Clearing that invisible phlegm from his throat, he added, 'I don't think that concerns you stepdaughter, though.'

'Can you fix the hearing for Monday or Tuesday? I'll book a room here and stay over.'

Dawson agreed on Monday, although he still seemed uneasy about something. When Judge Knox had booked himself a room, he thanked the other man and said he would walk to the prison.

It was what? – twelve, thirteen years since he had set foot in this prison. His QC days. The Grayson Farm murder. No body. Frank Critchley, the farmer, had either incinerated his pregnant mistress, burned her in acid or, most probably, fed her to his prize herd of Essex Saddleback pigs. Albeit without the body, he had secured a conviction, prosecuting for the Crown on circumstantial evidence alone. A triumph that had helped him earn promotion to the bench.

Things had not changed. Still there was the same malodorous atmosphere of stale bodies, unwashed linen, foul drains, urine, excreta overlaying the kitchen smells of stewed meat and boiled cabbage.

Presumably at Dawson's insistence, they had allotted him the prison chaplain's small converted cell with its enlarged window overlooking the courtyard. Julie was already there. Head bowed, fingers palpating each other, nervously. For the first time he noticed the heavy-smoker's yellow patina between the right index and middle fingers.

Hearing the assistant prison governor usher him into the room, she lifted her head. How pale she was! Skin like old parchment. Her fine, blue-grey eyes had regressed into their sockets. What were those bluish-purple bruises over her right eyebrow and left cheek-bone? Had the police brutalized her? Her upper lip, too, seemed swollen.

Judge Knox always felt uneasy in the presence of his stepdaughter. Indeed, with most women. Did he embrace her or kiss her cheek? He never knew, and Julie had never sought such signs of affection, even from the beginning. He had known her from birth and had brought her up from the age of three when he had married Joan.

Yet, both she and her mother had resisted any attempt to change her name to his. In memory of her dead father, she said, and he had understood. So, few people outside his restricted circle knew that Julie Armitage was his adopted daughter and his sole heir. On this occasion, perhaps it had worked to his benefit.

He stepped forward to grasp both her hands in his, shocked at how deathly cold they were. Her eyes had gone moist as she looked at him.

Putting his hands round her head, he drew it into his breast, feeling her shake with sobs.

'Julie, don't cry. Everything will be all right.' He fished for a hand-kerchief and wiped her tears with it. He sat her down in one of the two chairs, then moved round the small table to seat himself opposite her so that the light fell on her and he was in silhouette.

'Do you want to tell me about it?' he murmured.

'No, Papa,' she said, drying her tears. 'I didn't want you to know . . . I didn't want anyone to tell you or, involve you.'

'But why, when I'm your father, legally and in every other way?'

'Why? Because it was my fault and I have to take the consequences,' she whispered. 'I don't mind if they send me to prison . . . except. . . .'

'Except what?'

'What it would do to you and your career. Everybody says you'll get the highest office.'

'Julie darling' – he noted her surprised reaction at the last word – 'put that out of your mind and the idea of going to prison. With a good lawyer—'

'I don't want or need a lawyer,' she came back. 'Anyway, I'm plead-ing guilty.'

'You sound as though you want to go to jail,' he muttered and noted that she did not protest. Did she want to punish herself? He observed that she had bitten all her fingernails down nearly to the quick.

'But I am guilty,' she said.

'All right. But if a barrister made out a good case for extenuating circumstances, as a first offender you would get away with a fine or a short, suspended sentence.'

'Papa, why don't you just go away and let me handle things for myself.' Her head had dropped and she was talking, mumbling to the table-top.

'But Julie, it's the first time I've ever been able to help you in anything,' he protested. It was true. Even as a child or a schoolgirl, she had hardly ever asked him for anything, almost as a point of honour. She had won a scholarship to Oxford to read law and accepted only grudgingly the money he allowed her every month. If she butted against a tricky legal point in her studies, she resolved it herself rather than run to him.

'I owe you too much already,' she said, and his sharp judge's antennae caught a tinge of resentment in that remark.

'You owe me nothing,' he replied, and she lifted her eyes to look at him, wondering. Dull, slow eyes, he noticed as he went on, 'But you owe it to yourself to defend your own self, and I mean self, and to learn from the mistake you have made. You must agree to that.'

'All right,' she admitted reluctantly.

'Then I shall find you a barrister.' He thought for a moment. 'Dawson should know a good one.'

'Papa, I know somebody who works in chambers at Oxford.'

'Oh, whose chambers?'

'Hervey Longdon's.'

'Hmm . . . Longdon's a pretty good QC. What is he called, this barrister?'

'Barrett, Peter Barrett.'

'A friend of yours, is he?'

'In a way, yes.'

'Fine, I'll contact him today.'

She was looking at the fingertips of her left hand, then pressing each one as though they had lost their feeling.

'Papa . . . all right, but don't . . . well, don't. . . .'

When she dried up, he completed her thought. 'You mean, I must not, as you might put it, pull my rank on him.'

'I didn't mean it like that, but Peter and I were friendly once and he's very sensitive about some things . . . quite a few things. Especially about his appearance and. . . .'

'Don't worry, Julie, I shall make full allowance for his susceptibilities.'

He rose and went round the table to take her hands and kiss her on the cheek. 'Our time is up,' he murmured.

He had intended to interrogate her, gently and discreetly, but realized that Julie would tell him as little as she could and he might embarrass her. Anyway, Dawson would know as much if not more than she did about the case, and her barrister friend or the psychiatrist might tease the rest out of her.

'Anything I can get you for the weekend?' he asked. 'Books, magazines, cigarettes, that sort of thing?' She shook her head. 'I can have
food sent in from a city restaurant.' Again she shook her head.

'You know I'm staying over for the court case,' he said as he rapped
on the door for the assistant governor. He accompanied Julie and the
man to the prison hospital door before turning and heading for the
entrance.

What had he drawn out of her? Nothing. And yet, the bits and
pieces she had let drop as well as her whole attitude disturbed him.
English judges rarely had to intervene in the cut and thrust of court
battles, but they observed, they listened, they analysed, and they
judged everything and everybody. Twelve years on the bench had
deepened Judge Knox's insight into people and sharpened his psych-
ology.

Enough for him to realize that Julie was so obviously concealing
and camouflaging something she considered damning and too serious
to confess that it stuck out like an electricity pylon.

It was a day as grey as his own mood, so he decided to walk back
towards the town centre. It might clear his head and lift his spirits.
Oxford he knew well, having studied there and done two sessions as a
circuit judge.

For Judge Knox it had always been a source of regret that he had
never gone on circuit here before the Courts Act of 1971 abolished the
traditions of the assizes, when the judges were received like royalty,
had their own butler, cook and clerk; when they marched in full
regalia, including black cap for murderers in hand, preceded to the
court and followed by javelin men. But those days had gone with capital punishment and others changes he often deprecated.

Following the towpath along the Cherwell, he cut through Merton
Fields. How often had he bought his law books here with Jeff
Armitage on spring, summer and autumn days, for them to throw
problems at each other? That was twenty-nine years ago. They'd then
go and join Jeff's girlfriend, Joan Harding, at the teashop in
Cornmarket. She was studying modern languages at Somerville, and
Laurence Knox thought her the prettiest creature he would ever see –
though his friendship for Jeff prevented him from telling her, and

quelled any envy he might have felt for his best friend.

And now he had their daughter and his stepdaughter to look after – the only thing they had left him.

In the High Street at All Souls something turned his feet past the gatehouse and through the small quadrangle, where he noticed the hairy musk-leaves growing between the flagstones. At that Saturday afternoon hour, the fifteenth-century chapel lay empty and he entered.

Although not religious in the ritual or liturgical sense, Judge Knox had a profound belief that man's morality and the law based on it were inspired by some higher creation. Under pressure, however, he might have confessed that he was thinking of English law. Not Scots, or French or Islamic. Just English. Was it not Charles Péguy who said God had to create the French, for only they would ever understand his purpose? In that case, he had created the English to make the law which would fulfil his wishes.

For Judge Knox, the law was sacrosanct; no one was wiser than it, no one was above it, no one could flout it. English justice was not abstract like the Continental version with its search for absolute truth as though that were the holy grail. No, it was founded on the concepts of truth and morality innate in man. And these were elicited in the courtroom by a Socratic dialogue between the prosecution and defence, refereed by a judge. It might look conflictual, confrontational, adversarial, but it served true justice.

Standing there alone in the chapel, he wondered about God, whether someone or something like a creator really existed outside our minds. As a boy, he had believed. Indeed, he had invested everything with cabbalistic or supernatural significance: milometer figures, car numbers with 7s and 3s, pebbles sculpted by the roll of the sea or curious patterns of wild flowers. Had he really outgrown those childhood fantasies? Or had he clung to them like the old clothes he was always loath to throw away through attachment to them? Did superstition open the door to religion?

Judge Knox closed his eyes to the spectral light filtering through the stained-glass window, and the sight of the black-and-gold altar screen, and prayed for the souls of Jeffrey and Joan and their daughter, Julie.

Behind his closed eyes remembrance of his dead wife and friend filled his mind, then overbrimmed so that he turned abruptly and left the chapel before he was tempted to begin questioning the purpose of things that had killed Jeffrey and Joan and put Julie in prison.

III

That afternoon it turned fine, sunny with a light breeze and a scatter of cumulus against a blue sky. So Judge Knox strolled from his hotel up Banbury Road and beyond St Hugh's College to where the law directory had informed him that Peter Barrett lived. Perhaps he should have rung in advance to make an appointment, but he wanted to observe the barrister's first-hand reaction to the information he was given.

Barrett had the top flat of a villa set in a small, walled garden bursting with roses, phlox, delphiniums and annuals in every colour. Judge Knox heard him clump downstairs to answer his ring, then saw a figure dressed in a green-and-white track suit and running-shoes, as though he had just been jogging. Taken aback, the judge said, 'I'm Julie Armitage's father. I understand you know her.'

'Yes, I do. Nothing happened to Julie, I hope?'

'Well, yes. She's been charged with stealing a car, and I would like you to defend her.'

'Julie! Car-stealing! I don't believe it.'

'Can we discuss it elsewhere?' the judge said, irked at being kept on the doorstep.

'Oh, sorry. Of course. You'd better come up and tell me what you know about it.'

Barrett turned and led the judge upstairs into a large room where he had been watching a cricket match on TV. Glancing round, the judge saw that he used this as a study as well as his living-room.

Several solicitors' briefs lay on a large kneehole desk with law books either open or earmarked with coloured slips. To his astonishment, he noticed a pile of badly cut sandwiches on a plate weighing down another batch of briefs, a half-full beer-glass and two empty beer-cans holding down other papers.

'Sorry about the mess,' Barrett murmured.

Judge Knox said nothing, though privately wondering how well this man would defend his stepdaughter. His eye lighted on the blue cap on top of the bookcase. At least, Barrett had won a blue for something. As the barrister crossed the room to switch off the TV, the judge scrutinized him.

Rugged was the word his mind threw up. Barrett's chin had an outward thrust, and something had befallen his nose, which kinked near the bridge and seemed to have been broken and badly set. His mouth, too, appeared twisted out of shape and he spoke out of its left corner.

He must have forgotten Julie's injunctions and been eying these blemishes unconsciously, for Barrett ran an index finger over his nose, grinned and said, 'Afraid I didn't see that one coming.'

'Oh, boxing, was it? I thought it was a blue.' He pointed to the cap on the bookcase.

'I've one of those as well.' Barrett put a finger on his crooked mouth. 'And this to remind me to duck when a bowler loses his temper and chucks the ball face-high at you.' He shrugged. 'It broke my cheek-bone bone and left me with three missing teeth.'

'Do you still play cricket?'

Barrett shook his head. 'I've also given up blood sports like boxing.' Moving behind his desk, he motioned the judge to the chair on the other side and sat down himself. He picked up a half-eaten sandwich, took a bite and gulped some beer. 'Do you mind?' he asked. 'I get a bit peckish mid-afternoons.' When the judge shook his head, Barrett picked up a ballpoint pen. 'Now, about Julie.'

Briefly, the judge outlined the facts, observing that Barrett took no notes until he had finished. Looking up from his pad, the barrister then put question after question. Did Julie say she had stolen the car? How did she steal it? Where was she going at the time? And why Redhead's car? Wouldn't she have known it was his? What happened to the car?

Judge Knox could not answer most of those questions, but it reassured him that this curious young advocate had asked them.

'You'll have to request the prosecution or the police to give you their version of the story,' he said.

'I'll do that – but you say she's determined to maintain her guilty plea. Why?'

'Again, that's a question only she can answer, and perhaps she will tell you.' He shrugged. 'But if she persists in remaining silent you can at least make a plea for mitigation. It would seem to be an open-and-shut case, but as a first offender she'll get a suspended sentence at the most.'

Barrett was regarding him quizzically. 'You seem to know a bit about the law, Mr Armitage.' He took another bite at his sandwich. 'You know, I have a feeling I've met you somewhere before. Was it with Julie?'

'No, I don't think we've met,' the judge said. 'I should perhaps apologize for not introducing myself properly. My name is Knox, Laurence Knox, and I'm Julie's stepfather.'

That statement hit Barrett like another of those bouncers that had broken his cheek-bone. Then he laughed to hide his surprise and embarrassment.

'Mr Justice Knox,' he breathed. 'You're Sir Laurence Knox, the High Court judge . . . the Old Bailey . . . that's where I've seen you. Why didn't I realize it or recognize you? I know, the wig and gown.' He shook his head in disbelief, then his face registered a thought.

'Why didn't Julie tell me about you. . . ?' He broke off, the pause making his embarrassment more obvious.

'Perhaps you didn't ask her?'

'But I did . . . I remember . . . she said her father was a barrister.'

'He was. Jeffrey Armitage was a very good barrister. But he died young and I married his widow, Julie's mother.'

'Ah! that's it.' Barrett emptied his beer glass and poured the remainder of the second can into it. His strong jaws were working over another sandwich.

'But again, perhaps Julie thought you might not be favourably impressed by the fact that I was her stepfather,' the judge said, evenly.

'Perhaps,' Barrett came back, meeting the judge's gaze head on.

His reaction did not surprise or bother Judge Knox. So often when he introduced himself he perceived some implicit stricture in a word or phrase from the other person. Barrett's remarks, for instance. They threw off more undertones and overtones than a dozen brass bands. And all of them critical.

'I hope my name doesn't prevent you from accepting the case,' he murmured.

'But you could have Hervey Longdon himself, or any one of half a hundred QCs gratis.'

'When a judge finds a minor offence like car-theft defended by an eminent QC and two juniors, he often has difficulty remembering the principle of the presumption of innocence, which then, in his mind, might become a presumption of guilt. But if you really have to know why I came to you, my stepdaughter did not want any form of legal representation and only when I insisted did she express her wish to be defended by you and you alone. She knows and trusts you, it seems.'

'Well, I hope I can justify Julie's confidence.'

'You may only have to make a plea in mitigation.'

'Well, Sir Laurence, I'll do my best for her.'

Judge Knox looked at his watch and rose to leave. Barrett accompanied him to the front door and watched him walk away with that firm, purposeful stride. He was much younger than the forbidding character whose face glowered out from that full-bottomed wig on the bench or the front pages of the press, he thought.

He had a second thought: If Julie had gone off the rails, it was little wonder with a stepfather like Knox.

IV

On Sunday morning just after six o'clock, the judge's bedside phone rang and he heard the voice of the assistant prison governor apologizing for waking him. 'I felt I had to tell you, Sir Laurence, your stepdaughter is ill. According to the prison doctor, she's running a temperature and hallucinating.'

'When did this happen?' the judge got out, his mind still fuddled with sleep.

'Just before the night staff went off duty – about half an hour ago.'

'She has not had access to sleeping pills or tranquillizers, has she?'

'No, it's not attempted suicide or anything like that, Sir Laurence.'

Again, Judge Knox had that impression which he often experienced on the bench when a witness was evasive or prevaricating or lying. 'All right, I'll be there as soon as I can dress and find a cab.' he said.

'I can send the governor's car for you.'

He agreed, then rose, ran a razor over his face, had a shower and dressed quickly. A prison officer was waiting by the hotel entrance with a three-litre Rover. Within ten minutes, the judge was walking into the hospital wing.

They had placed Julie in a separate room, a small, ill-lit cell with a bed. She was lying asleep, quiet and motionless as though anaesthetized. A man in a casual suit with a stethoscope jutting from a pocket was scribbling something on a medical chart when the judge and the assistant governor entered. Introducing himself as one of the prison doctors, he explained that Julie's temperature was still a couple of degrees above normal and her blood pressure had dropped twenty points below her average level, but now there was nothing to worry about.

It was then that Judge Knox spotted the oxygen bottle and mask by the bed head. What did those mean – she had nearly died?

'Doctor, you must have some idea of what caused this crisis,' he said.

At that, the doctor flicked a glance towards the assistant governor, who nodded.

Without a word, the doctor drew back the bed-sheet and lifted the sleeve of Julie's hospital smock. Judge Knox followed the man's finger as it traced the pattern of tiny needle punctures in her arm veins, running from the wrist to a point beyond the elbow crook. Two veins had gone black where they had collapsed after repeated intravenous injections.

'There are about the same in her right arm. . . .'

Right arm? As the doctor continued, it flashed across the judge's mind that Julie was right-handed. Did that mean somebody had helped her to inject those drugs?

'. . . so she had started using her ankle veins,' the doctor was saying.

For several moments, the judge stared at the bluish-purple puncture marks and the ruined veins, black against the pallid skin. His head spun. He felt as if the walls of this tiny cell were shifting and contracting around him and any minute now they would topple inwards and engulf him, mind and body. An iron hoop tightened round his chest and his heart thudded violently against his ribs. To steady himself, he grasped the iron bedstead, aware the other two men were watching him.

Breaking the long silence, the doctor said, 'It started when she had withdrawal symptoms. She ran a fever, her blood pressure sagged and her heart slowed. . . . We had to use oxygen and steady the heart before we could sedate her. That's why we called you.'

So they had thought she might die! 'Thank you, Doctor,' he got out. Through his parched throat, he asked, 'Which drug is it – heroin?'

'That's what we assume,' the doctor answered. 'And from the number of puncture marks and the collapsed veins, she has been using it for some time, a year or more.'

A year or more! Julie had become a hardened addict. As counsel and judge, how many delinquency cases had he dealt with involving drug-addicts, those morally and socially fragile creatures who would commit daylight robbery, assault and even murder to satisfy their craving for cocaine or heroin? How had someone brought up like Julie fallen victim to something as potentially lethal as heroin?

'Can you treat my stepdaughter while she's waiting for her trial?'

'It'll be at least a week before she's fit to appear in a courtroom,' the doctor said, then added, 'I'll consult the psychiatrist this afternoon. We can probably start on a substitute drug like methadone in diminishing doses, but when she leaves here she'll still have to be weaned off heroin for good and that could take months rather than weeks – if she's willing to co-operate.'

'I'm sure she will.'

29

'Oh, we have quite a few addicts here who just don't want to throw away their heroin crutches,' the assistant governor put in.

'Some of them just can't,' said the doctor.

'Anyway, you can leave that to me,' Judge Knox said. He pointed at Julie. 'You said a week before she will be fit?'

'At least that.'

'In that case, I shall arrange to have her trial postponed for a fortnight.'

He thanked them both and left, refusing a lift. Although drizzling rain was falling through the grey day, he decided to walk back and reflect about what he had just learned and witnessed. His head throbbed and his face burned, even though bathed in the rain. But by the time he reached the Randolph he had charted what he had to do.

As he took his key, the porter said a Mr Barrett had rung to say he would meet Sir Laurence in the hotel lounge at 10.30 that morning.

On returning to his room the judge hung the do-not-disturb notice on the door. First, he rang Dawson, who agreed to the postponement. It hurt badly, but he dialled British Airways and cancelled his Marseilles flight. Fortunately he had the numbers of the hotels he had booked in Provence on his digital diary. He called each one and cancelled his reservations.

Finally, he contacted Gresham, his clerk, and asked him to pack a bag with clean linen, a couple of pairs of shoes, another suit, a raincoat and umbrella. He would be staying, he told the clerk, for at least a fortnight in Oxford.

Barrett was drinking coffee in the lounge when the judge came down, and was halfway through a large sugar-bun, his strong teeth and jaws chomping and chewing hard. Compulsive eating – was that also one of the peccadilloes Julie had hinted at? If so, what neurosis did it cover up or allay? Barrett had evidently heard nothing about Julie's illness, for he began by saying she had given him no information about the car theft and had not changed her mind about pleading guilty.

'But we're in other trouble, Judge,' he said.

'Oh!' That statement did not come as a surprise to him.

'Yes, the real reason the police are hanging on to the car is that it had drugs in it. One of their sniffer-dogs found them in the spare wheel and the underside of the back seat. A kilo of heroin done up in sachets, ready to sell.' He paused to look at the judge. 'Judge, are you listening?'

For a moment or two, the judge had the same sensation he had experienced in the prison hospital. Vertigo. As though he was losing his grip on reality. He lay back in his chair and shut his eyes, willing himself to relax until his mind and heart had regained some of their normal rhythm and calm. Was Julie not only an addict but a drug-pedlar as well? On this evidence how would he have sentenced her, even as a first offender? At least six months in jail without the option of a fine. Maybe more.

'Judge, are you all right?'

Barrett's voice penetrated his swirling thoughts. 'Yes, I'm all right,' he whispered.

'It may not be as bad as it sounds,' Barrett said, through another mouthful of sugar-bun. 'They'll have to prove a connection between stealing the car and the drugs being in it. That's probably why they didn't charge her immediately with the drugs offence.'

'No, I think they had another reason for not charging her,' the judge said. Dawson had mentioned on Saturday morning that the police did not oppose bail. Now he understood why. 'The police thought that when she was bailed she would lead them to the rest of the gang.'

'I see the argument – but why tell us now?'

'Because Julie will be at least a week in the prison hospital and we shall have to apply for a postponement of the car-theft cases. And we may have to defend the drugs charge, too.'

Barrett listened, incredulous, as the judge explained what had happened at the prison a few hours before. 'I don't believe it,' he gasped. 'I just don't believe they hooked a girl like Julie.' In his confusion and bewilderment, he was grasping and finger-combing tufts of his blond hair.

'I don't know how it could have happened, either,' Judge Knox said. 'But I mean to find out.'

'If I can help, Judge – that is, apart from handling the legal side. . . .'

'Thank you, I may need help,' the judge said. 'Anyway, what else did the police tell you? Have they seen this bookseller, Henry Redhead, who owned the stolen car?'

Barrett nodded. 'He seems to be in the clear, though, for he reported the car stolen the day it happened.' He balanced a sugar-cube on his spoon, half-immersed it in his coffee and watched the tawny liquid invade, undermine and finally dissolve the cube. That symbolized something, the judge reckoned, but could not guess what. 'Sure you wouldn't like something to drink, Judge?'

Judge Knox shook his head. He felt like ordering a double Scotch and downing it neat, but it ran counter to one of his rules – no liquor before lighting-up time. Anyway, it would blunt his intellect and physical acuity and he would need those a hundred per cent. Now he knew a couple of reasons for Judge Dawson's unease: Julie's addiction and the drugs in the stolen car.

His mind, programmed for thirty years to assemble, order, analyse and judge even the most complex facts, suddenly butted against a question, which he stated aloud: 'Why, when the car was stolen in this district, was Julie driving it there? She must have known the risk. If she knew it was stolen, with her training she must have known the police would have the number and description and would be searching for it.' He turned to Barrett. 'Had they changed the plates, did you discover?'

'No, and they hadn't doctored it in any way – same plates, same colour.' Barrett glanced at him. 'I see, do you mean somebody else stole the car and handed it over to Julie who didn't know it was a stolen car?'

'Something like that.'

Barrett fished a notebook out of his pocket and read off the number plate and the car details. His blond head came up suddenly. 'Funny thing, you know several hundred cars are stolen every week around here and the coppers get blasé about recovering them. But for this one they didn't even have to look, or at least they knew where and when to look. Somebody tipped them off.'

'And, of course, the informant did not give his name.'

'Right. When the duty officer tried to nail him about his identity, he hung up.'

'Did this Redhead know the mileage when his car was stolen.'

'Only to the nearest couple of hundred miles, he said.' Barrett consulted his notebook. 'But he or somebody else must have put the three-figure milometer back to nought, for that showed ninety-four miles.'

'So, they think that was the last journey the car did?'

'Hmm. London and back, for instance. It might even be all the car had done in the two weeks since it was stolen.'

'How would they know that?' the judge came back. 'That gauge might have been set at zero on every trip.'

'It's only an assumption,' Barrett answered, 'but Julie called at a garage on the London road with a soft tyre, the nearside front one. It needed fourteen pounds of pressure. That tyre is still losing a pound of air every twenty-four hours according to the police.'

'Losing it how?'

'A leaky valve.'

'A pound a day ... fourteen pounds, fourteen days,' the judge mused aloud. 'Nobody would drive a car too long with a soft tyre, so it looks as if it was stolen and hidden for all or most of the time. That means it was stolen for a purpose.'

'You may be right.' Barrett looked at the judge with much more respect. He rose, saying he would see Julie the next day and apply officially for a postponement of her trial.

He left the judge pondering what information they had: Who would steal a car from the area in which they meant to use it, stow it away for two weeks without changing the plates or appearance, then get someone to use it and tip off the police? It looked to him as though Julie had at least one enemy who wanted to ruin her life. If, indeed, they had not already ruined it.

Even if she was cured, a big *if*, she would still carry the nightmarish memories of those drug sessions. People were in bond to their memories, and a memory stamped chemically by drugs on the body might never be erased. Even he found it hard to efface from his mind those bluish-purple needle-marks, those smashed veins he had seen that morning.

At that moment, he had conjured up Joan's face and could imagine her anguish at the sight of her daughter in that degraded state. He had been almost glad she was dead and not having to suffer as he was suffering now.

V

He had occasionally written to Julie at Grantham Hall, Cedar Grove, and she had sent him photos of the building. Now, actually seeing the place disillusioned him on two counts: some vandal had felled the half-dozen cedars that had existed and he lamented the loss of his favourite tree with its pagoda spread of branches; and Grantham Hall was no more than an Edwardian redbrick building on three floors complete with privet hedge, worm-eaten front lawn and ageing, wilting rose bushes.

A boarding-house for female students at Lady Margaret Hall and Somerville College, the place let six rooms and provided the women with an evening meal and a common room where they could study, chat or watch TV. It was owned and run by Mrs Stafford, widow of an RAF wing commander who suffered from schizophrenia and had finally shot himself.

On Sunday evening, she opened the door to the judge, had him identify himself, then said, 'I'm so sorry Julie's ill. Such a pretty girl with good manners.' He followed her scrawny, angular body and stick legs upstairs to the second-floor room that Julie had rented.

'She hardly ever used it over the past year, but since she paid the rent. . . .' Mrs Stafford shrugged.

'The letters I wrote,' said the judge. 'She must have collected those?'

'Yes, she called once a week to pick them up – except the last one.'

'Did she get many letters?'

'Oh, mainly correspondence from the university from what I saw.' She opened the door and handed him the key to close it when he had finished. 'It's just as she left it,' she said.

'So you have no idea of where she was living.'

'No, and I don't think any of my girls have, either.'

Left in the room, he gazed round at the table and two chairs, the single bed under its patterned quilt; his eye scanned the bookshelves with their rows of law books, reference books and a collection of paperbacks, fiction and non-fiction. Not many clues about the girl who had lived there. Yet one thing struck the judge with force: she had paid the rent and kept the place tidy, so she had intended to return and perhaps resume her studies.

He saw she had cut and filed *The Times* law reports and kept copies of the *Law Journal* and the *Law Times*, presumably to analyse certain judgments that had made legal precedent.

But wherever had she unearthed a late eighteenth-century edition of Blackstone's *Commentaries on the Laws of England*? She must have spent her pocket-money for two whole terms on those. Other books confirmed her serious interest in the law. Sir Henry Maine's *Ancient Law* and *Early Law and Customs*, and Roscoe Pound's *Jurisprudence*. All vintage stuff.

Hooking the second volume of Blackstone free, he turned its pages, then abruptly thrust it back as though it had scorched his fingers. Start to browse through law books and he'd be here until midnight.

But in that moment he had noticed something! He slid the book out once more and turned to the flyleaf. Stamped Henry Redhead, Bookseller, Cornhill Road, Oxford. Both Maine and Roscoe Pound volumes had the same stamp.

Then surely she would have known Redhead's car, the one she was supposed to have stolen!

Last year's calendar dangled on the wall. Julie had used chrome highlighter on several September days. After that, nothing. That squared with the time she had quit the room according to the old buzzard, Stafford. Why? Why no forwarding address? Why the stolen car? Why the drugs? Why the guilty plea? Why the complete reticence about everything?

How, where, when and why had he failed Julie? For if he had not failed her, she'd never have turned to drugs.

Mrs Stafford showed him out. 'Did she have any special friends among the girls?' he asked.

'None in particular. Or maybe Irene Farmer, who's since left, and Jane Birkinshaw, who's still here.'

'Anybody else?' Something prompted him to put that question.

That clamp of her lips and the hiccup of hesitation signified something. 'There was a girl, Katie Gamble, who was here for nine months. She was a year or two older than Julie. They were friendly.'

Mrs Stafford obviously did not approve.

'Miss Gamble left when. . . ? After the summer vacation last year, was it?'

Those curious seaweed-green eyes focused on his face. 'You know about her, then?' she said. He raised his eyebrows a fraction but said nothing, an old courtroom ploy. 'Well, I decided she could not stay.'

'For any specific reason, Mrs Stafford?'

'You would really have to put that question to the person concerned.'

He had encountered witnesses like Mrs Stafford, who would have defied a Marshall Hall, a Patrick Hastings, the rack, thumbscrews, the thousand cuts, the lot when their moral sense decreed silence.

Four o'clock was tolling from St Michael's as he passed. He needed a break, so he found a tea-shop in the nearby Cornmarket and ordered tea and toast; he opened the map and guidebook he had bought with his Sunday paper that morning.

Already, he had listed the garages along the London Road, and although he felt weary, he must try to find the one where Julie had stopped. He was drawing a long bow, making so many assumptions, but he had a hunch the stolen car had lain hidden for two weeks before making that London journey after dark on Thursday.

Refreshed by his tea, he set out to walk to the London Road, marking off the garages that shut at five or six in the evening. Beyond where the road forked left to London, he quizzed the girl in denim blouse and blue jeans in the all-night garage. No, she hadn't seen any girl on Thursday in an Escort with a flat tyre.

Two garages further on, at the second all-night service station, he struck lucky. There, the proprietor, John Higgins, had seen such a girl just before nine on Thursday. 'Another half-dozen miles on the motorway and that tyre would have blown out,' he said. 'What happened – she have an accident?'

'No.' Something in the man's attitude prompted another question. 'Did the girl seem nervous or harassed?'

'Wouldn't say that, like. But in a helluva hurry. Looking at her watch all the time I'm checking the valve and blowing up the tyre. She tore off at the rate of knots, so I thought she might've hit something.'

Trudging back to the Randolph, the judge weighed this evidence. Julie had never acted like someone driving a stolen car. Her intelligent head would have warned her to pick a garage further from town with an airline she could use herself. She would never have drawn attention to herself as she had done.

Why that particular garage? Probably because the flat tyre forced her into the first one on her route. In that case, she could not have passed the first two garages.

In his room, he spread his map on the table. With a pin, a piece of thread and a ballpoint pen, he drew a circle using the Higgins service station as its centre and the first all-night garage as the radius. A rough conjecture perhaps, but the stolen car had probably come from somewhere inside that circle. According to Higgins, the Escort had a full tank, which made it look as if someone had stolen and prepared it for Julie.

His phone rang. A male voice asked, 'Are you Mr Justice Laurence Knox?'

'I am.'

'This is the *Oxford Mail*. Is it true that your stepdaughter, Miss Julie Armitage, has been remanded, charged with stealing a car?'

'Yes, that is true.'

'Can you say anything further about the case, Sir Laurence?'

'No, and since my stepdaughter has been charged and the case is therefore *sub judice*, neither can you unless you want to risk being in contempt of court.'

'Do you know at least when it will be heard?'

'No. If I did, I would inform you, but the police or the crown court authorities will give you those details.'

'Thank you, Sir Laurence. . . .'

'Just a minute. Can I ask you this? How did you hear about the case and the fact that Miss Armitage is my stepdaughter?'

For a second or two, the reporter hesitated as though suspecting the question might be some sort of trap. Eventually he said, 'We had a tip-off.'

'From police sources?'

'No. I shouldn't tell you this, Judge, but it was an outside caller. He didn't give his name.'

'But he told you I was staying here?'

'Yes . . . yes, he did.'

Replacing the handset, Judge Knox reflected that anonymous tip-offs seemed the order round here. Probably the same man who had tipped off the police about Julie.

He rang Barrett and told him about the reporter and his fear that he would be molested by the press now. Did Barrett know of a small hotel in Oxford where he might stay incognito?

'If you don't mind staying with an aunt of mine, I'm certain she'd be glad to have you, She runs a place called the Penn Lodge Hotel, half a mile from the Randolph, on Woodstock Road. If you like I'll ring and fix a room for you.'

'Thank you, I'm grateful,' the judge said, then asked, 'Do you happen to know where this bookseller, Redhead, lives? He's only listed in the phone book under his shop address.'

'I'll make enquiries and ring back in half an hour.'

When he rang, Barrett said his aunt was keeping her best room for him the next day. 'She's delighted to have you, and she knows Julie well.'

'And Redhead?'

'He lives in Bramall Lane on the north side of the town, off the Banbury Road.'

Judge Knox thanked him. Bramall Lane was well outside his magic circle. Dammit, he could have sworn the man lived within that radius.

As he packed his papers and some of his clothing in his hold-all, the judge suddenly felt bone-weary. His day had begun at six and he had not even stopped to eat lunch; now he had no appetite for dinner, he had gone beyond hunger. Undressing, he stood in the shower sluicing himself with alternate hot and cold water, then went to bed.

Too tired to dream of Provence or anything else, he knew nothing until his alarm pulled him out of his sleep at seven the next morning.

VI

Barrett's aunt he had pictured as another version of the raw-boned, pinched-faced Mrs Stafford; but the woman who welcomed him at the Penn Lodge Hotel had grey, laughing eyes in a candid face framed by blond hair tumbling in waves to her shoulders. She also had a no-nonsense manner; she took the case his clerk had fetched that morning and conducted him upstairs to the first floor, saying the lift was more bother than it was worth. He put her in her late thirties, early forties.

As Barrett had promised, she had given him her best room. Large with a bay window overlooking a park and a cricket field, it also had a direct-dial phone, TV and a large bathroom. And, if a minor consideration for the judge, he nevertheless noted that it cost half of what he had paid at the Randolph.

'I knew Julie through Peter, and I'm fond of her, so make yourself at home here,' she said, showing how things worked. 'You can either use the dining-room or have your meals served in your room, and if there's any special service you want, just let me know.' She handed him a card. 'It's my personal extension number if you need me.'

Margaret Denham was, as Barret had told him, the widow of a heart surgeon at the Radcliffe Infirmary. Five years before, on their sixth wedding anniversary, they had gone to Venice for a week; on their second day they were sightseeing when Frank Denham complained of violent indigestion; she sat him down at the nearest table, outside a hotel on the Riva degli Schiavoni. He died there in front of her eyes from a massive coronary attack. Their savings and his life insurance money had paid for half this hotel. Margaret had mortgaged the other half and decided to run the place herself

Barrett also informed him that the hotel rarely had an empty room, and soon the judge realized why. Margaret Denham supervised the kitchen herself and the cuisine was a mixture of good English, French, and Italian with variations. Nothing could have been further from the English boarding-house or Swiss pension.

An hour after settling in, he was leaving for the prison when she stopped him with a box tied in pink ribbon. 'A cake for Julie,' she said. 'Peter says the food there is awful.'

Perhaps he looked askance at the gift or hesitated slightly, for she laughed and said, 'I assure you there's nothing in it but eggs, flour, cream and dried fruit.'

'I didn't suspect anything else.'

'I should hope not,' she came back with mock reproach. 'Anyway, nobody could possibly suspect an eminent English judge of smuggling a file or a gun into prison inside a cake to aid and abet an escape.'

At that they both laughed, and he thanked her.

'Tell Julie I'll come and see her in a day or two,' she said, then turned her grey eyes on him. 'Do you think she might get off?'

He shrugged, wondering how much she knew about Julie, how much Barrett might have let drop. At last he said, 'I don't think she'll go to prison, but she will probably receive some form of suspended sentence.'

At the prison, when he entered the small cubicle they had allotted Julie and him, he noticed she looked better. More relaxed. However, she would still say nothing about how she came to steal the car and why it had been carrying drugs. Evidently she was persisting in her intention to tell him and Barrett as little as possible; she even repeated that she would have herself to blame if the Oxford judge sent her to prison.

'But at least you're getting treatment here, Julie.'

'I suppose so.'

'The doctor – what's his name, Marsh? He's very pleased with your progress.'

'He's not bad,' she admitted. 'But Sanderson, the trick-cyclist, the head-shrinker as they call him here, he bombards me with silly questions . . . about losing my father, then my mother.' Julie smiled, wryly. 'I think he'd read *The Importance of Being Earnest* and thought, like Lady Bracknell in the Wilde play, that to lose two parents was criminal negligence.'

'Don't forget he has to make a report, and that's important for you.'

'Oh, I know. But I've told him I'm of sound mind, though a bit deficient in wind and limb, and I don't want him saying I've a mental age of fourteen, or that I was momentarily insane when I stole the car and therefore not responsible before the law.'

'He's acting in our best interest, Julie.'

'Papa, that's the first time I've ever heard you have a good word for a psychiatrist,' she retorted, and her flash of humour and show of temperament heartened him.

However, she was right; he had little or no time for psychiatrists, who brought their convenient moral and medical judgments into courts to persuade juries that sadistic and perverted murderers like Smith, Heath, Haig, Christie and others tortured and mutilated, murdered and robbed their victims because their mothers read Dracula and Frankenstein to them at bedtime, or beat them or did not give them their ration of kisses and cuddles. Or they were latchkey children. Or from broken homes, spurned, emotionally blunted. How many normal murderers had he met in twenty-five years at the bar or on the bench? Not one. At both extremes there were black-hearted villains and saints; in between, the middling good.

'What does your friend, Barrett, say about the psychiatric examination?'

'Peter? He's all for it. He says if we can prove I didn't understand what I was doing because of some temporary nervous crisis, I might get off.' She looked at her stepfather with defiance in the set of her features. 'I have told him to forget that sort of plea.'

'That is your prerogative, Julie.'

'And Papa, I . . . well, I don't want any string-pulling or fixing of my trial with your friends.' A flush of shock and anger in his face pulled her to a halt, and she added quickly, 'Oh, I'm sorry, I know it's against all your principles, and mine, too. But the psychiatrist is putting ideas into Peter's head and it might be better if I didn't see him.'

'No, you must see him, and whatever you do, don't try to fool him,' the judge said. 'You must tell him the truth.'

'The truth, the whole truth and nothing but the truth,' she murmured, placing her hand on her heart, then turning her eyes to gaze through the small window placed high on the cell wall. 'I see how people can tell the truth and nothing but the truth and I've always tried to do that. But the whole truth!' She turned to look at him. 'Papa, does it exist, at all?'

'Oh, it does,' he said, though he knew what she meant, for he, too, had difficulty with that bit about the whole truth. 'Truth exists all right, even if it is only a personal truth.'

'What's the personal truth about us?' she murmured. 'Of course, he had to ask me about that – what my relationship was to you, my step-father.' Julie was scanning a point on her left thumbnail, peering intently at it, rubbing it with the ball of her right thumb, polishing it. 'You see, he was trying to find the flaw in my psyche – some would say in my character – that had destroyed my ego and made me depend on this.' She held the top of her smock-sleeve and slid her left arm forward to show the needle-marks and the ruined veins that had so upset him on his previous visit. Even now, he averted his eyes and sucked in a deep breath.

Julie had lifted her own face from looking at them and said, 'Don't you want to know what I confessed to him?'

Confessed? Her choice of that word disturbed him. 'If you want to tell me,' he said, his mouth dry.

'I said you frightened me.'

'Frightened you! How could I . . . how did I frighten you?'

'Oh, it was when I was very small. Know what I thought – you'd killed my father and married my mother.' She shrugged her shoulders and gave a half-smile. 'A sort of mixture of Oedipus, Macbeth and Hamlet.'

'But that was when you were only a child,' the judge protested.

' "The child is mother to the woman," the trick-cyclist thinks. He said it was important and went on and on about it until I got tired and a bit angry.'

'I didn't frighten you when you grew up, did I?'

'No, not in the usual sense of the word, but . . . but you were remote and hard to reach.' She stopped talking and fumbled in her smock for a packet of Gitanes which Barrett must have procured for her. She lit one, the match-flame wavering as her hand trembled violently. It reminded the judge that Marsh, the prison doctor, had warned him not to tire her too much, for she was losing weight and sleep as they reduced her drug intake.

She was talking again. 'Papa, from where I stood, even growing up, you were a sort of god who sat on Mount Olympus, handing down punitive justice in the form of thunder and lightning, fire and brimstone, dark dungeons, that sort of thing. And that was kind of scary, too.'

'Julie, I'm sorry. . . . If I had only known that was how you saw me. . . .'

'That's the trouble, Papa,' she whispered. 'We can never step into the other person's skin and feel and see the way they do and share their experiences.'

'No,' he admitted. 'But perhaps I did not try hard enough.'

She nodded her head slowly. When he saw how weary she seemed, he conducted her along the corridor to the hospital, taking her hand in his. After she had disappeared with one of the orderlies, he stood there for a long moment, deep in reflection.

He realized he knew little or nothing about his stepdaughter and she was twenty-two years old. And yet he loved her. Oh, perhaps he had never declared it – admitted was the better term – in so many words. That would have embarrassed him, just as much as telling Joan how much he loved her. Had she, too, felt like Julie – that he was remote, Olympian? Standing there, in the prison corridor, the judge also realized it had taken a crime, an arrest and a psychiatric examination in prison before he and Julie had begun to reveal something of what was in their hearts.

As he walked away from the prison Barrett's Rover drew up alongside him, pointing towards the prison gate. 'Judge, are you going back to the hotel?' He nodded and the barrister said, 'I've got to have a word with Julie, but I've seen the two prison quacks. Maybe you'd like to hear their opinion.'

'If you think it is helpful.'

'I do. Say I meet you in half an hour at Penn Lodge.'

Judge Knox nodded and walked on. He did not go straight back to the hotel. For the first time in years, he entered a small pub on the

London Road. No one, he hoped, would ever dream of meeting Mr Justice Knox, a High Court judge of the Central Criminal Court, in a suburban tavern in Oxford. And if anyone did, well it was just too bad. Here, they still casked their ale and the tang of hops, malt and tobacco smoke seemed ingrained in the wooden bar and chairs and rafters. The judge approached the bar and ordered a double whisky.

'Any particular brand, sir?' the landlord asked, running off several names.

'Johnnie Walker,' the judge said, though it hardly mattered since he wanted the liquor for its alcoholic content rather than its bouquet. As an afterthought, he asked for a half-pint of the local ale. In a corner seat, he gulped the whisky down and sipped the ale slowly; in a few minutes, he felt the strong liquor taking effect, releasing the tension that had built up during his talk with Julie. How much had she told the psychiatrist, and Barrett?

Barrett was waiting for him when he returned to the hotel, sitting in the lounge drinking coffee, which he seemed to consume by the gallon, and forking cake into his twisted mouth from a slab on his plate. 'Present from Julie,' he mumbled. 'She didn't feel like eating it all.'

'How did you find my daughter?'

'That's what I wanted to see you about. Do you mind if Dawson remands her for another week, or even a fortnight?'

'No, but why?'

'Both the prison quack and the sick-tricyclist think she should have a bit longer to dry out, and give her a chance. It isn't easy for her, or them.'

'What do you think? It's your case.'

'I say she should stay in the hospital until they've broken the back of her drug problem. If the case went against us, and they. . . .'

'. . . sent Julie to prison for drug offences, she'd suffer too much and relapse, is that your reasoning.'

'Spot on.'

'Then I concur. She should stay where she is for at least a fortnight.' He paused, wondering whether he should put the question, then decided he would. 'Apart from that, how did you find her?'

'A bit shaky, but otherwise OK.'

'Did you make any progress with why she stole the car, or how they came to find drugs in it?'

'Julie admits to stealing the car, but denies knowing about the drugs.' Barrett shrugged. 'But it'll be hard to convince even a humane judge like Dawson of that.' He fastened his teeth on another hunk of his aunt's gift cake and chewed on it, reflectively. 'Anyway, the police mean to press the drug-possession charge,' he murmured.

'So they think Julie's still hiding something.'

'Uh-huh, and so do I. And I only hope she comes clean before the trial.' Barrett polished off the rest of the cake, gulped down his coffee, pleaded another rendezvous and departed at the gallop.

Left to himself, the judge pondered that morning's evidence. Julie was accepting her punishment to protect someone. Of that he felt sure, and Barrett evidently had the same notion. But whom was she protecting? He must find out.

Somewhere along his genealogy, the gene that had inspired Redhead's name and probably given his antecedents red hair, fair skin, clear eyes, had been dominated by another gene, probably that of a rogue. That had darkened the bookseller's hair and beard, had turned his eyes a tarry black and caused one of them to squint upwards.

So the judge meditated, peering over the top of a book at the man behind his desk in the rear of the shop where he traded in new and second-hand books.

As he approached, he noted the cigarette between saffron fingers, and the nicotine stains on the mouth and black beard.

'Yes sir?' Redhead queried.

'I've had a look through your shelves, and I wondered if you ever came across a late eighteenth-century edition of Blackstone, or even a first edition. His *Commentaries on English Law*, I mean.'

'*Commentaries on the Law of England*,' Redhead corrected, lifting his head to gaze at the judge.

Confronted by a man who squinted, which eye did he look at? 'I'm sorry, that is what I mean. Do you ever get a set?'

'Sometimes, not often,' Redhead murmured.

'What would they sell for, say, a late eighteenth- or early-nineteenth-century edition?'

Redhead pulled his beard. 'Let me see . . . anything between five hundred and fifteen hundred pounds, depending on their condition.'

'As much as that!' Judge Knox noticed the rogue gene had also endowed the man with a neck twitch that was hard on his shirt collar.

'Hmm,' Redhead grunted. 'And I have a waiting-list of half a dozen for the same thing. If you put your name and address on this postcard, I'll inform you when I have what you want.' He watched the judge fill in the card, then he filed it.

'Do you mind if I have a look round?'

'No, go ahead – but we shut for lunch in half an hour.'

The judge pushed through to the rear, where he glanced at the biographical section. Apart from Lord Denning, Megarry and a couple of old circuit judges, his colleagues had sparse representation. As it should be. Judges should confine their words of wisdom to the court-room, he thought.

He was still observing Redhead, who turned to hook three books out of a shelf behind him with a bent index finger. As anyone with any reverence for books knew, that way you broke the spine and ruined the book. Curious, that a bookseller who sold rare and costly books had so little respect for them! How would this man have reacted if, instead of asking for Blackstone, he had whispered that he had a penchant for hard porn and dirty pictures; or a slight ache for a pinch of cocaine, crack or heroin?

From his observation post, Judge Knox noticed the small utility van sitting in the back courtyard; it bore no name, but one of Redhead's assistants was loading books into the back, so it probably made deliveries or collected second-hand libraries for the shop.

As the assistant carried out the last load and shut the van doors, the judge left the shop discreetly and posted himself in the small alley leading to the back courtyard. When the van appeared, he stood in its path, then went to the driver's window.

'You wouldn't by any chance be going to Mr Redhead's other place, would you?' he said.

'The depot, you mean? Yeah, I'm going there.'

'I live just nearby. Would it be very much trouble to give me a lift?'

'Naw, 'course not. Hop in.'

They turned along High Street, crossed two bridges, then forked left at the London Road.

'Where you say you live?'

'Just by your depot.'

At Hale Lane, the driver turned left and stopped by a two-storey building with its windows bricked up, a front door in heavy metal and a large garage door. Thanking the young man, the judge slipped him a one-pound coin, got out and walked off. At the corner, he stopped to watch as the man slid open the garage door to reveal space enough for at least four cars.

Was that, the judge wondered, where the car containing the drugs had been hidden for a fortnight after being reported stolen? That depot lay well inside the circle he had drawn round the garage where Julie had stopped with her flat tyre.

Judge Knox prided himself on divining with better results than any truth drug or lie detector, the quantum of lies or truth, good or evil in people. He had not needed to exercise his sixth sense on Redhead. That man figured somewhere in the story of Julie's arrest and whatever plot revolved round it.

At one o'clock, when he had put the CLOSED sign on his shop door, Redhead shut and locked his office, picked up his phone and punched out a London number. Realizing straight away that he had made an error, he pressed the cut-off button. With shaky fingers, he lit himself a Gauloise and started again. This time it rang and the bookseller heard a voice he recognized at the other end before speaking.

'He's been here,' he whispered.

'Good, he's taken the hook. What did he want?'

'An early edition of a book on the laws of England.'

That evoked a low, throaty guffaw at the other end. 'What for,' the voice asked, 'when he knows them backwards? Oh, I know why – the rotten bastard's thrown his law books at so many people he's run out and has to stock up.' Again, he laughed, this time a cackle that irked Redhead.

'You know why he came here. He came about the girl, that's for sure.'

'What's he like these days?'

'He's pretty spry for a man in his early fifties. He's in good shape mentally and physically. I hardly recognized him without his bench gear, his fur-trimmed bed-jacket and his horsehair head-warmer. But he's no fool, I tell you.'

'You don't have to tell me. He's as cunning as a jailhouse rat – and I've known a few.'

'Look, Cliff, it's none of my business, but I hope you know what you're doing tangling with somebody like Knox. He's pretty powerful and I'm sure he suspects something.'

'Look, Redhead, point number one: it is your business. Point two: what if Knox does suspect something? Point three: what can he do about it?'

'He's the law, isn't he?'

'Only when he's in court surrounded by coppers and legal flunkies. Outside, it's different.'

'I don't like it.'

'Hmm, so you don't like it.' His voice rasped louder down the line. 'Well, Redhead, now he's found you, you'll just have to lump it. And if you won't lump it, I'll have to send a couple of my boys down there to burn that beard of yours off with a blowlamp. Get it?'

Redhead heard the dead click on the line. Putting down the phone, he stared at it muttering curses into his beard. In a pocket, he found the judge's postcard, turned it over to look at the address he had written. It said: *Charles Marshall, c/o Randolph Hotel, Oxford.*

That false name and the request for Blackstone's *Commentaries* added up to the fact that Knox suspected or knew that he, Redhead, had something to do with the way his stepdaughter had been set up.

Redhead might have a left-eye squint, but he had none the less sized up Judge Knox in his shop. For a man who had spent almost all his working life in courts, he looked trim, active, alert. But it was his face that had stamped itself on the bookseller's mind: that way Knox had of impaling you on the stare of those blue eyes.

This man would never stop until he had nailed the truth. Whatever that was. For Redhead himself had no idea why Cliff had it in for the judge and his daughter. Knox would trace the girls, who would lead him to the club and Massey. And from there, he would arrive at Cliff and some sort of show-down.

Just to imagine what might happen then cut Redhead's appetite for lunch.

VII

Julie gave absolutely nothing away. Even when the judge dropped hints about how much he had discovered and tried every cross-examination trick he knew, she refused to be drawn. Mrs Stafford was a venomous shrew with a face like an old mop and a head full of gall and wormwood. Redhead? He was only a bookseller who had offered her a bargain of the Blackstone volumes. Yet, she seemed nervous about the enquiries he was making.

Then he mentioned Katie Gamble. Now to that name the judge noticed she did react. Her cigarette glowed more brightly and the way she held on to the smoke and expelled it in a deep sigh convinced him that he must find the girl who had been her fellow-lodger at Grantham Hall.

He enlisted Barrett's help. At his suggestion, the barrister sifted through the crown and police-court records over the past two years and contacted various CID officers whom he knew. Within a couple of days he arrived at the hotel with a big smile on his crooked face.

'She's quite a number, Julie's friend.'

'Do you have evidence enough to advance the statement that she is Julie's friend?'

Barrett glanced at the grim face. 'Well . . .' he tweaked the bridge of his broken nose between his thumb and index finger as though it pained him, '. . . not exactly, but almost.'

'Then let us confine ourselves to what is adducible.'

Adducible, you antiquated old fart . . . you're not in the Old Bailey now,

Barrett said, but to himself.

He produced his notebook and held it up to prove that he had the evidence, He intoned in his best courtroom style: 'Miss Catherine Jane Gamble, aged 22 or 23, pleaded guilty to one charge of soliciting men in the street two years ago, and two charges of soliciting men from a car in the interests of her trade of prostitute. She received fines of ten pounds. . . .'

'Never mind the fines. Any other convictions?'

'No, but she has changed her style.'

'Meaning what?'

'Just that from what they tell me she's moved up-market,' Barrett said, grinning. 'She now picks and chooses her clients according to how fat their wallets are and she has a posh flat off New Road among the dons and *haute bourgeoisie* of Oxford. Katie's pretty exclusive, since she has an unlisted phone and doesn't appear as a phone-box pin-up or in any of the who's-and-what's-on magazines.'

'How did you find her, then?'

'I shouldn't tell a high court judge this, but through a bent copper who keeps a fatherly eye on what he calls girls who go off the rails on the streetcar named desire, in return for favours financial or. . . .' He braked to a halt, noting the hard set of the judge's features and those blue eyes glowering at him in the way they subjugated prosecuting and defence counsel who stepped over the line. Barrett realized that he would have to modify his slang as well. 'Sorry, Judge, but they do exist, bent coppers.'

'If so, I have been fortunate never to meet any.'

Barrett bit back the retort on his tongue, aware that Judge Knox had the steadfast conviction that all British policemen unswervingly upheld the virtues of duty, morality and truth, and that they were incorruptible.

'Do you have this young lady's number, Barrett?'

Barrett hesitated. 'It's just . . . I was thinking I'd have to go and see her myself rather than—'

'No, I'm sorry, I shall do that.'

'But Judge, even if I give you her number you'll never get within a cable's length of her, especially if you tell her who you are. You can't go with a notebook and pencil and interview a pro like Katie Gamble.'

'I'm not such a fool, Barrett. Just tell me how she plies her trade.'

'By personal recommendation.'

'Then who was recommending you ... or don't you require a recommendation?' Acid dripped from that statement, and Barrett bit his tongue on the remark he would have liked to throw back at the judge.

'My police informant said he could fix things.'

'Well, in that event, he can arrange for me to visit Miss Gamble.'

'But not under your own name, Judge. Think how that would look on the front pages of the *Sun* or the *Mirror*.'

'I see what you mean, Barrett.' For a minute or two the judge stood, thought constricting that small furrow above his nose. 'Well, let us say my name is Smith.'

'No, not Smith. Katie must get fifty a week of them.'

'Then Spencer,' said the judge, who even toyed with the notion of calling himself Spencer-Smith in honor of his bête noir, the Attorney-General.'

'Fine. I'll tell my friend to buzz Katie, then we'll let you know which night she can take you.' He nearly added, 'Or vice-versa.'

'Night? Night?' the judge repeated, then nodded his comprehension. 'Of course, I suppose it is a night calling.'

Barrett could see and hear that Judge Knox was far from attempting a pun or any other form of humour. As he went downstairs and through the hotel lobby, he tried to imagine that incongruous rendezvous between the high court judge and the high-class call-girl.

I hope she takes the old bustard's pants down for him, he said to himself. *And throws them out the window – and him after them.*

When she opened the door to him, the judge stood for a moment as though mesmerized by the sight. Like an expert photographer, Katie Gamble had used the brilliant backlighting of her room to project her body into silhouette; she had put on some gauzy, translucent creation of organza, tulle or voile. And the judge, standing in the hall shadow, saw every contour of her breasts, her thighs and even the darker valleys between her breasts and legs.

'Mr Spencer?' she said, and he nodded, having already announced himself on the intercom at the entrance to the block of flats.

He followed her into the flat, already impressed with her lifestyle. From the letter-box names, he had inferred that two doctors, one knight and a canon shared the apartment block. What would they say if they learned they had a high-class call-girl among them? But perhaps some of them knew and even used her services.

Half a glance told him Katie was pretty. Prettier than Julie, he noted with a pang. Long, oval Modigliani face with blond hair framing it to the neck and curling inwards there. Those aquamarine eyes of hers were inching over him, missing nothing; but they had laughter behind them, as though something about him amused her.

He kept his own eyes off that body shifting sinuously inside that fine cloth web. How did a girl like this, somebody with elegance and dignified good looks, sell herself body and soul in such a profession? Perhaps she was asking similar questions about a middle-aged man who needed to keep this rendezvous, to buy her body for an hour or two.

Her flat must have cost a fortune to decorate. But then at the £500 it cost for one night with this *poule de luxe*, she earned enough to pay for all those well-framed Impressionist and Cubist reproductions, all out of Bond Street. Her decorator had a passion for glass and mirrors: glass-topped tables, glass or Perspex bookshelves, wire and Perspex chairs were everywhere. Along one wall a full-length mirror faced a smaller one to give a sort of *Galérie des Glaces* effect. Was she narcissistic, or did people like performing with mirrors?

'Have a look round while I get you a drink, Mr Spencer,' Katie called over her shoulder, then added, 'I can't keep calling you Mr Spencer, now can I? What do I call you?'

'It's Philip,' he murmured.

'Well, what'll you have, Philip – whisky, gin, vodka, champagne, sherry, beer? You name it.'

'A sherry, please.'

He looked round. Half the flat was taken up by the bedroom and bathroom, connecting with the living-room through double doors. A bubble-bath with room for two, even three people, was embedded in panelled mirrors with marble steps leading up to it. A huge bed occupied most of this suite; and again, the designer's obsession with glass had run away with him. Mirror were on the wall and ceiling, with a crystal chandelier as a centre-piece.

As he stood gazing, an arm came round his shoulder and switched on the chandelier, which threw bits of sequined light all over the room.

'Quite a sight, isn't it?' Katie said, proffering the sherry she had poured, then withdrawing the glass to place it on a bookshelf. 'Here, it's a warm night and you must be steaming in that jacket.'

Before he could stop her, she had undone the front button and pushed her hands across his chest and nearly into the sleeves which she manoeuvered off his shoulders. Freeing her left hand, she cleverly caught the jacket. 'That's better,' she whispered.

A *frisson* of excitement passed through the judge as he felt her fingers and pointed nails parade over his skin through his cotton shirt; even in those few seconds, he felt a strange impulse and could readily imagine himself being seduced by this girl, even making love to her.

He stifled the urge, watching her as she handed him the sherry. Was it just groundless suspicion, or did that wary, leery look imply anything? Not for the first time since his involvement in this affair did he have the impression that someone was leading him by the nose. When he had called Katie Gamble to confirm the rendezvous, she seemed to know more about him than Barrett had told the police contact who recommended him.

Katie took his hand and led him over to the sofa, one of those that moulded itself round you when you sat down. She curled herself up like a cat beside him. After a minute, she looked at him.

'How d'you like it?' she asked.

For a moment, his mind wrestled with that ambiguous question. Was it vague on purpose, or did she really mean what he thought she meant?

'I . . . er. . . .'

Her laugh began as a gurgle and ended an octave higher. 'I meant the sherry,' she said, pointing the champagne glass at it.

'Oh . . . I see,' he said, then caught himself. 'I thought you meant the flat.'

'Well, how do you like that?'

He nodded. 'It's an impressive example of contemporary décor,' he said.

Katie gave another of those laughs. 'I know what you are, you're an Oxford don.'

'What makes you say that?'

'It's the way you speak, your perfect English. And only a don would come back at me with an answer like that – when they were thinking of something different.'

'But you don't have to know who or what I am,' the judge said.

'Uh-huh, you're dead right.' Katie offered him a cigarette from a coloured glass box. When he refused she put back the one she had chosen for herself.

'No names, no questions. If I meet you in the High tomorrow, I walk by you and you me. That's the way it has to be.'

She rose to refill their glasses, then pirouetted before him so that the flimsy material she wore moulded against her body. When she came to rest, she wriggled her shoulders to bare her prominent breasts, their nipples standing out, hard. Involuntarily, he sucked in a deep breath.

'What do you think of them . . . my tits, I mean?' She pulled in her stomach to push her breasts out even further, then turned so that they were in profile. 'Come on, what do you think?' she insisted.

'Anatomically speaking they're . . . they're prodigious.'

'What does that mean? You don't like them?' A laugh burbled in her throat. 'They haven't been done, you know.'

'Done?'

'Pumped up with plastic foam, that sort of thing.'

'Oh!'

'Haven't you seen them before?'

Her question perplexed him. 'Do you mean your breasts in particular?'

' 'Course I do. They were all over page three in the *Sun*. Three times they did them, and that's a record.'

Judge Knox, who never even glanced at any page of the tabloid newspapers, murmured that he had must have missed those occasions when they flaunted her charms. But his remarks glanced off her mind which had darted to something else. He wondered what sort of mind Katie had. Probably sheathed in that sort of stuff with which they coated non-stick pans – nothing adhered.

'You don't smoke anything, then?' Katie was saying.

'No, I never have.'

'I don't mean cigarettes. I mean, no pot, no grass, no coke, nothing like that?' When he shook his head, she opened another glass box, a black one, and the judge saw a dozen cigarettes, obviously home-made, though rolled by a machine. 'Egyptian grass,' Katie said, twirling one in her fingers. 'The best.' She lit the cigarette and dragged deeply on it, though the judge noted it burned slowly. Its acrid, heady tang hit his nostrils and the back of his throat.

'Sure you won't?'

He shook his head. 'It would make me sick,' he said.

'I know just what you need – a pinch of coke.' Bouncing off the sofa, she disappeared to return with three small plastic sachets of white powder which the judge recognized from his many trials as cocaine, or perhaps "crack", the latest variant of cocaine and a danger-ous hallucinant. He was aware that those sachets of powder at fifty pounds a gram, were worth several hundred pounds on the open market; he also realized that this so-called friend of Julie was probably an addict and almost certainly a drug pedlar.

'Try this,' Katie said, tapping powder into a line on to the table. She offered him a straw, then mimed how to suck the powder into one of his nostrils.

Clumsily, purposely, he blew instead of sucking and spilled the powder on to the carpet.

'No, silly, you've got to shut one side and suck,' she cried. 'Look, I'll show you.'

Building another mound, she inserted one end of the plastic tube into it, the other end in her nostril. With her left index finger, she held the left nostril closed, took a strong pull on the straw and the cocaine flew upwards into her nose. Her blue eyes blinked with the impact of the drug.

'Now you,' she insisted. 'It's easy.'

Judge Knox took his time, knowing that in a minute her powder would begin to act. Sniffing a little of the cocaine, he sneezed violently expelling most of it, then trying again with just as little success.

Yet, he had sniffed some of the cocaine and within minutes even those few grams of the potent drug had begun to take effect on him, who had hardly ever taken an aspirin.

His head and body seemed to have drifted apart from each other; he was floating a yard from the floor and his feet were treading air; his head seemed full of coloured glass beads with prismatic light or sparks shooting through them; this light resolved itself into figures and faces. Julie's. Joan's. Lannagan, the West Indian he had sentenced a week ago.

Then the face of Katie Gamble. But this one was real, and she was kissing him, clutching him round his bare chest. To his astonishment, he found his trousers and underpants round his ankles.

Had he or she undone them?

He clawed himself back to reality, felt his mind clearing and his feet once again on the carpet. How long had he been under the spell of that powder? Seconds, minutes, quarter of an hour or more? Katie Gamble was still on what she would call a 'high' – he could see that. Her eyes? They'd gone dark blue and were blazing as they focused on something far away that only she could perceive. Her unsteady movements gave him the impression that she was levitating, as he had done.

Gently he wrenched himself free. Reaching down, he gathered and pulled his underpants up and his trousers round his waist. He sat Katie on the sofa while he went to the bathroom and sluiced his burning cheeks with cold water.

Katie was still lying on the sofa, her mouth open, a dreamy expression on her face. Something or someone – God forbid, not himself – had torn her gauzy dress and exposed those monumental breasts. He had difficulty keeping his eyes off them.

She was smiling and her lips were moving as though she was talking to herself, or hallucinating.

It took her a full half-hour before she turned her eyes on him and seemed to see him as he was.

'How did it feel?' she asked in that equivocal tone of hers. 'Wonderful, isn't it – but kinda scary.'

'Yes, it undoubtedly is,' he agreed, while vowing there would be no repeat performance. It had scared him that, for the first time in his life, he had lost control, he had no mental or physical record of what had happened during that period when the cocaine was warping his brain and his senses.

Although fairly sure he had not attempted carnal intercourse with this girl, it disturbed him to think he might have tried had the drug not worn off. He shivered, thinking he might have done worse, even occasioned her bodily harm.

'What sort of feeling?' she insisted.

'As if I was floating.'

'Me? I was inside a big plastic bubble, away from trouble, falling upwards with coloured snowflakes bouncing off our big coloured balloon on the way to the moon, or the mountains of Venus. That how you felt, too?'

'Yes,' he said to humour her, realizing she was still woozy from the drug.

'Good wasn't it?'

'Yes.'

'Your first time?'

'Yes.'

'It's better second time.'

'Maybe – but not tonight.' He pointed to the two sachets of crystalline powder. 'Where do you procure those drugs?' he asked.

'We said no questions, no names, no memory, remember?'

'Sorry. I mean where could I get some?'

'I'll tell you next time,' she said.

Watching her closely, the judge recalled from trials over which he had presided that when coke-sniffers came off their 'high' they plunged into a sort of reverie where they felt their minds and bodies voided of everything. Katie seemed that way – bewildered, disorientated. Indeed, he himself was experiencing the curious backlash of what little coke he had absorbed; he seemed uncertain of his co-ordinates in time and space.

Perhaps this was the moment, if ever.

'I have a confession to make,' he murmured.

'What sort of confession?' Katie asked, suspicious.

'I really wanted to date a girl called Julie whom I met once some time ago.'

'Julie?' That name seemed to increase her bewilderment. 'Julie Armitage, was it?'

'I never knew her other name. Just Julie.'

'If it's Julie Armitage you can stop looking. Julie's finished.' Her bright, feverish eyes fixed on his face and she mimed injecting something into the crook of her arm. 'They hooked her.'

Judge Knox wanted to ask, to shout: 'Who are *they*? Who hooked her?' His legal sense warned him not to upset his witness. 'Such a pity,' he murmured. 'She seemed such a nice girl.'

'Who, Julie. Yeah, she is . . . or was.'

'You knew her well, then?'

'We were in the same digs . . . she got into a jam about money.'

'In debt, was she?'

'Yeah . . . in deep.'

'But couldn't she borrow from her family or friends?'

'Yeah, she could've. I believe her old man was rolling in it, but she wouldn't go near him. His money was tainted, she said. So, she went to them.'

'Who, the people who turned her into a heroin addict?'

'That's them, the bastards.'

'But why did they hook her?'

'Search me. She got Massey into trouble, somehow.' She paused for a moment, then said dreamily. 'And Bert had a big yen for her, so she must've done something really bad.'

'Massey's still there, though?'

'In the Greensward? . . . 'Course he is, and it's still like a money-press.' She gave that throaty laugh. 'Greensward . . . grass . . . get it?'

He got it. Nothing to tax the mind of a *Times* crossword expert in Katie's clue about where she and others procured their drugs.

'Know what I'd like?' Katie pointed a finger at the champagne-bottle in the ice-bucket. 'A glass of bubbly.'

Judge Knox rose and poured a glass of champagne, which she quaffed in two gulps, holding out the empty glass for another. She had adjourned the case, and if he came back, cold, to the cross-examination, it might arouse her suspicions.

'I have to go, my dear,' he said.

'Oh, I thought you were staying the night.'

'Another time,' he said, and went to make himself look respectable in the bathroom.

He deposited a bundle of twenty-pound notes on the glass table, thanked her and said goodbye. She hardly heard, being almost asleep on the sofa.

'No names,' she murmured.

'No names,' he repeated.

Katie was still curled up on the sofa when the two men let themselves in with a key. One of them spotted the bundle of notes lying where the judge had left them; he counted out £200, which he threw back on the table and pocketed the rest.

His companion was rousing Katie. When she did not respond quickly enough, he slapped her several times with the flat and back of his right hand, holding her head up by her blond hair to add power to the blows. Katie gasped, then yelled and covered her face with her arms, shouting at him to stop.

She recognized both men from the Greensward Club, though now they wore leather jackets instead of dinner-jackets. Bernie and Spinks, Massey's bodyguard, someone had whispered to her. They looked more like young thugs to her.

'Wake up, hophead,' Bernie, the older man, shouted at her. 'You know why the old gaffer didn't stay the night?'

'I don't know,' Katie mumbled. 'I gave him some coke and I think it knocked him over, went to his head.'

'Wasn't where it was supposed to go, so you missed the target,' Spinks said.

Bernie slapped the money in his pocket. 'Didn't get his pay-dirt, poor old sod.'

'He didn't seem all that interested,' Katie said as she swivelled her legs off the sofa and stood up unsteadily, running a hand over her bruised face.

'What was he interested in then?' Bernie asked.

'Like a lot more of his kind, he came along to have a look . . . that was all.'

'He sure got an eyeful,' Spinks chuckled, fixing leery eyes on the rent in Katie's dress and her bare breasts.

'What do you think he was after?' Bernie said.

'How do I know? Struck me he was a don on the loose from his wife for the night.' She stared at them, startled. 'You don't think he was a copper. They'd have let me know, wouldn't they?'

'No, he wasn't a copper,' Bernie assured her. 'Did he ask you any questions?'

'Questions?'

'Yeah, questions. Come on, clear the coke out of your skull and think,' Spinks said, grabbing her arm and squeezing until she yelled with pain. 'Bernie wants to know, did your old gaffer ask anything?'

'No, but he said he'd fixed to see Julie.' She thought for another moment. 'He was more interested in Julie than me.'

'I bet he was,' Bernie said.

'You tell him anything about Julie?' Spinks said, squeezing hard and twisting her arm behind her back. 'Did you tell him anything?'

'I don't tell anybody anything . . . you know that. What else do I know to tell?'

Bernie caught her by the shoulders and shook her until she was screaming with pain. 'Did you tell him anything about Bert or the club? Think, you stupid bitch. Did you say anything about Bert or the club?'

'No, he didn't ask,' she sobbed. 'He didn't ask. Let me go.'

He shoved her, sending her flying backwards and over the back of the sofa on to the floor where she lay crying. 'If he shows again, Bert says to ring him. Understand?'

They heard her whimper a 'yes' then Bernie gestured to Spinks and they left her, still sobbing, and made their way through the block by the back stairs.

VIII

His umbrella raised against the drizzle, the judge walked across the prison courtyard towards the hospital wing. Spotting Sanderson, the psychiatrist, leaving the doorway, he lowered his umbrella to shield his face, trusting that the man would not notice him. But twenty yards on, there he was confronting him. 'I hoped I would see you, Sir Laurence,' he said. 'I thought we might have a word.'

'Is it important?' the judge said, curtly.

He despised the whole brood of psychiatrists, considering them cranks who invented arguments in their curious jargon for exonerating criminals, from the petty thief to the serial killer. If such charlatans spent just a month in his court listening to the horror tales he heard daily, it would transform their warped beliefs about criminals and how to punish them.

As a judge, he felt unconcerned about the mainstream and its tributaries of human conduct; he dealt with crime, took account of the facts and how the law applied to them. Where would things end if they started using Freud or Jung as the touchstones of guilt or innocence, if rape or murder were excused on the grounds that somebody's mother hadn't cuddled him or his father had beaten him senseless or his aunt had seduced him aged five, or her uncle had pawed her at the same age.

Why not go back to genetic antecedence and blame great-great-grandfather for having passed on a rogue gene that might have come down to him from Cain?

This man, Dr Sanderson, he would have disliked anyway for his lugubrious face, open mouth, weepy, red-rimmed eyes, saffron fingers and that irritating mannerism of twirling wisps of grizzling hair round his finger as he spoke, as though dialling his own number, whatever that was.

'I think it could be important,' Sanderson replied. So the judge nodded reluctantly and followed him along the corridor to the small cubicle which did duty as his office. His gaze fell upon an untidy desk, papers with tea and coffee rings on them, dusty files and a stained white overall hanging on a nail driven into the bookshelf. Outside, the judge observed a couple of dozen prisoners at exercise with a couple of prison officers overseeing them. Under the drizzle, they looked miserable.

He refused the rickety chair the psychiatrist offered, to imply that he did not intent to prolong the interview.

'I believe Julie is making some progress,' Sanderson said.

That 'Julie', with its overtone of familiarity, irked him but he stifled his annoyance. 'Do you think you can cure her of her addiction?' he asked.

Sanderson looked at him, winding a strand of hair into a curl with his finger. 'Nobody but the addict can cure addiction,' he replied. 'And unfortunately, no addict is ever completely cured. They're only one whisky, one shot of heroin or one cigarette' – he held up the one he was smoking – 'away from a relapse. And that applies to Julie, like everybody else.'

'But surely most of it is chemistry,' the judge said, sharply. 'When the body is free from the drug and the physical craving ceases, you can say somebody is cured.'

'I wish it worked that way. But we've got to ask what caused the drug problem in the first place, then tackle that. And that is normally some mental or emotional crisis.' He stopped dialling for a moment to look at the judge. 'Can you think of any emotional crisis in Julie's life?'

'Offhand, no.'

'Her mother's sudden death,' Sanderson prompted. 'That was a shock, wasn't it?'

'I suppose so,' the judge admitted. He was watching Sanderson's Adam's apple bobbing up and down like a ping-pong ball on a water jet. Fascinating.

'On that occasion, didn't Julie disappear for a week without ever saying why or where she went?'

What was this man driving at? All these leading questions. You only asked leading questions when you knew most if not all the answers.

Had Julie told this quack something she would not even confess to him about that incident?

'It was a brutal way for her mother to die, and of course it shocked our daughter. So, she fled blindly, instinctively, like a wounded animal.' Why did this man interrogate him with those moist, raw eyes?

'Didn't you think that flight was very strange – and the fact that she didn't appear at the funeral?'

'Of course I thought it strange, but I put it down to shock and grief.'

'Did Julie ever say anything to you about her mother's death?'

'No, and to spare her feelings, I didn't dwell on the circumstances.'

Sanderson scribbled several notes on a yellow pad, head down, murmuring as he wrote. 'It might have been better for her if she and you had emptied your minds to each other.' When he had finished writing, he raised his head.

'Do you mind, Sir Laurence, if I ask you a few personal questions? Oh, they have a bearing on your daughter's case.'

'What sort of questions?' the judge asked, guardedly.

'Well, for a start, what kind of childhood did you have?'

'Normal.'

'You were an only child, I believe.' Judge Knox nodded curtly. 'Did you have a happy childhood?'

'It was normal, I said.' He glowered a the man behind the desk. 'I never felt like strangling my father, nor did I lust after my mother, if that's what you mean?'

A wintry grin crossed the psychiatrist's face. 'The Oedipus complex? It gets us a lot of criticism, and a lot of laughs – but it can happen.'

'In Greek tragedy, maybe.'

'No, in real life. And its opposite, the Electra complex – I suppose you've heard of that.'

'Vaguely,' the judge said, then added with undisguised irony. 'And, of course, in twenty-five years at the bar and on the bench I've met hundreds of cases where girls stabbed their mothers through the heart for the love of their fathers, or because they lusted after them.'

That provoked another wintry grin. 'It doesn't always work as crudely as that, Sir Laurence.'

'For me it doesn't work at all.'

Sanderson leafed through his notebook before lifting his eyes to look steadily at the judge. 'Could I ask you a little bit about your background?' He began that hair-twirling trick that now set the judge's teeth on edge. 'Forgive me, but I looked up your background in *Who's Who* and a newspaper-cuttings library.' He smiled. 'There really isn't much about your personal life in either, is there?'

'I'm a judge, and English judges don't go in for personal publicity.'

'Your father was a country solicitor?' Judge Knox nodded. 'In Repton, Derbyshire, wasn't it?' Again, the judge nodded.

'But something happened that changed things in your family,' the psychiatrist prompted.

Judge Knox took a deep breath and expelled it through his nostrils.

'Look, if you're trying to establish a connection between the fact that my father was struck off the roll of solicitors and the problem my daughter has now, I am afraid I cannot follow your line of analysis.' Despite himself, his voice had risen in pitch and volume and he had to tamp his anger. 'My father took the blame for the peculations of his partner, who forged documents implicating my father in his dishonest dealings – that was the long and short of the matter.'

'You were just a boy when it happened.'

'I was fifteen.'

'What did you want to do at that age?'

'If it is of any relevance, I wanted to write novels like Somerset Maugham's based on his travels and personal observation – or the sort of iconoclastic biographies Lytton Strachey wrote.'

'But you chose the law. Why?'

'You mean, when the Law Society had made such a gross error of judgement about my father? Who knows? That might have been the reason.'

As he made the comment, the judge reflected that perhaps this horse-faced fellow might have placed his finger on something. Maybe he had chosen the law and risen to become one of the most eminent judges in the land because of the injustice done to his father and because he wanted to prove something to himself. But what? His mind made a rapid scan for the answer – though in vain.

'Have you ever made any errors of judgement yourself, Sir Laurence?'

'In twelve years I've had no more than two appeals upheld against me, so I suppose you can say I have been wrong at least twice.'

'There might have been others you didn't know about, though.'

'If there were mistakes, they were honest ones.'

'I've no doubt about that, Sir Laurence.'

Sanderson muttered a 'thank you', folded his notebook and rose. He opened the door for the judge and accompanied him along the corridor to where another passage led to the hospital As they parted, he said: 'If Julie mentions anything that might have some bearing on why she took her first dose of heroin, you'll let me know, won't you?'

'Of course.' Judge Knox nodded to the man, then stepped along the corridor that went through the admin offices towards the hospital.

Watching the quick-striding, straight-backed figure recede, the psychiatrist was thinking that judges and doctors had a lot in common; they only saw people when they were in trouble, mentally, physically, socially; it often gave a black tinge to their view of humanity in general, and often distorted their relations with their families and friends.

In his book, Judge Knox was that sort of case.

As he strode along the prison corridor, the judge was cursing himself for playing that quack's game, and for his own weakness. Why had he lied in his teeth? Why had he compounded the lie by with-holding information that might have helped Julie? Who knew better than he that his father had been as guilty as Lucifer of embezzlement and abuse of trust in stealing his clients' money. That he had realized, even as a boy, and later on when he had studied the Law Society papers on the affair. Had he himself judged his father, he would have been much less lenient than the Law Society.

In a sense, the scandal that had hit his family began his obsession with the law. Sanderson was right about the way it had influenced his choice of profession, but wrong about the motive. He did not mean to redress a wrong, but perhaps to place himself where the law could not touch him.

A normal childhood! With a father who was a drunk and an adulterer as well as a thief? And a mother who was Chapel Welsh. Eighteenth-century fire-and-brimstone Wesleyan Methodism running out of her ears. By living a hell on earth and sharing it all round, she thought you earned your ticket to Paradise.

He could have given that quack of the rueful countenance enough to fill two or three of his notebooks with Freudian, Jungian and Adlerian claptrap.

But those psychiatric clues pointed to him as well. Where did he get his sense that religious and moral sin were equated with crime? From his mother, of course, with her washed-in-the-blood-of-the-lamb mentality. All those compulsive rituals that sprang from her religion.

She kept a washer woman working several hours a day washing and ironing their sheets, their underclothing, their handkerchiefs, socks, everything. She washed her own hands so often he wondered they had any skin left on them; he and his father followed into the ritual bath or under the ritual shower every morning before grace and their fruit juice and cereal.

Until he turned seventeen, he underwent an inspection of his hands, fingernails, neck and ears. Their bathroom drill was timed to the second, regardless of the natural function of the small or large intestines. And yet, never once did he catch either his father or mother undressed or anywhere near naked. Wasn't that what had caused the Fall – nudity? All for want of a couple of fig-leaves!

Ritual cleansing dominated their whole lives. Their diet, for instance. There was no meat. Fish, cheese and milk she allowed with qualms. She drank herb tea herself but permitted his father and himself to have Indian tea. No coffee. Not that drug! Dirt she chased everywhere – Hoovering, dusting, polishing, scalding, scrubbing, scouring. Where, he asked himself, was all this dirt? He needed no psychiatrist to help him answer that question. It was in her mind. She lived by a simple equation with no unknowns: DIRT=SEX=SIN

How would Sanderson have marked his mother's card in Freudian terms? Probably as a galloping case of penis-envy, castrating towards her husband and trying to emasculate her son.

To think he had inherited or acquired some of her compulsive actions and attitudes. At times, she seemed to have programmed him as though she had trepanned his skull and implanted microchips governing his behaviour. For some reason, out of these flashbacks, a Vedic poem surfaced that had struck him in reading Hindu literature:

These five are fixed for every man
Before he leaves the womb:
His length of days, his fate, his wealth,
His learning and his tomb.

His father had secretly rebelled, but too late; it was her influence that turned him into the high-spending drunk who eventually had to put his hand in his clients' pockets.

Often, the judge wondered whether his mother ever rumbled his father's small stratagems of the covert tippler. He had bottles everywhere as his son discovered when he unearthed a half-bottle of White Horse from the garage toolbox.

Now he knew why his father had to slip out and see that his car was covered on frosty nights, or to couple the trickle-charger to his battery. His breath always reeked of those little cashews tobacconists sold to counter smokers' halitosis. Bottles in the attic, under the bath, on top of the wardrobe. Everywhere.

And she unwittingly abetted his clandestine drinking by forbidding him to smoke in her living-room, so he smoked and tippled everywhere else. Since they had ceased to share a bedroom, she never noticed if he was drunk.

During his second year at Burton Academy, his history master arranged for his class to visit Derby and study some of its churches. Laurence wanted to look at one he had missed off the list, St Werburghs, where Dr Johnson had married Mrs Porter. So he broke away at lunch-time and spent half an hour there.

Returning along Friar Lane at half past one, he passed a small restaurant and happened to glance through the window. A mental flash pulled him to a halt. That profile. Snug nose, fleshy chin, tortoiseshell specs, ruddy, whisky-blotched face. His father! And he was with a woman! He passed the window, discreetly, three times.

They were sitting at right angles to each other, their knees touching. She was facing the window. He noticed her blond, bobbed hair, her laughing face. A double string of pearls dropped into her low neckline. She ten years younger than his father, at least. And nothing like a client!

On his third passage he noticed the ice-bucket with a bottle sticking out of it. But something else was even more damning. On his father's plate was the thickest steak he had ever seen; he could almost smell the blood exuding from it. His mother would have fainted at the sight of that blood effusion.

At that moment, he envied his father. Had he possessed the courage to go and order himself a pork or lamb chop, a steak or even a wing of chicken and wash it down with beer or wine, his face would have confessed his guilt; anyway, it would have lain in his conscience.

Even at this remove in time and space, thirty-five years on, he still felt pity for his father. Lonely, lost, unloved by the woman he had married.

He recalled that day on his sixteenth birthday when his father had taken him aside and pressed an envelope into his hand. 'Don't for God's sake open it in front of her, or tell her,' he whispered, the slurred s's hinting that he had tapped one of his hidden bottles. 'Now listen hard, Larry (who called him Larry now?) to what I'm going to tell you.' Judge Knox could still feel that grip on his shoulder and it set his heart hammering again with nostalgic tachycardia. 'Get out of here, get away from here.' Or was it 'her' he said?

'But how . . . where?' he had stuttered.

'Anywhere but here.' His grip tightened. 'Look, Larry, you're a bright boy. Your grammar school has half a dozen scholarships to Oxford. You can win one.'

'Oxford? Oxford?' he had repeated, uncomprehending.

'Yes, Oxford. . . . 'S where they speak the best dialect in the country. Establishment jargon. Upper crust stuff.' He sniggered. 'Know who the upper crust are? A lot of crumbs held together by dough.' His snigger became a guffaw. 'Go and learn about them, take your time from them, learn their way of working and they'll open every door and you can choose which one to walk through.'

When he opened the envelope in his room he found a cheque-book

in his own name and a bank statement from the Midland Bank informing him he had £200 in his account. A small fortune.

For a long time he wondered whether to accept the money, or use
it. After all, his father had just been struck off for allegedly embezzling
between £3,000 and £5,000. Was this some of the stolen money?

It niggled at his conscience so much that he went to his father and
asked him point blank if the money had come from the amount he
had embezzled. His father had looked at him with indulgent eyes and
a quizzical smile on his lips. 'Look, son, money can't talk, it has no
smell, no taste, no family tree.' He thrust the cheque-book back into
his son's hands. 'Even if it has come from that money, I've paid for it,
every penny and more with what they've done to me.'

So he took both the money and his father's advice. He defied his
mother. He won an Oxford scholarship, then another two years at
Oxford which enabled him to study law more deeply. Gradually he
buffed away the rough vowels and garbled consonants of his
Derbyshire speech, replacing them with upper-crust Oxford, even to
the nasal timbre and slight drawl.

Indeed, he modelled his voice and even his courtly manners on
Jeffrey Armitage to the point where even Joan confused their voices on
the phone. Perhaps that was why she had married him after Jeffrey's
death: he reminded her of her first husband.

Once and once only did he return to Repton. To bury his mother.
His father sold the house and moved in with a woman he afterwards
married. She lived in Derby and looked like the woman in the restaurant, although he was never sure and asked no questions.

'Write your life in your own hand, m'boy,' his father had advised
him.

Well, so far he had written and acted out his own script.

He arrived at the hospital office and asked if Julie was in the interview
room. A male orderly disappeared along the corridor and returned
with one of the nurses, who shook her head when she saw him.

'Afraid Julie's a bit under the weather and we had to give her something to calm her down,' she said.

'She's not ill, is she?'

'No, but she's always a bit uptight and feverish after she's seen Dr Sanderson, the psychiatrist.'

He thanked the nurse and retraced his way to the gate. He knew exactly how Julie must feel after a session with that man. A pity. He had so many question to ask her after his session with Katie Gamble. Who was Massey and what did he mean to her? What had she done to turn him against her? And above all, why did she consider his money tainted?

Tainted with what?

IX

An hour after lunch, his clerk rang with the information he had requested. Michael Gresham had examined the Stock Exchange and company records for the ownership of the Greensward Club and found it to be privately owned. He read off the names of the directors: Derek Clifford Strang, Arthur George Bates and Herbert Hugh Massey.

He had also checked with the Criminal Records Office and only Massey was listed there, with two convictions. His first was for receiving stolen gold and jewellery from a Hatton Garden robbery; for this, he had done six months in jail; the second time he was given a year for possessing 186 grams of heroin and about half a pound of cannabis.

'Where was he convicted?'

'First in Knightsbridge Crown Court, the second time in Southwark Crown.'

'Not by me in Southwark, though?'

'No, Sir Laurence. His Honour Judge Duckworth first time and His Honour Judge Dimsley second time.'

'And he served these jail terms where and when?'

'The shorter sentence at Brixton four years ago, and the longer one in Pentonville two and a half years ago.'

'Do these people have establishments other than the Greensward Club?'

Yes, Gresham said. Strang, Bates and a third man, Charles Albert Fox had two similar gambling and night clubs in Southwark and Victoria, and Strang and Bates had five betting shops all south of the river around Lambeth, Brixton, Battersea, those areas.

After he replaced the phone and closed his notebook, Judge Knox sat for some time staring through his window. On the playing-field, a Rugby crowd was yelling encouragement and his eye caught the parabolic flash of the oval ball. Saturday afternoon! He hardly realized he had been here for more than a week.

Where would he have been? At the Pont du Gard, that wonder of a Roman aqueduct between Avignon and Nîmes? Or in Aix, sitting on the Cours Mirabeau watching the crowd go by?

Turning the notebook in his fingers, he studied the names, addresses and figures he had written there.

Why didn't he hand the whole thing over to the police and let them deal with it? Barrett would cope adequately with Julie's trial and she might escape with a fine and a suspended sentence. He might even persuade her to fly out and join him for the rest of his holiday.

But mentally he crossed out the whole idea. Two things damned it. First, Barrett had obtained his information about Katie Gamble from a senior police officer who was aware of what was going on with her and the Greensward Club and yet was sitting on his hands. Neither he nor Julie could expect much help from such corrupt authority.

Secondly, he as well as Sanderson, the psychiatrist, needed to nail the real reasons and motives for Julie's conduct. Oh, he agreed with her that nobody ever arrived at the whole truth and nothing but the truth; yet he would come much closer to it working on his own than a whole battalion of detectives impersonally picking over the facts.

It was risky, he realized that. Hitherto, he had kept his enquiries private, but now he must venture into places like the Greensward. He could well envisage flaring tabloid headlines: OLD BAILEY JUDGE IN GAMBLING JOINT. Or A FLUTTER THEN STRIPTEASE FOR M'LUD. No one would ever accept or imagine that he was there to study certain crimes at first hand, and he would be forced to resign from the bench.

Well, regardless of the risk, he would go it alone. For it had become a challenge, this search for the deeper meaning of Julie's behaviour. If it concerned him in some way, he must know; if it ruined his career, well that was the price he must pay.

There was nothing private about the Greensward Club. Anybody who wanted could play roulette, blackjack, chemmy or throw dice; anybody who wanted to spend his winnings or sweeten his disappointment at losing, could take in the night club with its hostesses and floor show next door. Anybody, that is, who knew about the Greensward, which did not go in for advertising and lay behind a thick barricade of masonry, trees, rhododendrons and other shrubs. Nothing on the entrance gate indicated the casino and night club.

A taxi dropped the judge at the club door and he pushed through, aware the doorman and two other men in dinner jackets were scrutinizing him. Leaving his hat and coat with the cloakroom girl, he wandered into the casino.

In the panelled room under diffuse lighting, some 200 people sat or stood round the various gaming-tables. To the judge, it looked not unlike the two casinos he had visited, at Monte Carlo and at Divonne in the Jura.

For half an hour, behind the onlookers, the judge watched the roulette play. Some people were on a winning streak at two tables, their chips piling high before them. Two men at one table had, by the judge's reckoning, amassed some £20,000 pounds. One of them picked up his winnings and left, throwing a twenty-pound chip to the croupier.

What check was there on this money? It had never dawned on him before how easy it was for casinos like the Greensward to fake their profit-and-loss accounts. Who could tell how much cash changed hands? Anybody could bring in several hundred thousand pounds, buy chips, lose at the tables and the money was legalized. Alternatively, they could win as much out of the illegal money already in the club. A nice way of laundering drug money, he thought.

Glancing round, his eye caught the reflection of a TV camera hidden in the ceiling cornice, watching the play and the players. Had they spotted him and did they already know who he was?

A door led from the casino across a foyer to the night-club entrance.

Judge Knox strolled through to find himself in a large, dimly lit room with about fifty tables deployed round a dance floor on which a dozen couples were dancing to a five-piece band behind them. A bar ran almost the length of one wall with stairs mounting over part of it to the floor above, where presumably the offices were, and perhaps a few bedrooms.

A waiter escorted the judge to a corner table and asked if he wanted to eat or drink. He ordered champagne which arrived in an ice-bucket accompanied by a salver of toasts and savoury biscuits layered with caviar, foie gras and smoked salmon.

One of the hostesses approached. She was pretty, allowing for the diffused light, she was dressed in a long frock which seemed to be supported only by her large breasts and left her shoulders bare. 'Like to dance?' she asked and he shook his head. 'Would you like me to keep you company, then?' she said with a smile. He nodded and she sat down. 'I'm Caroline,' she said.

A waiter materialized with a second glass which he filled with champagne. 'You're new here,' Caroline said, sipping her drink.

'You don't get many new faces?' he asked to avoid answering her directly and prompting more questions.

'No, they're mostly the same types – businessmen and their friends on expense accounts and couples out for the evening. They all know somebody who knows the place.' She was nodding her blond head at the salver. 'Do you mind?' she asked.

'No, go ahead.'

In five minutes, she had polished off the savouries as though she had not eaten for weeks. He beckoned for another tray on which she started straight away. She had a thirst, too, which accounted for three full glasses of champagne while he was still sipping his first. But then, she was under orders to sell the stuff at their extortionate prices.

He wondered about a girl like this who carried herself well and spoke the Queen's English – how did she land up as a night-club hostess? Would this girl have known Julie, who had taken a similar road? He checked his impulse to quiz her, for that would give him away.

'Do you live in Oxford?' he asked, instead.

'I have a room here in the club. If you want to see it—'

'Not tonight,' he said, quickly, realizing that this was an invitation to spend the night with her, probably at the same tariff as Katie Gamble.

'Your boss?' he queried, pointing to the man in a dinner-jacket who had just come downstairs and had started chatting to some men at the bar.

'Yes, that's Bert Massey,' she said. 'He always does the rounds at this time.'

'What is he like to work for?'

'All right, if you don't step out of line.' Catching his puzzled look, she added, 'I mean shooting your mouth off and moonlighting.'

'Moonlighting?'

'Doing overtime with the clients on the quiet, see?'

Massey was heading towards their table, so Caroline excused herself and went back to sit at the bar. 'I'm Bert Massey,' he said, smiling at the judge and putting out a hand which the judge shook. 'I run the place.'

He sat down, flicked a finger at a waiter, who brought another bottle of champagne. 'You're new,' Massey said, 'and I kind of like new faces.' He grinned. 'It's my chance to give them a drink on the house and have a fly one myself.' Expertly, he popped the cork and poured the champagne himself, lifting his glass. 'I hope you'll come here often.'

Judge Knox sipped his champagne. So this was the man who, Katie Gamble said, had seduced Julie and turned her into a drug addict, presumably to tie her to him and keep her working for him. What had possessed her to fall for this smooth villain with his Bermondsey accent and barrow-boy line of patter?

Even in a dinner-jacket and black tie, he couldn't disguise what he was, an East End spiv. He had seen so many during his time at Southwark Crown Court and in the Old Bailey. When he thought of Julie and this man, anger formed a hard ball in his chest and constricted his throat. He had to fight back the urge to face this rack-eteer with what he had done to his stepdaughter.

'Somebody tell you about us?' Massey was asking.

'Yes.'

'Can I ask who?'

'Sorry, I forget . . . a friend of a friend, I think.'

'But somebody in town.'

'Yes, somebody in town.' Was Massey fishing to find out whether he was a policeman or just somebody who wanted to gamble, drink, pick one of his girls and perhaps buy a few grams of heroin or cocaine?

'I hope they said nothing uncomplimentary.'

'No, just the food and the floor show were good, the girls pretty and the gambling on the level.'

'Well, I hope we live up to that recommendation,' Massey said. 'Enjoy your evening.' He wandered off.

Now the judge had to wait and see the floor show. Caroline joined him and drank the free champagne and another bottle as well. Although he did his best to pump her gently about Massey, Strang, Bates and Fox, the other owners, she refused to be drawn.

Their floor show bored him when it didn't deafen him. The bill included a black American woman crooner with flame-red hair and frayed vocal cords, a brace of Cockney comics, a folk singer and a rock band that set the place thrumming and vibrating with their ear-dinning sound. Only one turn had any originality: a striptease done by a couple, the woman in mid-eighteenth-century crinoline and the man in brocade coat, knee-breeches, silk stockings and buckled shoes of the same period. It finished with both naked inside the crinoline hoop and got the biggest hand of the evening.

Just after midnight, the judge retrieved his hat and coat and ordered a cab. When the girl told him there was half an hour to wait because of the rush on late-night taxis, he decided to walk. It was a clear night and his hotel was no more than a mile away.

Outside, he marched briskly, the air and exercise clearing his head of the few mouthfuls of champagne he had drunk. He heard the racket of the odd vehicle along Woodstock Road, but nothing much stirred in this street. However, a car came out of the club drive behind him and went past, travelling fast.

At Harwell Road, he turned to head for Penn Avenue and the hotel. It was a tree-lined road, poorly lit with part of the playing-fields on one side and a few houses sitting twenty to thirty yards back from the kerb behind wooden or iron railings.

Half-way along, he noticed a house with an estate agent's FOR SALE board at its gate. A tree in its front garden overhung the wooden fence. As the judge reached the tree, he saw the silhouettes of three men emerge from its shadow. Even then, he did not suspect they would attack him. And when they spread out and jumped on him, it was too late to run or put up much resistance.

They said nothing. They wore masks. They were not after money or valuables. They were professionals. They were taking no chances.

One man seized the judge's arms and pinioned them behind his back while another clamped a broad strip of sticking plaster over his mouth to gag him. They pushed and pulled him into the garden of the deserted house.

There, they set to work on him. Silently. Methodically.

First, they ripped off his coat and knocked off his hat, throwing them aside. A fist sank into his stomach, winding him and driving the breath out of his lungs. With his arms twisted behind his back, any resistance was limited. But he did kick out and heard a yell of pain as he landed on a shin-bone.

'You old fucker, I'll do you for that,' the victim shouted, then swung a fist that caught the judge on the cheek-bone, dazing him. Another blow from the same fist hit him full on the mouth and he tasted the salt tang of blood. His head whirled and he would have dropped sense-less to the ground if the man behind had not propped him up for more punishment.

'Not on his fizzer, you stupid git, not there,' the man behind him shouted at the figure in front who was aiming at the judge's face.

'Bastard kicked me.'

'Kick 'im back.'

Judge Knox sucked in air through his nose and with it a curious smell. Leather. From their blouses . . . that was it. That smell was among the last thing his senses really took in.

Pain exploded in every part of his as the man he had kicked drove his knee into his groin. Then both men in front started throwing punches at every part of his body – his stomach, his gut, his ribs, his shoulders. After the first dozen blows he had no feeling left. He sagged, putting his full weight on the arms of the man behind.

'Let 'im go.'

'No, kick the old bastard stupid.'

'Kill 'im and you're in for life.'

'Yeah, kill him and Cliff'll do us in, too.'

That raucous voice and the name, Cliff, were the last things he heard as he was falling.

He was elsewhere, his head full of flashing images like some video clip running backwards, madly at first then slowly.

He was falling, falling, falling.

One thought expanded in his mind, almost to bursting point: Fall much further than this and I'll never climb back on to the planet. A parabola with no beginning, middle, or end.

Vivid pictures flickered across his fuzzy mind. Down there was hell-fire under clouds of soot and sulphur. There was a judge consigning him to that pit. Spencer-Smith in ceremonial scarlet and ermine and full-bottomed wig, sword in one hand, scales in the other. '*Domine dirige nos*,' he screamed. 'To be burned at the stake.'

'Your black cap,' the judge shouted back. 'You can't condemn me without your black cap. It's against the law.'

Other images so fugitive he could make no sense of them flitted across his mind. Joan's face in fish-eye distortion. Julie's light-years away.

His life was a gossamer thread, a slender thing vibrating like those shorthand scribbles the heart and brain trace on hospital cathode tubes.

The thread was snapping.

X

A ripple of voices filtered to him through the half-open window and he wondered what they were for several seconds. He opened his eyes and panned them round the room until he came to the case and valise above the wardrobe. They were his. And the voices had now amplified into shouts that came from the playing-fields. How had he managed to get back to his room at the Penn Lodge? Had he lived through some terrible nightmare, or was his experience real?

It was real, all right. His head throbbed and he felt as though every bone between his neck and thighs was crushed or broken.

Slowly it fell into place in his mind. Those three thugs who had set about him as he walked home from the Greensward Club. But why hadn't he died? He had been sure they were going to kill him. No, something had stopped them. Through the pain in his head and body he tried to recall what had stopped them. It was important. But it had gone. It would surface again sometime. Like the words and music of a forgotten aria, it would break surface. There was a dream, too. That had probably lodged in the same cerebral recess and would come round again. Like a comet.

For half an hour he lay there trying to reassemble the fragmented bits of that nightmare experience, but in vain. He looked for his watch but could not find it. However, sunlight on the patch of wall opposite his bed told him it was mid-afternoon.

He had just decided to try reaching for the phone when the door opened and Margaret Denham put her head round it.

'Ah! You're awake.' She entered, shutting the door behind her. 'I wondered if you were ever going to wake up.'

'How long have I been here?'

'Since yesterday morning. Our doctor gave you a strong sedative injection for the pain.' She punched up his pillow and smoothed the bedcover. 'You were pretty badly knocked about.'

In response to his questions, she said a passer-by had discovered him early the previous morning lying moaning in the garden of a deserted house and had dialled the police. Margaret had already alerted the police when she realized she had not returned from the club. As soon as the police informed her that they had found him, she phoned Peter, who arranged for him to be brought to the hotel, reasoning that it would avoid awkward police questioning at the hospital. Peter wanted to keep the police and press out of things, she said.

He listened, absorbing the information slowly. Whatever the doctor had injected still left him drowsy, so Margaret Denham let him doze until just after six when she arrived with a tray containing soup and sweet rice-pudding. Drinking the soup out of a cup made him wince when it touched the raw spots in his mouth where they had hit him. But he managed a cupful and several spoonfuls of rice-pudding.

When he was drinking the coffee she brought, Peter Barrett appeared with a cup of coffee in his hand and his mouth full of the apple-cake he was holding.

'How're you feeling, Judge?'

'Like the idiot I am.'

Barrett squatted on the bed while the judge recounted his visit to Katie Gamble and the Greensward Club and his brief meeting with Massey.

'She sounds quite a dish, Katie,' Barrett said, suppressing his amusement at the way the judge related the visit. 'Did you? . . . did you. . . ?' He sipped his coffee and looked at the judge.

'What are you trying to imply, Barrett?'

'Sorry, Judge . . . crumb in my throat. Did you get anything out of her, I was going to say?'

'What I told you.'

Barrett pointed to the bruising on his face. 'You should have told me you were going to the Greensward and I'd have come along as another pair of hands. Did they try to sell you any coke or crack?'

'You mean, the authorities know about those drugs and do nothing?'

Barrett shrugged. 'Some top policemen think that by knowing how the drug scene operates and the people involved, they can contain the problem. Close the Greensward and let drugs on to the streets and it would be more difficult.'

'It's a viewpoint,' said the judge, 'but one in which I certainly do not concur.' He turned in bed, wincing at the pain in his ribs. 'That place turned Julie into a drug-addict and God knows what else besides.'

'I saw her this morning and she's much better. Even the quacks say she'll beat her drug problem and they'll be able to straighten her out.'

'Straighten her out! What do they mean?'

'Remove the underlying problems, the kind that made her pick up a syringe in the first place.' Barrett fell silent for a moment, then said, 'Judge, did Julie ever tell you anything about me – I mean, why she chose me to defend her?'

'Only that you were friends.'

'That's putting it too simply. We were more than friends – until she suddenly left her digs and took up with Massey.'

'You knew nothing about her addiction, then?'

'No, nothing.' Barrett paused, drew a deep breath and expelled it slowly. 'I wish I had.' As though to end that line of conversation, he finished his demolition of the apple-cake and washed the crumbs down with his coffee. Leaning over to the judge's tray, he dug out a couple of mouthfuls of rice pudding with his coffee-spoon and savoured them. 'Hmm, I bet the other residents aren't getting anything like this. Aunt Meg has the touch, hasn't she?'

'Your Aunt Margaret is a splendid woman.'

Barrett looked at him through his blond eyebrows, and his face wrinkled into a grin. 'Don't for God's sake tell her that, Judge. It might go to her head.'

'Mrs Denham is not so easily swayed, Barrett.' That cutting edge in the judge's tone warned the barrister he had gone far enough. 'Did the doctor say when he thought I'd be fit to resume my activities?'

'No, but he said you were lucky to be alive after the hammering you took and lying out all night. He wanted to have you X-rayed but I stopped him. He said only somebody with a good constitution and in good nick would have shaken off that beating. You have a cracked rib, he said, but it will heal on its own.' He picked up the judge's tray, placed his own cup and saucer on it and was about to put it outside the door when the judge called.

'Barrett, don't you want to finish the rice-pudding?'

Barrett brought the tray back and ignoring the heavy irony, he nodded and said, 'Thank you, Judge, I feel a bit peckish and Aunt Meg's rice-pudding is out of this world.' He resumed his seat and attacked the pudding, then looked at the judge. 'You are pretty fit, aren't you? I thought judges only exercised two parts of their anatomy – top and bottom.'

Judge Knox did not laugh. He said, 'I suppose that assumption applies to most of us judges.'

'So, how do you keep in trim?'

'I play golf badly enough to make it a very long walk, I swim in the club pool at weekends or I take the train as far as the Lake District and walk ten miles a day. I eat and drink sparingly. Enough about me.'

For quarter of an hour, he subjected the banister to the sort of cross-examination Julie might face during her trial which would now take place in ten days. Barrett must try to get Julie to change her plea to not guilty which might mean an acquittal or would at least give Dawson the opportunity of imposing a fine or a suspended sentence on the drugs charge.

When he rose to leave, Barrett could not resist saying, 'Watch Aunt Meg, Judge,' then he slipped through the door before the retort hit him.

Downstairs, his aunt was sitting at her desk entering some bills in her accounts book.

'There's something different about you, Aunt Meg,' Barrett said, peering at her.

'What do you mean, Peter?' she said, rising to the bait.

'Ah, that's it, you've changed your dress,' he exclaimed, eying her floral-silk frock. 'I haven't seen that one before. Is it new?'

'No, I've had it for years,' she replied, somewhat defensively, he thought.

'Stand up and let's have an eyeful,' he said, and she complied while he cocked his head from side to side, pursing his lips approvingly at the way it clung to her figure, emphasizing her breasts and hips. 'Fetching,' he murmured. 'Very fetching.'

'You like it, then?'

'Who wouldn't?' A thought clouded his face. 'But Aunt Meg, you'd better not wear that in front of the judge.'

'Oh, why not?' Disquiet erased the pleasure at his compliment from her face.

'Well, he's an invalid and that would certainly raise his blood pressure.'

'Peter, you're teasing me again.'

'Only a mite,' he said, then looked at her squarely. 'You're not setting your cap at Judge Knox, are you?'

'For heaven's sake, it hadn't entered my head.' She hesitated, then fixed him with her frank grey eyes. 'But if it had . . . entered my head . . . is there any reason why I shouldn't?'

'Noooh . . . noooh, except he's the terror of the Old Bailey.'

'I had heard all that,' she said. 'But if he's that bad, why doesn't he let Julie bail herself out of the mess she's got herself into?'

'Good point, Aunt,' he conceded. 'I asked myself that very question and concluded he was trying to save his own career. You know, they whisper he's going up to the appeal court, and that's one of the biggest deals in the country, legally.'

'Well, I don't agree with you. He loves Julie or he would never have risked facing those gangsters and taking the sort of beating they gave him two days ago.'

'Hmm, maybe you've got something there,' he murmured. 'It's a wonder they didn't kill him, those thugs. They came pretty near.'

'They didn't kill him because he willed himself to survive,' she said. 'He's a remarkable man, Judge Knox.'

Barrett had to agree, silently.

Later that afternoon, when she carried tea into the judge's room Margaret was astonished to observe him propped up in bed with several sheets of paper round him; using a gold pencil, he was covering another sheet with words half an inch tall. She could not help noticing several of the words. DOMINE DIRIGE NOS (Wasn't that the legend above the bench in law courts?) SPENCER-SMITH; JOAN; JULIE; HELLFIRE; STAKE; BLACK CAP.

He must have caught her puzzled frown, for he said, 'It's a little game I'm playing.' He explained that, in his view, the brain did not work like some computer by scanning every bit of data until it matched the right piece by an elimination process. No, the brain was triggered by emotion and intuition as well as its scanning system. It took short cuts and he was injecting words and pictures he'd remembered during his mugging to help the brain find the answers to several questions.

'I do something like that when I'm stuck with the *Telegraph* crossword,' she said, putting down the tray on the bedside table and manouvering it to where he could reach it. 'Sugar, milk?' she queried.

'Both, and I'm a one-lump man.'

'That reminds me of Dr Johnson.'

He stared at her and a smile crossed his face which turned to a grimace with the pain it caused him. 'You mean, when he asked Boswell if he was a one-bottle or a two-bottle man?'

Margaret nodded as she stirred the tea and handed it to him. 'I often wonder who was the greater man – Johnson or Boswell?'

'Neither – though my judgement is purely subjective. They were like lock and key, lost without each other.'

'It's a nice way of putting it.'

That small fragment of dialogue helped to establish a bond, a sort of complicity between them. For a minute or two, Judge Knox sipped his tea, then put down the cup as though he had reached a decision.

'Look, Mrs Denham—'

'It's Margaret, Judge.'

'All right . . . Margaret . . . then you must stop calling me Judge . . . I'm Laurence.' She nodded and he went on, 'I've been wrestling with this problem' – he pointed to the papers – 'for hours and I need a rest and somebody to talk to. Why don't you get yourself a cup and share my tea?'

Margaret needed no other invitation. When she returned with another tray, she noticed he had inked in another word on a blank sheet:

MOUNTAIN

'Is that the word you were searching for?'

'No, but I think it's close.' He explained that one of his attackers had shouted something which his mind had registered as important. It seemed to be associated with the word, mountain.

'Sometimes if you think of something entirely different, your lost thought will pop up,' she said. 'You were going on holiday before all this happened, weren't you?' she prompted.

He nodded, then told her about his projected walking-tour of Provence which would now have to wait until next year; he explained how free and unburdened he felt when he had discarded the trappings of the Old Bailey and put the Channel between him and England; he could travel the length and breadth of France and Italy without once bothering about whether someone would recognize him as Sir Laurence Knox, Mr Justice Knox of the Old Bailey.

'It must be an extraordinary life you lead as a judge.'

He shrugged. 'I suppose it is,' he said. 'But when you become a judge you give up any idea of living like an ordinary person.'

'You mean that?'

'I do, because it's true. It's a vocation that has restricted, even ruled out my social life. As a judge you can't be seen with people who might come before you in court, and these days that means pretty well everybody. You can't go to the theatre in a party or play golf except with your equals, or go to Epsom Downs on Derby Day, even in the royal box, or dine in restaurants where you might be accosted by somebody you've tried or might be about to try.'

Margaret gazed at him, wide-eyed. 'Oh, I knew judges were a race apart, but I never imagined them in that sort of purdah, so to speak.'

'It's even worse,' the judge said. 'God help the High Court judge who is found reading *Lolita*, the *Sporting Life*, comic cuts or is caught with a Greenpeace or CND badge at a demo. I don't vote in case somebody accuses me of political bias, I don't drive a car in case I commit a criminal offence which might preclude me from judging other motorists, I can't run an overdraft or get behind with my taxes. It's that sort of life.'

'It's almost like the priesthood.'

'Not for me.' He smiled. 'Giving up those things wasn't much of a problem since I was never one for making the social rounds and politics leaves me cold.'

Margaret reflected for a moment. 'But you move around here without anybody recognizing you, and I wouldn't have thought that even in London more than one in a thousand people would identify you if you strolled down the Strand.'

'Perhaps not,' he admitted. 'But you always *think* the other nine hundred and ninety-nine do as well.'

'I never looked at it that way.' She shook her head incredulously. 'So you, a pillar of the law, have the same sort of feeling of being watched that the people you judge must have.'

'It hadn't struck me that way either – but I think we do.'

She looked at him, inching her frank grey eyes over his face. 'I bet a good many judges don't practise your form of priestly self-denial.'

'That is their problem,' said the judge.

'But it must be even harder for someone on his own – like you.'

With another woman, he might have suspected that that statement was leading him on to ground where he might not want to venture; yet, Margaret Denham seemed too sincere for that, too open.

'It's like everything else, you get used to it.'

'How did your wife adapt to it?'

'Oh, she knew the law and lawyers from way back and understood the restrictions on our social life and accepted them.' He surprised himself by going on to tell her about Joan, how they first met, how they married after Jeffrey's death and how he adopted Julie. Never before had he talked to anyone about his dead wife. Not even to Julie.

'You mentioned that she died,' Margaret prompted.

'Yes, in one of those idiotic accidents that makes you think of fate. Joan had just done some shopping at a big West End store and had her hands full when she stepped on to the down escalator. Half-way down, the escalator stalled and stopped abruptly and Joan fell to the bottom with another person on top of her. When they got to her she was already dead with a broken neck.'

'What a dreadful thing to happen. It must have been a terrible blow for you and Julie.' She did not continue, noticing that the judge had closed his eyes. She waited for him to speak again.

'It is five and a half years since it happened, but I still think of it most days,' he murmured. 'Of course, the store acknowledged their liability and paid me a generous amount of compensation.' He shook his head, sadly. 'But what is compensation? What does money represent except what you want to buy with it? I could think of only one thing, and no money could buy that.'

'How did Julie take it?'

'Very badly. Too badly even to put her feelings into words. She never even cried. She just appeared to go numb with the shock.'

'She would be what . . . fifteen, then?' He nodded and she went on,

'Poor girl, losing both. . . .' She broke off, thinking she might offend the man who had become Julie's second father. He broke the silence.

'Julie never even attended the funeral,' he murmured as though to himself.

'I can understand that.'

'Not me. I confess I found her behaviour hard to understand. She ran away for the week in which Joan was buried and came back without a word of explanation of why or where she had been.'

'And you never discovered why or where?'

'No, she always refused to discuss it, and I never pressed her.' His voice faltered and he sipped some of his tea before going on. 'You see, I want to forget it as well.'

He looked at Margaret and again shook his head as though perplexed. 'Judges in England aren't supposed to have feelings like everybody else. In the courts, especially the criminal courts, they listen to every sort of villainy from shop-lifting to violent robbery, rape, sexual perversion and murder – and all this criminality is supposed to be erased like words or figures or music from magnetic tape when it's cleared. All our cerebral or corporeal molecules go back into neutral after each case, so that we revert to being the perfect judicial measure, what I once called the perfect benchmark. But we are human, we do feel, and I knew what Julie was suffering, for I was suffering just as much as she was for the loss of her mother – and for her as well.'

'Poor Laurence,' Margaret whispered. 'And you couldn't tell anybody.'

'No, and I don't know why I've told you, in that long summing-up – but I feel better for it.'

She sensed that he was tiring from the pain of his injuries and the effort of making that confession. She mixed the sedative that Dr Grey had left and made him drink it. When she had drawn the curtains to shut out the late-afternoon sun and was going to the door, he called out her name and she turned.

'I just wanted to say what a pretty dress that is you're wearing.'

XI

Barrett was right, Julie did look better. Her skin had lost that jaundiced tinge and her hands seemed much steadier as she smoked one of the Benson and Hedges he had bought for her on his way to the prison. It was his first visit for six days, and he still felt weak even after four days in bed. He had warned Barrett to avoid any mention of the mugging, and fortunately no one in the media had picked it up.

They had given them Sanderson's small cubicle, and Julie glanced at the psychiatrist's white coat and his hotchpotch of medical books, novels and files.

'They call him the shrink and the sick tricyclist, but he's all right,' she said. 'I think he has helped me a lot.'

'All we have to do is get you out of here, Julie darling.'

'Where do you think they'll send me after the trial?'

'Back home if Barrett does his part as he should.' He quashed the protest she was going to make by adding, 'Oh, he won't get you off, especially if you persist in pleading guilty. But with the right plea, he can shorten the sentence and the judge may suspend it.'

Her trial would begin on 1 September under Judge Dawson. She was still pleading guilty, but he knew now from what she had hinted to Barrett that this was her way of ensuring that very little evidence was called that might embarrass him and his career. Because of their different names, not many people would link her with her stepfather.

As they sat facing each other across the psychiatrist's table, she stared at him. 'Your lip's puffed and you have a bruise on your forehead. What happened?'

'It's nothing, I tripped and fell.'

'Is that why you're wearing dark glasses?'

'Yes, that's why,' he replied, hoping she would not see the bruise round his right eye.

He wanted to question her to clear up some of the mysteries. What relationship, for example, did she have with Redhead? Had she got into debt, then sold drugs to pay it off? Who had turned her into an addict? Was it Massey? But Julie, with her law training, would easily duck those questions.

So he began with an innocuous remark. 'Julie, the police are pretty certain you drove to London and back the night they stopped you. They have some notion you picked up the car just off the London Road, near Hale Lane. Are they right?'

She turned both questions over in her mind for a long moment before nodding her head. 'Yes, they're right,' she admitted.

'Did you know the car belonged to Redhead, the bookseller?'

Again, she reflected about that question. 'Yes, I did,' she said finally.

'But what you didn't know was that he had reported his car as having been stolen to the police nearly a fortnight before you were given it. Did you?'

'No.'

'Why would Redhead want to trap you in that way?'

'I don't know. . . .' She stopped suddenly and drew a couple of times heavily on her cigarette, setting the end glowing brightly in the dusky room. 'Well, that is, I have an idea why.'

'Why, then?'

Julie did not reply at once; she sat silent, smoking her cigarette down to its filter then lit another from the smouldering stub. 'I thought they wanted to ruin you and your career through me.'

'Who are *they*?'

'Don't ask me that . . . anyway, I probably don't know who might be behind it all.'

'But go back to the beginning. You did it for the money, didn't you?' She nodded, and he went on, 'And these people who trapped you were paying you for what you did for them, is that so?'

'Yes,' Julie cried. 'But they got it back.' She bared her arm and pointed to the crook with its constellation of needle punctures. 'I was in a downward spiral,' she said in a whisper. 'Another few weeks and I would have killed myself, I felt I couldn't go down any further.'

'But Julie darling, why didn't you ask me for money if you needed it. You knew I have more money than I need and could have given you what you wanted.'

'I couldn't ask you.'

'But why?'

At last he had arrived at the question he had come to ask her the day before he was attacked; the day she and he had both seen Sanderson; the day she had pleaded she was too sick to meet him.

'I don't know and don't ask me . . . I couldn't and that's all I know.'

'Julie, I don't need to ask you. You didn't want to have anything to do with my money because you thought it was tainted. That's why, isn't it?'

She turned moist eyes on his face and he could see she was nearly in tears. Her hand went to the pocket of her smock, groping for a handkerchief. Not finding one, she drew the smock-sleeve across her eyes and nose. Watching her, the judge was about to offer his own handkerchief, but desisted. Too often he had seen witnesses distracted by something irrelevant like a handkerchief or a glass of water, and their real evidence was lost for ever.

'The money was tainted,' he prompted.

'It was insurance money,' she mumbled.

'Insurance money?' he repeated, momentarily at a loss. 'But even if it was insurance money, that doesn't affect its quality or its value.'

'Maybe not.' Julie lifted her head to gaze at him. 'Papa, do you remember *The Monkey's Paw*?'

'*The Monkey's Paw*?'

For a moment that question fazed him before he realized what she meant. Then he recalled that night many years before, when they had listened to W.W. Jacob's eerie, powerful tale in a dramatized radio version. One evening very late, wasn't it? Now it was coming back. Joan and he on the living-room sofa. Empty coffee-cups. Julie sitting by the fire flickering in the dimly lit room. Hand cupping her chin, rapt face. She'd be what, then – fifteen?

They were all caught up in the story. Living inside it, even. As some books when you felt they'd changed everything for you, you weren't the same person. It had been in the house they'd bought in that square just over Campden Hill. A pretty Georgian house that he'd had to sell a few months later after Joan's death. He'd got it all! It had been not many weeks before Joan's fatal accident. Why had Julie picked on that scene? He almost blurted out the question, but his professional voice censored it in his throat. *Let the witness tell the story*, it said.

'It's a story, isn't it?' he murmured, casually.

'It's more than a story . . . but Papa, you must remember. We listened to it on the BBC one night after dinner in Campden Hill.'

'Yes – but what about it?'

'But you must remember,' she said, as though anguished. 'It's about a poor London family who're given a monkey's paw by an old soldier back from India . . . it's a talisman, he says, and will grant them three wishes . . . though it also brings unhappiness . . . despite the warning, the father wishes for a fortune, thirty thousand pounds.'

So fast did the words tumble from Julie's lips, he could scarcely follow them. So fast that he imagined they had been rehearsed a thousand times until they became a sort of conditioned reflex. Here, she was faltering.

'Did he get his wish?' the judge prompted, though aware of how the story ended. She nodded, dumbly. 'How was that? He won some lottery?'

'No, he got thirty thousand pounds compensation for his only son, who was crushed in a machine at his factory . . . crushed . . . crushed.' She moaned the last words, then said, dismally, 'The mother wished for him back . . . but as she went to meet him at the door, the father wished him dead, knowing how disfigured he was.' Julie was sobbing. 'Too late . . . too late.'

She put her head on the table, buried it in her arms, still sobbing. Bewildered now, the judge leaned over the table to stroke her head.

'Julie darling, don't take it so much to heart,' he murmured. 'It's only a story.'

'No, it isn't,' she said in a strangled voice. 'And don't keep saying it's only a story . . . it isn't just a story . . . it's true.'

'What do you mean, it's true?' Even as he put the question, he surmised the answer. Intuitively, he realized that Jacob's spooky tale was Julie's parable of her own story, and that somehow this was connected with her behaviour afterwards. 'Julie, tell me why you say it's true.'

'Because I didn't wish Mummy dead . . . you must believe that, Papa . . . I didn't wish her dead . . . I just wished, well . . . well, I wished she wasn't there that night, sitting with you on the sofa . . . and that's all . . . that's all I wished. . . .'

That was all! In a flash, the judge grasped the whole picture and how it related to her garbled, breathless version of *The Monkey's Paw*. She believed it, the more so since her mother had been killed by a machine which had disfigured her.

Now he realized why Sanderson, the psychiatrist, had interrogated him in this very room a week ago, why he had insisted on analysing the relationship between him and his stepdaughter. Did he suspect there was some carnal relationship? From his sessions with Julie, had he concluded that she had been so much in love with her stepfather that she had wished her own mother to disappear?

He had even mentioned the Electra complex. A daughter jealous of her mother and willing her dead so that she could possess her father. And in this case, Joan went on and completed the girl's scheme. Julie had rubbed the monkey's paw and felt she had to pay for having her wish come true.

Sanderson evidently believed that everything Julie had done since had one overriding motive: expiation for the guilt she felt for her mother's death. She could not touch the compensation money, for that was tainted with her guilt; she had to earn her own money and what better way of paying the price of the monkey's paw than debasing herself with drugs and playing the night-club hostess.

He helped Julie to her feet and put his arms round her, feeling her convulsive sobbing against his chest. He did not attempt to argue her out of her belief in the confession she had made, or persuade her she was blameless.

'Julie darling, everything will come out right for us, you'll see,' he whispered in her ear.

Waiting until she had calmed down, he led her back along the corridor to the hospital door and handed her over to an orderly with whispered instructions to keep her under strict surveillance.

'I'll come and see you in a day or two,' he said, then kissed her.

He walked back to the hotel, his mind as grey as the overcast sky.

Was Julie merely a pawn in some sinister game that someone was playing to avenge themselves on him? He was convinced of one thing:
Whoever was plotting to ruin Julie or himself or both of them, did not
intend to kill him. At least not yet. If they had, those three thugs
would have finished him there and then.

XII

At mid-morning when he returned from the prison, Margaret
Denham had a message for him to ring his clerk in his Old Bailey
chambers. What was Gresham doing in his chambers, which were
locked up for the long recess? His clerk took the call, explaining that
someone had rung the Old Bailey that morning and asked for Judge
Knox's clerk in order to give him an important message. Gresham had
gone to the chambers to take the message when the man called back.

'And this message?'

'The man said, and I noted his words: "If Judge Knox wishes to find
out the truth about his daughter, he should go and see Connie
Blackwell. She lives in Egmont Street, Brixton".'

'Did he say who he was or who originated this message?'

'No. When I asked for his name and a phone number, he just
laughed.'

'Have you looked for this Miss Constance Blackwell in the directory?'

'I did, but she either doesn't have a phone or has an unlisted number
– though I would very much doubt that she's unlisted.'

'Oh, why?'

'Egmont Street is one of the more sordid streets near Brixton
Prison.'

'That's no good reason, Gresham. Ring directory enquiries and ask,
and if she is unlisted, the police will find the number for us.'

'What do you intend to do, Sir Laurence?'

'Go and see her, of course.'

'Would you like me to accompany you?'

'No. Nor would I like you to tell anybody about this call.'

When he informed Margaret Denham that he was catching the next London train and might have to spend several days in the capital, she said she had planned to drive there herself that afternoon. Why didn't she advance her trip by a few hours and give him a lift? He agreed and packed a suitcase with items for a stay of three days. In half an hour they were on the motorway and less than an hour's run from London.

She drove much faster than Joan and had surer hands.

'Did you ever own a car, Laurence?'

'Yes, when I was a barrister, I had second-hand souped-up sports cars like the Singer Le Mans and a Morgan, then when I took silk I treated myself to an Alfa Romeo. But when they made me a judge, I put up my car in case I was ever tempted to drive.'

In London, he asked her to stop in Baker Street, where he could find a cab, but she insisted on driving him to his flat since her appointment was not until that afternoon.

'But you'll have to eat lunch somewhere.'

'Oh, I won't bother with that,' she said. 'I'll buy a sandwich and coffee somewhere.'

'I was going to do the same thing – buy a sandwich and make coffee in my flat. Why don't you join me?'

Did he guess that she had been angling just for that? She said 'yes.' He directed her to Fleet Street and from that bustling thoroughfare into the cloistered calm of the Temple where he found her a parking-place near his flat.

She eyed the immaculate lawns, the flower-beds and ornamental trees with wonder. They walked through the Temple archway to the Feathers pub, haunt of lawyers and journalists, and bought their sandwiches. Then they followed the twisting alleys, lawns and cloistered courtyards to his flat.

'But it's another world,' she exclaimed, stopping to look at an ancient building. 'It's like stepping back two centuries.'

'Two?' he said. 'You mean five. Bits of masonry are still standing from the fourteenth century, and the practice of law hasn't changed much since. We're often taken to task for creating our own spurious little world and yet making new laws which govern everybody else.'

'It reminds me a bit of Oxford where you get that time-warp feeling, moving from the street into the colleges.'

'True,' he conceded. 'I moved from Oxford into the Temple here, and hardly felt the change.'

They climbed the fifty-two steps to his flat and he thanked God Mrs Evans had left it tidy.

Looking round, Margaret saw how simply he lived. His furniture was mostly good antique pieces; a Georgian lyre-legged table, an eighteenth-century writing desk, Chippendale dining-chairs and a Chesterfield sofa. Legacies of Joan's time, she imagined. Books were everywhere: encyclopedias and law books in tooled leather bindings, sets of Scott, Dickens and the Lake poets, but little modern fiction.

She noticed mementoes of his dead wife in pictures, both studio portraits and enlarged snapshots, and the tapestries she had worked for the chairs. Julie was there in pictures at every stage of her development. Margaret noted only one indulgence – the stereo compact disc and cassette system and the small library of classical recordings, all tabulated.

They ate their sandwiches and the judge made them coffee which they drank by the window overlooking the Temple gardens; she listened to him describing how he'd go there to read briefs at lunchtime, fearful of how he would plead them that same afternoon in the law courts or at the Central Criminal Court.

'I can't imagine you being afraid of much.'

'Oh, but I am. Only fools are without fear.'

She rose and poured them more coffee, remembering he was a one-lump man. When she sat down, she looked at him. 'Laurence, this woman you're going to meet in Brixton – aren't you scared to keep that sort of rendezvous after what happened at the Greensward?'

He hesitated. 'Yes, I'm scared,' he said.

'Then why go?'

'Simply because I'd be more afraid of living with myself if I didn't go. I owe it to Julie.'

'I don't like the thought of your being there on your own,' she said. 'Couldn't you take someone as a bodyguard, even Peter.'

He shook his head emphatically. 'That's another reason for going alone – with the police or a bodyguard accompanying me, I would never find out what really happened to Julie.'

He came downstairs to see her off. At the street entrance she turned. 'Laurence, will you ring me to tell me you're safe and well when you get back?'

'As soon as I return I'll call you.'

'Take care of yourself,' she said. Impulsively, she kissed him on the cheek, and before he could recover she had gone round the corner, leaving him still blushing at that kiss.

Gresham had not exaggerated. Sordid was the word. When his taxi dropped him in Brixton, he found himself in another world. Twenty-odd years ago he had known the district slightly as a young barrister visiting clients in Brixton jail half a mile away. Now, it had become part of multi-racial, multi-cultural, multi-coloured Britain. Black Africans and Caribbeans, Indians, Pakistanis, even Chinese jostled against him as he headed for Egmont Street. He should have known who Egmont was, but couldn't place him.

Nor the street. 'It's jes' behine th'stayshun,' a black man informed him. He avoided the street-market with its fly-blown fruit and vegetables, Asian spices and knick-knacks. How many pubs did he pass? A dozen or even more on that short walk. And betting-shops? Orwell's Prole Sector from 1984, only bleaker, more squalid.

Egmont Street was a small cul-de-sac cut off by the railway wall. In its fifty yards it had two pubs, a coin-laundry, one betting-shop. Against the wall, a dozen children were playing soccer with a small, rubber ball.

Judge Knox located the address his clerk had given him. A woman emerging from the dingy entrance directed him to the third floor and he climbed, breathing through his mouth to avoid the stench assailing his nostrils. On the third landing there were three doors. No names. He rapped on the middle one and a black woman opened it.

'Miss Constance Blackwell?' he said.

'Constance! Constance, is it?' She gave a gap-toothed grin, giggled, thumbed towards the left-hand door and said, 'She be all yours, man.'

When he knocked, the door was edged slightly apart and he discerned a white face.

'Miss Constance Blackwell?' he queried.

'Who wants 'er?'

'I have a message to come and see her.'

'A message. Who from?' She was scrutinizing him in the wedge of light spilling through her door on to the landing as if imagining he had come to possess her furniture or run her in.

'It was a telephone message advising me to come and see you.'

'Some geezer recommend me, that it?'

'Exactly.'

A chain rattled and the door opened and she beckoned him inside. 'Seein' as you're here, come in,' she whispered, then slammed the door shut behind him. 'Them black bastards count the flies through my door, they do,' she muttered.

His eye took in both her and her surroundings. Connie Blackwell he placed in her early thirties. Her bonde hair was teased out in a spiky halo, her face was powdered and daubed. She wore a flimsy, cutaway blouse and tight skirt that left nothing to the imagination. No prizes for guessing her trade, the judge thought.

She had been drinking beer. On the table stood a litre bottle of cheap ale and a half-full glass. A scarlet-tipped cigarette smoked in a saucer. Dishes lay piled up in the sink from lunch-time, probably from breakfast. Her colour TV was showing a race-meeting though she had doused the sound. What a contrast between this and Katie Gamble's luxury flat!

Connie Blackwell switched off the picture, lifted an early *Evening Standard* open at the racing-pages off the one easy-chair and said, 'Better take the weight off your legs. Them stairs!'

A detached spring twanged under him as he sat down. She took the hard-backed chair by the table. 'So you'd a message to come and see me, eh! What did this geezer trying to take the piss out of us tell you about me?'

'Nothing about you, madam,' the judge replied. 'He merely said that if I wanted to know the truth about my stepdaughter, Julie Armitage, I should come and see you.'

He was watching her face, which lay in profile against the murky light from the window.

This woman he knew! Somewhere, somehow he had met her. It was not only her face under its make-up mask that seemed familiar. Her attitude struck a chord; those small, head-tilting gestures, that way of running her thumbnail over her bottom lip, pushed out by her tongue. All that added up to some form of identity. But where, how, why and when? At the same time, he noticed she was glancing at him as though scanning her own memory.

'Julie Armitage . . . Julie Armitage. . . .' Her tobacco-stained index finger traced a zero on her forehead. 'Mister, somebody's havin' the both of us on. If I'd met a name like that, I'd put a face to it in less than that.' She snapped her fingers. Her thumb made another pass over her lip. 'This stepdaughter o' yours . . . she work this beat?' He shook his head. 'No, I can see she wouldn't, not with Blacks and Paks and the Chinks around here.'

'My daughter lives in Oxford.' That stopped her thumb and set her wondering. Judge Knox decided he would have to explain things. 'Perhaps I should tell you, madam, my name is Knox, Sir Laurence Knox.'

That hit her between the eyes and jerked her backwards in her chair with such force she nearly broke its back.

'Knox . . . you ain't His Honour Judge Knox?'

'Yes, I am.' He looked at her. 'Do you know me, and do I know you?'

' 'Course we know each other, though it's nearly eight years since I seen you and you were wearing your wig and red jacket.' She pulled at one or two blond tufts. 'You wouldn't know me now I've gone blond and 'ad a haircut.'

'So, you saw me in Southwark Crown Court about eight years ago,' Judge Knox prompted. 'What was the case that involved you and me?'

'The case?' Connie was almost rubbing the skin off her lower lip and looked as if something had seized up her mind. At last she said, 'Your Honour, you see . . . well, I can't tell you what . . . I mean, I can't tell you till we've seen Gus.'

'Who is Gus?'

'Gus Wilkins . . . we were wiv each other then . . . it was 'im fixed the whole thing . . . and I wish to God he never 'ad.' She halted again, pressing her lips together as through to remind herself to keep her mouth shut. 'Sorry, Your Honour . . . I 'ave to see Gus.'

'When can we do that?'

She glanced at the cheap quartz clock on the sideboard. 'He comes on in an hour's time, six o'clock . . . He's potman in the Liar in Uniform round the corner.'

'The Liar in Uniform?'

'It's a pub, the Lion and Unicorn.' She shrugged. 'It's what they think o' uniforms round here.'

As the judge was wondering what a potman was, she rose and filled an electric kettle. 'We can have a cuppa, Your Honour.' She gave him a yellow-toothed grin. 'Not every day I've a judge to tea.'

So black and strong was her brew that even diluted with milk its fumes cut his breath. Sipping it cautiously, he let her prattle on, and by piecing together the fragments she let slip, he concluded that she and Gus had appeared as defence witnesses in some case he had tried in his old court, Southwark Crown.

But at nearly eight years' remove and with hundreds of repetitive cases in between, how could he remember the one concerning this lady? He would have to wait until Gus illuminated his memory.

They walked the 200 yards to the Liar in Uniform, one of the sleaziest pubs in that squalid area. As murky inside as outside, it had a spit-and-sawdust bar and a larger saloon-bar with half a dozen tables and a dozen chairs; it had not seen paint for twenty or thirty years and the wooden partitions had a thick patina of grime; it also stank of spent tobacco smoke, stale beer and bodies. In his city suit and collar and tie, Judge Knox felt incongruously overdressed among the black and white customers in sweat shirts, jeans and Punjabi dress.

Connie went and fetched the judge a lemonade and also brought two vodkas and two beers; on her way back she beckoned with her head to a man in denim trousers and an old cardigan who was collecting the empty glasses. When he threaded between the tables and gave Connie a peck on the cheek, the judge saw that he was a bit older than Connie and had four days' growth of beard on his face.

'You know this gentleman, Gus?'

Gus peered at him in the dim light. 'Not as I can put a name to,' he muttered.

'It's His Honour, Judge Knox . . . you remember 'im.'

'Cor!' Gus exclaimed then drew back to peer with narrowed eyes at the judge's face. 'Cor!' he repeated. Watching this manoeuver, the judge noted Gus's pinpoint pupils in the dirty light and wondered how many heroin needle-marks he had under those frayed cardigan sleeves.

' 'Ave a drink, Gus.' Connie pointed to the vodka and beer.

Gus downed the vodka in one then gulped some of the beer, fixing the judge with those gimlet eyes in that blotchy red face. He turned to look at Connie. 'How'd he know where to find you?' he asked.

Connie explained that a man had phoned the judge giving her address and a message to go and see her about his stepdaughter, Julie Armitage. That was all. No other reason.

Gus pulled a small cigarette stub from his cardigan pocket, so small he had to watch his nose when he applied a match to it. He dragged on it. 'And you couldn't guess who it was phoned?' he said to Connie, who shook her head.

Gus pointed to the judge. 'You couldn't guess the bastard's after him, too?'

'You mean, Cliff?' Connie's thumb was going again. 'Even Cliff wouldn't try to do a judge, 'e wouldn't run that risk.'

'Wouldn't he, just?'

Cliff? Cliff? Where had the judge heard or seen that name before? Suddenly, it wrote itself in block letters across his mind, the phrase he had been seeking for the past week. 'For Chris' sake don't kill 'im or Cliff'll murder us.'

Gus was swivelling his chair round, slowly, his weak eyes tracking across the room.

'Who's to say he hasn't got somebody here tonight, watching us?'

'Who are you talking about?' the judge asked.

'Cliff Strang,' Connie said before Gus could stop her. 'You'd 'ave known 'im as Flint. Changed 'is name and everything else when 'e came out o' stir.' She turned to face Gus, who was glaring at her. 'Look, Gus, ain't no point in keeping it to ourselves any longer. We got to tell 'im.'

'I'm tied up here to closing-time.'

'How much do they pay you?' the judge put in.

'Twenty quid a night.'

'Gus!'

'Well, fifteen anyway with the perks.'

'I shall pay you twenty pounds if you can arrange to leave now.'

'I'll fix for somebody to take over.' Gus finished his beer, then went round both the saloon and the snug bars, picking up the empty glasses, voiding the ash-trays, swabbing up the spilled beer and fetching fresh drinks for customers, who rewarded him with a cigarette or the small change.

'You don't remember 'im at all, Your Honour?' When the judge shook his head, Connie said, 'No, you wouldn't. Them days Gus was a snappy dresser, good-lookin' and a good talker. But now he's snowed up to here.' She pointed above her head.

'Snowed?'

'Snow . . . coke . . . cocaine,' she whispered. 'That's all he works for here – enough to buy his daily fix.' She mimed the action of injecting the drug. 'Cliff hooked him on hash, then coke, and now he's going on to heroin, and that's curtains. But Cliff works that way.' She sipped her beer, wiping off the froth on her upper lip with her tongue-tip. 'He tried it with me, but I said No and kept saying No. But he still runs me.'

'Why do you let him run you?'

'Why? 'Cos he'd have me done in if I didn't kick back three-quarters of everything I make.' She sighed. 'Folk does anything to stay alive.' She shushed his question with a raised finger, flicking her eyes at a young Indian or Pakistani who had entered the pub. 'Watch 'im,' she hissed.

Having bought himself a lager, the well-dressed Indian sat down at a corner table, lit a cigarette with a match from a box which he tossed on the table, casually. He left half his beer untouched, nodded at the two Jamaicans at the table and sauntered out. One of the Jamaicans picked up the box.

'How the snowman makes his rounds and supplies 'is customers,' Connie whispered. She said Strang sometimes came to the Liar for a drink, but really to watch Gus picking up fag-ends and drinking the beer and spirit dregs. 'He gets a kick out o' that,' she said.

'But Gus can't be making money for this man, Strang,' the judge said.

'That ain't the name of 'is game, Your Honour. Cliff's paying us out for what we did to 'im. He knows Gus and me hate what we're doing. Knows we don't like Blacks and Paks and Indians, red, white or brown. But Gus and me 'as to serve them, like.'

Judge Knox was beginning to see part of the picture, although it still puzzled him why this man, Strang or Flint, wanted him to meet these two wretches. There had to be some link between them, himself, Julie and Strang, yet what it was he could not imagine. Evidently, it had something to do with a case at Southwark Crown Court, from what Connie had let drop.

Gus was talking to a Jamaican and had made a bargain with him, for he hooked his jacket off the peg and crossed the pub, lugging six cans of beer in one hand. 'We'll go to Connie's place,' he said. 'Mine's being used.'

'Gus, they'll raid you one o' these days,' Connie said, digging an elbow into his ribs. 'If they find your pals cutting and mainlining and sniffing coke and crack there, they'll shove you in stir and that'll finish you.'

At Egmont Street, she led them upstairs. Once in the flat she put the kettle on to make them tea. Gus disappeared down the small passage-way to the bathroom and she gazed after him, shaking her head. When he returned, his eyes were brighter and he had lost that droopy expression. He gulped the tea that Connie handed him, so hot it would have taken the roof off the judge's mouth. Then he broke open a can of beer and swigged that.

'Gus, we'd better come clean wiv His Honour.''

'You got the newspaper cuttings, ain't you? Show him them.'

Connie nodded and went through into the bedroom, to return carrying an old album with scuffed, dog-eared covers. Flipping over the pages of snapshots, she halted at several cuttings with yellowing edges folded into the album. She pushed them over the table to the judge.

As he unfolded the cuttings, brittle with age, he saw they were mainly from the local Brixton, Clapham, Bermondsey and Lambeth press, though there were snippets from national newspapers like the *Mail*, *Express* and *Telegraph*.

They all concerned a trial seven and a half years previously, over which he had presided. His official picture was there, though almost unrecognizable in the poor half-tone reproduction and in that full-bottomed wig he had worn for his swearing in as QC.

Their pictures appeared, too as the main prosecution witnesses: Miss Constance Blackwell, aged twenty-five, and James Augustus Wilkins, aged thirty-six. These, too, he could hardly identify with the blond strumpet sitting opposite him, or the weedy drug-addict peering over his shoulder.

'That's Strang, or Flint as he was then,' Connie said, placing a lacquered fingernail on another picture.

Derek Clifford Flint, 32, of Borough Road, Lambeth, the caption read. Accused of raping Constance Blackwell, shop-assistant, from Emery Street, Lambeth.

As the judge ran his eye down the accounts of the case, it came back to him in flashes. He recalled the smooth-faced, smooth-tongued, smoothly dressed man arguing and shouting from the witness box, even insulting the prosecution counsel and witnesses from the dock.

It was a rape case where consent had been pleaded, Flint's counsel contending that the lady in question had acceded to his client's advances and had even conferred her favours on him a dozen times before the alleged rape. So, where was the rape if she consented? There was no case, Flint's counsel affirmed. Another scene crossed the judge's mind – the tall, robust figure of the man, Flint, yelling his innocence as he was sentenced to ten years, then led downstairs.

It must have been an open-and-shut case, for the jury stayed out no more than twenty minutes and returned a unanimous verdict of guilty. As he read through the two days of the trial, he could see that the evidence given by Blackwell and Wilkins was damning, something he had hinted at in his summing-up.

No judge could have imposed anything but a severe sentence, since all the testimony pointed to the fact that Flint had not only raped

Constance Blackwell but had done so at knife-point in front of her boyfriend, James Augustus Wilkins, whom he had first beaten, then tied and gagged. Miss Blackwell had described in minute detail how she was forced to undress with a knife at her throat, then submit to Flint.

When he had finished reading the cuttings, the judge closed the album. 'Well, I remember something of the case, and it would seem to me now, as it did then, to have been a straightforward trial.'

'Straightforward,' Connie Blackwell said, giggling.

'Straight as a dog pissing in snow,' Gus whispered hoarsely. He had gone quiet, his head sagging as though the heroin effect was wearing off. 'It was fixed, Judge.'

'Fixed? What do you mean?'

'He means we set Flint up, like,' Connie put in. 'It was like this, see. Gus 'ere was running me and I was pulling in good money across the river in Westminster. I'd a car and a place in Lambeth to bring them back. Everything couldn't 'ave been better until Flint comes along and says it's 'is beat and tried to take me over. He gives Gus a licking in front of the pub crowd and said I was 'is and hands off, like. And that's when we decided to fix 'im. It was Gus's idea.'

'But he raped you, didn't he?'

'Noooh, it ain't what I'd call it since we'd had it off before.' Her lipstick left a scarlet ellipse on the teacup which gave the judge a queasy feeling about his own cup, as he looked at the unwashed dishes. 'Cliff didn't rape me, but said he'd fix my face if I didn't work for 'im instead of Gus.' She fell silent, sucking nervously on her cigarette. 'Well, he's done me since he came out o' stir – but not the way that got 'im put in stir.'

'So, how did you do this – go to the police and lodge a complaint? Was that it?'

She shook her head. 'There was this copper, a CID inspector who had it in for Cliff. It was him set it up. Told us what to do and what to say in court. Even togged me out in an off-the-peg suit to wear in the witness box. Gus got a new set of duds, too. We'd to look the part, the copper said. We got our story off like some stage act, didn't we, Gus. Talking real proper, weren't we, Gus?'

'Couple o' twits, we were,' Gus mumbled, his head still on his chest.

Putting all this and the pictures together, the judge could now see them both, even if seven and a half years had fudged their image slightly. Connie Blackwell, her dark hair swept back, face lightly made up, a sober grey two-piece suit over a white blouse. In that garb and with her small, precise voice, she would have cruised past St Peter. And Wilkins shaved, hair slicked back, in a decent suit looking very much the aggrieved party. No wonder the jury had brought in a guilty verdict and he had given Flint ten years.

Judge Knox could hardly bear to look at them both. His anger was threatening to boil over and it took an effort to check it.

'So you made everything and everybody, including truth and justice, look silly,' he got out at last.

'Sorry we had to fool you, Judge,' Gus said, still subdued.

'It was really the prosecutor and the jury you fooled first.'

'Yeah, maybe,' Gus retorted. 'But it was you sent him down. Ten years. Nobody ever thought he'd get a stretch in stir like that. It changed Flint a lot. Made him vicious and sour about everything and everybody. And Cliff fights dirty, always did and even worse now.'

'Tell him about the jury foreman, Gus.'

'How do we know it was Cliff had him done?'

'Oh, come off it, it was Cliff all right did 'im or 'ad 'im done, the foreman was sure.' She turned to the judge. 'Ran a grocer's in Bermondsey, did the foreman. Well, the shop was firebombed twice, then they mugged Jim so bad it paralysed him and he's in a chair.'

'I suppose you both knew you were committing perjury and perverting the course of justice?'

Connie gave a long sigh. 'You know how things are, Your Honour. Once you've made a statement you can't go back on it. We'd 'ave been done by the same cooper if we'd ratted on him.'

Yes, how well he realized that once the law machine ground into action, nothing short of the Apocalypse could arrest it. How many cases had he tried that should never have come to court and wouldn't have but for a corrupt or overzealous police officer, a negligent public prosecutor and mercenary barristers? But how could this ease his mind about this case where an obvious injustice had been committed?

And one that involved himself? 'Is there anything else you wish to tell me about the case?' he said, coldly.

Connie looked at Gus, who shook his head slowly, wearily. 'No, Your Honour, nothing.' She hesitated a moment, then said, 'What are you going to do – have us arrested.'

'I don't know.'

As he rose to go, Connie got out of her chair. 'Do you want Gus and me to go with you, Your Honour?'

'No thank you,' he said, feeling he could no longer stand the sight of either of them.

He blundered through the door she held open and groped down the three flights of stairs in the dark.

Outside, he stood for several minutes to collect his wits and find his bearings. A man had been sentenced to ten years in prison for a crime he did not commit. All right, he might argue it was the jury's fault, a defect in the judicial system, a crooked policeman and a gullible prosecutor. He had merely sentenced the man. But ten years! And the stigma of prison. Those thoughts made him feel sick.

Enough light remained in the sky for him to walk through these streets without fear of being mugged. Breathing the fill of his lungs even of this polluted, vitiated air might clear his head and give him room for reflection. He headed for Clapham and the tube station, marching quickly through the crowds and turning over and over in his head what he had read and heard.

What could and what should he do about it?

As one of Her Majesty's judges, he must redress the wrong he had done this man, Strang or Flint. Such evidence as he had just heard he must place before the Court of Appeal and request the Director of Public Prosecutions to indict Wilkins and Blackwell for perjury. Regardless of how it affected his career, he must obey his duty and follow his conscience. Truth and morality were, as he had often said, all or nothing concepts. It didn't matter that the man wronged was a villain himself.

Now he knew that this man, Strang, had pulled all the strings and he, the puppet, had twitched this way and that at his command ever since Judge Dawson had informed him about Julie's arrest.

Strang had settled scores with Blackwell and Wilkins and, it seemed, had even paid out the jury foreman; he had used and abused Julie and had ordered his, Knox's, mugging by those three young thugs. Now, what other punishment did he have in store for the judge who had sentenced him to ten years?

How glad and relieved he was that people were thick on the streets of Brixton at that evening hour. It gave him a more secure feeling. For, since the moment he had stepped out of his taxi, he had sensed that someone was following him. Yet he did not think Strang would choose even a deserted Brixton street or this particular moment to even scores with him.

Back in his flat, before he rang Margaret he looked at his answering machine. That afternoon, from habit – or perhaps from a sense of fatality – he had cleared the machine and switched it on.

Now he saw there was the expected message on it, timed at 8.45 p.m. Just five minutes after he had left Blackwell and Wilkins in the Egmont Street flat.

A toneless, grave voice – probably the one Gresham had heard – said:

'Judge Knox, if you want to know the other half of the truth you've just heard, come along to Pitt Street, Number Eleven, third floor. Nine o'clock tomorrow night.'

He caught the click as the handset slotted into place, then the machine hissed before it went dead.

XIII

Just before nine, a taxi dropped the judge at the entrance to Pitt Street which lay on the other side of New Bond Street from Hanover Square. A choice area of the West End. It was a short street, full of smart shops, a couple of office buildings and four blocks of expensive flats. Number Eleven had only ten occupants in luxury flats with their front rooms set back behind ample terraces. No doubt high-priced property was yet another of this villain's stratagems for legitimizing drug money, the judge reflected as he sought the interphone button opposite Strang's name.

For long hours the previous evening he had lain awake, wondering if he should at last bring in the police, or at least tell Barrett where he was going. Eventually he had decided, scared or not, to come alone. After all, it was his problem. He also reasoned that if Strang intended to kill him, no one could stop his hired thugs.

If this blackguard's idea was murder, he seemed altogether too clever to turn his plush flat into the crime scene. No, he would handle it with much more subtlety, with his brand of sadism and style. By the same reasoning, the judge had dismissed the idea of taking the revolver the City police had given him for his protection when he tried IRA terrorists or members of the mafia.

No one answered his ring, but the front door burred and opened at his pressure. A lift in the foyer took him up three floors. There was one door only on the landing, which indicated that the flats were built on split levels. He thumbed the bell.

A few seconds later the door opened, a figure appeared and a voice said, 'You took a long time to get here, Judge, didn't you. Nearly eight years. Come in.'

In the concealed lighting of the flat, he saw that Strang was a big man, fully two inches taller than himself. And he was just short of six feet tall in his socks. Elegantly dressed, he wore a Bond Street mohair suit and a silk shirt and tie, obviously tailored for him. He sported a gold tie-pin, and a gold ring on the left hand little finger. Meeting him socially or passing him in the street, the judge would have assumed he was a successful businessman, a member of one of the liberal professions or, at worst, a yuppie who had made his pile.

'Now you know I've waited nearly eight years for this moment,' Strang said, pointing the judge to a sofa, one of a pair bracketing a glass coffee table.

Judge Knox sat down, aware that Strang was watching him in the way a boxer or a fencer might observe his opponent in the initial round, inching his eyes over his face.

'Does my face fit?' Strang asked in that cool, neutral tone.

'With certain adjustments, yes,' the judge replied. 'But then you were a man called Flint, not so well-groomed and sitting between two constables in the dock at Southwark Crown Court. Also, if I remember rightly, you had dark hair.'

'Right on all counts, m'lud,' Strang said, softly, running a hand over his blond hair. 'Eight years makes a difference. Especially in jails like Wandsworth and Pentonville. You learn little tricks, like changing your hair, your name, your garb to cover your tracks. . . .'

'Well, that you've managed brilliantly – not even Scotland Yard's Criminal Records Office could find you.'

Something like a sardonic chuckle arose in Strang's throat. Levering himself up from the other sofa and strolling over to a painting hanging on the wall, he nudged it aside, opened a small safe behind it and pulled out a folder, which he threw on the coffee-table.

'That's your CRO file with the rape story you had your police search for.' He shrugged. 'How did I get it, you wonder? I bought it from a copper, and I also bought another copper to erase my name from the Yard computer.' Lifting an onyx cigarette-box, he extended it to the judge, who shook his head. Strang took a cigarette, lit it and watched the smoke spiral slowly upwards in the air-conditioned room.

'Does that knock you back, Your Honour? Haven't you met lowly-paid detective-constables with two of everything – houses, cars, mistresses, TVs, DVDs, videos and other Japanese electronic toys? Or their bosses, specialists in crime, who lift their winnings and are absent-minded about their losses at my betting-shops and live high, spending ten times their yearly screw on booze, high-priced whores and the other goodies life offers?'

He rose and shrugged then crossed to the drinks cabinet where a bottle of champagne sat in an ice bucket. He wrapped it in a napkin, popped the cork and poured two glasses, bringing them and the bucket over to the table where he had already laid out a salver with caviar and smoked-salmon savouries on it.

'It isn't poisoned,' he murmured, handing the judge a glass.

Judge Knox accepted and sipped the frothy liquor, glancing round the living-room. It was large and led to a corridor off which lay the bedrooms, bathroom and kitchen, he assumed. Everything breathed opulence; the expensive reproductions and lithographs on the walls, the period furniture, the Persian and Turkish carpets on the parquet floor, the diffused lighting behind the expanse of brocade curtains at windows separating the room from the terrace.

His eye returned to two curious objects which stood on the coffee-table before them. At first glance, they seemed to be modern sculptures done in glass coloured bluish-green, reddish-violet, ruby, agate and opal. Dissimilar in every way, one resembled an armless boy sitting on a plinth, the other looking more like a miniature Christmas tree grow-ing out of a piece of red rock. Spectral light filtered through them from bulbs embedded in the glass and fixed to the ebony base.

'Flint-glass,' Strang said, following the judge's gaze. 'Flint, like who I was.' He grinned. 'Maybe that's why I bought them. They tell me they're the bits of flint-glass left in the furnace after they make coloured optical glass. They're much the same way as they were broken out, sharp edges and all.'

'Quite striking,' said the judge.

'Yeah. Before I was old enough to realize that nobody ever made their fortune by working, I did a stint in a glass-works making that sort of glass.' He cast a hand at the rest of the living-room. 'They're the only things I bought, apart from the TV and video equipment. I bought all the rest with the flat as a job lot from a businessman on his uppers.' He gave a mocking laugh. 'That's another thing you learn in stir – cash'll buy anything, and anybody.'

Judge Knox held up a hand at the drink he proffered. 'You wanted me to see Miss Blackwell and Mr Wilkins,' he said. 'I saw them last night.'

'I know.' Strang nodded. 'So, now you know the story and you've seen how a couple of rats like those two live.' His face went into a hard set as he leaned over to grind out his cigarette stub in the onyx ashtray. 'I could have them tortured and rubbed out tonight or tomorrow just by picking up the phone – but if I did that, I wouldn't see them squirm in their little black hole, would I? Death's too good for their kind, and if I killed off my real enemies I'd have nobody to hate.' His voice had become a snarl.

'I'm sorry your term of imprisonment affected you so badly,' the judge murmured, knowing such a comment would mean nothing to this man. From what he had seen of his treatment of Julie, his revenge on Blackwell, Wilkins and the jury foreman, from what he had learned about him, from the man's attitude now, he realized prison had warped him to the point where the mainspring of his life was vengeance. Cold, calculating vengeance.

That perverse motive had probably spurred him to make money quickly through drug-dealing and gambling-clubs to settle his psychopathic grudge against anyone who had been involved in his trial.

Indeed, Strang ignored him and his remark. He rose and went to the Georgian bookcase which reached from the floor almost to the high ceiling of the flat. Opening the base to reveal a large-screen TV set, he returned holding half a dozen video cassettes and the remote control apparatus for the TV and video recorder. He left the cassettes and the apparatus on the table, filled his champagne-glass and used a swizzle-stick to froth off most of the gas before sipping the liquor. He had obviously prepared the event scrupulously and meant to savour every moment of it.

'Nice pad, isn't it?' he said, his hand and the champagne-glass describing an arc to embrace the room. When the judge made no reply, he went on, 'Nicer than the pad you gave me in Pentonville and Wandsworth jails.'

'Mr Strang, a jury of twelve men and women found you guilty and my duty was to pass sentence on the facts we had.'

'Facts?' he sneered. 'Those two bastards and a bent detective called Symmons set me up and you put me away for ten years. I kept a clean snout and got a third off. It still left two thousand four hundred and thirty-five days. Ever had a day without meat or drink, m'lud? That's how long those days were.'

Strang took a gold pen from his pocket and scrawled the figures upside down on his CRO file so that the judge could read them off. 'I ticked them off, day by day, the two leap-year days as well. And I cursed you and those two rats and the jury foreman every day of the two thousand four hundred and thirty-five I did. And I vowed that, if I did nothing else with my life, I'd make you all pay back those days when I came out. That's what stir does to you as well.'

'I'm sorry all this happened, Mr Strang, and you've proved to me there was an error of judgment. So, why don't you seek redress through the courts which erred in the first place.'

'You're joking, Judge.'

'On the contrary, I'm deadly serious. You have enough evidence to go before the appeal court, accuse Blackwell and Wilkins of perjury and clear your name. They may even pay you compensation for wrongful imprisonment.'

'I've cleared my name, Judge. My own way.' He picked up the CRO file to make the point clear, then he shook his head, sourly. 'If I did appeal and win, which isn't likely with characters like you making the decisions, what'll they do – hand me no more compensation than I make in one day and send me home?' His hand whitened as it tightened round the champagne-glass as though he meant to crush it; his other fist he banged on the glass table, setting the ice-bucket and the cassettes rattling. 'I'll take my compensation my own way as well.'

'Then you risk falling foul of the law again.'

'Not the way I operate. The law doesn't touch the big players. Ask them in Oxford. Too many heads would roll if the law started meddling.' He refilled his champagne-glass and lit another cigarette with the mechanical precision that the judge had remarked in everything he did. Even his speech seemed robotic.

This man reminded Judge Knox of a triple murderer he had tried and sentenced to life imprisonment, who killed for money which he squandered on whores. Same flat, remorseless voice. Same automatic actions. Same immobile face. Probably the same heartless attitude to women, who were there merely to be used and abused for his financial and sexual appetites and discarded like his spent cigarette stubs. No sign in this flat of a woman's presence or hand.

'If I fell, I'd take a good dozen top coppers with me,' Strang was saying. 'Yeah, and maybe one of Her Majesty's eminent High Court judges.' He lifted his glass, sardonically. 'Here's to ermine and horsehair.'

'So, you invited me here to blackmail me.'

'Tut, tut, m'lud. Not one of your better leading questions. You know why I invited you, since you picked up most of the clues I left lying under your feet, even if I had to give you a hand now and again, and a small working-over. You know very well we have to discuss the future – Julie's and yours.'

'What have you got to do with our future?'

'Well, I take it you want to stay where you are, at the Old Bailey. And believe me, Judge, my friends and I would like you to stay there, too.'

'I fail to see that my future or where I exercise my profession is any concern of yours,' Judge Knox said, though now he was aware of why this man had set the traps for him that he was about to spring.

'But it does concern me, Judge. Indeed, it's very important for me that you're in the right job.'

Picking up the remote control apparatus, Strang fiddled with it and the judge noticed the TV set come alight. A blur of incoherent images streaked across the screen. Strang switched off the lights in the two flint-glass sculptures to heighten the picture contrast.

'Sorry about the picture quality, but they're candid camera shots, where the subject doesn't know she's performing,' he said.

It was Julie, almost naked, sitting on a bath-rim. A sort of tourniquet was cuffed round her left upper arm. There was a syringe in her right hand. Judge Knox could scarcely bear to look as she rubbed up a vein in her elbow crook and plunged the needle into it with a little 'ah' of pain as it pierced the vein and she pressed the piston to send the drug into her bloodstream.

He felt sick. Waves of nausea were rising from his stomach, lapping over his chest and forming a hard ball in his throat that threatened to choke him. Thank God this paranoiac, this sadist had dimmed the lights and could not see his distress. Raising his hand slowly, he unbuttoned his collar and sucked in air to the bottom of his lungs. His heartbeat was pulsing and throbbing rapidly in his throat and head.

Another sequence appeared: Julie in a bedroom with another girl, both of them injecting each other. A man who looked like an Indian arrived and the three of them were filmed cooking up and injecting heroin.

Judge Knox could not look any longer. It was too painful. 'Stop it,' he croaked. 'Stop it.'

'Yeah, I know how you feel,' the colourless voice said. 'There are dozens of different poses in the cassettes, miles of them – but when you've seen one you get the general idea.' He pressed a button and the screen went blank, 'What do you think of them, Judge?'

'I think you're a black-hearted villain, Strang,' the judge said, fighting to quell his urge to vomit. 'You took an innocent girl and turned her into a drug-addict merely to take your revenge on me.'

'The sins of the father. . . .'

'Have nothing to do with my stepdaughter whose life you've tried to ruin.'

'Tried!' He uttered the word with a sneer on his face. 'Your little bitch of a daughter is anything but innocent – and she's hooked up to here.' He tapped the crown of his head. 'When she comes out of jail, she'll be round here in a couple of days for a new fix.'

'Julie will never do that. She's cured.'

'She'll be the only one I've ever met, then,' Strang said. 'But if she doesn't come back begging for her fix by herself and looking to be screwed by anybody and everybody, we'll be there to help her.'

'In that case, I will see the law prevents you.'

'Your law isn't going to stop anybody.' Strang turned those hard, bleached-blue eyes of his on him. 'Who says I had anything to do with selling the little bitch the drug in the first place, or taking all these dirty pictures?' He thumbed at the pile of cassettes. 'Who's to say I didn't buy these from somebody just for the fun of looking at them?'

'So, you mean to blackmail me into buying back these cassettes, is that your game?'

'Blackmail? It's a word I dislike. Let's say I bought these cassettes and I'm offering them to you rather than sell them elsewhere to protect your interests. If I sold them to somebody who didn't have your interests at heart, you'd have to resign from the bench, wouldn't you? And we'd all be unhappy.' As the judge remained silent, Strang went on, 'Let's look at it as just a transaction like any other, providing you're willing to co-operate.'

'It's still blackmail, an indictable offence and one to which I can never be a party, and you know it.'

'Oh, don't let's get het up about a word – let's say I've got something you want to buy, put it that way if you like.' He picked up several cashew nuts from a dish and flicked them one by one, expertly, into his mouth, chewing them while regarding the judge with a cynical smile on his face.

'I've been reading up on you, Judge. You're a rich man. What are you drawing down – well over £100,000 a year. You're single, a low spender with a low profile. Your Campden Hill house fetched you half a million. And what did they pay you for your wife's accidental death – another half-million wasn't it?' He tossed a few more nuts into his mouth and chewed on them, contemplatively, before aiming a finger at the cassettes on the table. 'You could afford to pay, say, two hundred thousand pounds for a couple of these.'

Judge Knox tried staring him out, but those ice-blue eyes did not flinch. Pay this man even ten pounds for one of these cassettes and it would be the start of a long torment which would leave him even more debased than Blackwell, the prostitute, or Wilkins, the potman, more in hock to this man than they or Julie had ever been.

He might retain his place on the bench, but as Strang's lackey, handing down justice tempered by this villain's demands, and subservient to him and his criminal gang. Strang would bleed him white. Even if he retired, Strang would blackmail him for his pension and gloat over his misery just as he went to gloat over the wretched existence he had created for Wilkins and Blackwell.

What a mistake it had been not to put his own trust in the law and ask the police to deal with Strang and his whole brood of thugs and racketeers! Pride and ambition had caused him to err. To save his name and his career he had acted alone and stumbled blindly into every elephant-trap this vile creature had dug before him. At all costs, he must preserve his calm.

'Not a penny,' he said.

'But Judge, you haven't begun to see what I have to offer you for your money,' Strang said in a mock plaintive voice. He pointed to the pile of cassettes.

Without waiting for the judge's reaction, he picked up the remote-control handset and pressed two buttons, stopping the second at the right number after the blur of colour on the TV screen.

When the picture stabilized and started running normally, the judge sat up, stiff and erect, as though someone had driven a stake through his heart.

Like a rabbit confronted by a stoat, his mind and senses had frozen. To look, he knew was fatal. Yet, he could not help himself. Flee, just flee. Anywhere. Blindly. But just flee, he tried to order himself. How could he? That horror in the corner showing those odious pictures acted like a curare-dart or nerve-gas on him. He was hypnotized, paralysed, petrified by what he saw: Julie and Strang wrestling and tussling with each other in every conceivable sexual posture.

Through his mental turmoil, he heard that smooth, bland voice saying, 'I had to rape her first, but she came to enjoy it – like the drugs.'

Strang had run the tape forward several sequences. Now, he saw Julie in a dozen orgiastic embraces with different men. Mouth open, breathing hard and fast, uttering small cries. Whimpering at times. Lying on her belly, or sitting astride Africans, Jamaicans, Indians and even Chinese. All on a double bed like the one in Connie Blackwell's squalid flat.

And he, who had never seen his father or mother naked, had to watch Julie in every sexual position that he had imagined from his bench experience. And some he could never have imagined. Whoever had taken these sickening pictures left nothing to the imagination. Focusing on a face between her legs, dwelling on the penis she was taking in her mouth. Sometimes, the camera caught her face in a tortured grimace and once or twice she cried out in pain under a thrusting body.

He felt her pain himself, felt like crying it out aloud. But he suppressed that impulse, converting it into hatred against the evil perverts who had plotted this revenge on someone as innocent as Julie.

Julie, the baby he had adopted and reared and loved through all her stages. Child, schoolgirl, adolescent. Watching this sordid, nauseating cinema, he would have felt revulsion even as an impartial spectator. But watching his own kin! It was the worst form of torture. A pulse hammered in his head. He thought: What would Joan have felt? Or Jeffrey, her natural father? God be thanked, they were both dead.

These dreadful images would live in his mind for the rest of his life.

'Good, aren't they, Judge? Well worth what I'm asking.'

The judge looked at the pervert who had plotted all this, who had used his money, cocaine and heroin to corrupt his daughter into debasing and defiling herself as a common prostitute and an addict, who had shamed her to the point where she wanted to kill herself – Strang was watching these loathsome pictures with no sign of repugnance, indeed with hardly any emotion at all.

He must stop those obscene, revolting pictures of Julie debasing herself. He must stop this evil sadist from gloating about what he had done. He must stop this paranoiac from thinking that he, a High Court judge, was for sale.

Those thoughts expanded in the judge's mind, filling it to the point where something snapped inside it and, with that, his self-control.

Judge Knox seized the first thing that came to hand, one of the flint-glass sculptures from the table. He tore it free of its flex and hurled it with all his force at the TV set, hitting the screen. He saw the set burst into fragments, scattering glass everywhere. He heard the tube implode with a loud bang that obliterated everything else in his mind.

Afterwards Judge Knox had no recollection of anything else he did in the following minutes. No recall of the fact that he had picked up the second glass lamp and used it as a bludgeon to beat Strang to death.

In the minutes immediately after his brainstorm – and long afterwards – he tried to piece together his actions. But they seemed lost for good. His mad frenzy, his rage to kill had erased that whole episode from his mind.

When his madness abated, his senses began to return and his mind to clear. He noted the various clues to what had happened.

Strang was lying on the sofa, legs and arms limp, spread-eagled. His scalp had been ripped open, his face was mashed almost beyond recognition and oozing the blood which covered it. His mouth was still twisted into something like a cruel smile.

Without awareness, the judge had overturned the glass table and scattered the cassettes, the ice-bucket and bottle, the salver with its nuts and savouries, the CRO file that Strang had shown him.

Champagne still frothed on the carpet.

A sharp pain broke through his confusion and he looked at his right hand; it was dripping blood from a deep gash where he had gripped the sharp edge of the flint-glass figure of the armless boy.

For several minutes, the judge sat on the sofa binding a handkerchief round his injured hand to stanch the blood flow. Reflecting.

He had committed murder, the most heinous crime in the calendar; he, who had rebuked, condemned, punished so many murderers, had flouted every principle he had lived by and murdered a man.

Well, he would take his punishment.

His lifetime of training had taught him that nothing must be touched now that the deed was done. Nothing, that was, except the video-cassettes. They must be destroyed. Even though they were his motive for murdering Strang. Even though they would undoubtedly influence the jury in his favour. No, he would destroy them without a qualm, without considering that this would implicate him more deeply.

He noted the time, five past ten, at which he had killed Strang, then went to the bathroom to wash his gashed hand under cold water. In the medicine cabinet he found a strip of adhesive dressing with which he covered the open wound.

When he rang Barrett at his home, the barrister had just returned from his squash club.

'I have bad news for you, Barrett. I have just murdered someone.'

Dead silence. 'Barrett, are you still there?' he said.

'Yes, Judge, I'm here.' Barrett seemed to be talking through a mouthful of something, though it might have been confusion clogging his tongue. Judge Knox heard him suck in a long breath before he said, 'Sorry, Judge, but could you repeat what you've just told me?'

'I have just murdered somebody.'

'Murdered? Who?'

'Never mind who. I am in a third-floor flat at Number Eleven Pitt Street, Mayfair. Take a note. I would be grateful if you could get here as quickly as possible and accompany me to the police station where I shall have to make a sworn statement. How long will it take you?'

'About an hour and a half, two hours at the most.'

'As quickly as you can.'

Replacing the handset, the judge searched Strang's pockets and found his flat-keys. He then began a systematic search of drawers, bookshelves, the bedroom wardrobe and other corners, looking for cassettes. Satisfied that there were none, he picked up the five from the floor and the one from the TV-set video.

In the kitchen he unearthed a plastic sack and placed the cassettes inside it, then took the lift down to the entrance hall. He tried all the keys until he identified the one which opened the main door, just in case he locked himself out.

In Bond Street, they had put their rubbish out for the night, piled in sacks and cartons against shop-fronts or placed in plastic bins. He chose a plastic bin and stuffed the cassettes under a heap of small cartons and plastic bottles. He hoped they would crush or incinerate the lot.

Back in Strang's flat, he sat and calmly wrote out his statement on a sheet of the victim's notepaper from which he cut the name and address. He wrote:

I, Sir Laurence Knox, judge of Her Majesty's High Court, aged fifty-three, of 15, Middle Temple Alley, state that I have unwittingly murdered Derek Clifford Strang of 11, Pitt Street, Mayfair.

That said it all. He dated and signed the statement, looked up the number of West End Central police station, then sat back on the sofa, closing his eyes to shut out the sight of Strang's mutilated head.

An hour later Barrett buzzed him from downstairs. The judge let him into the flat. His eyes darted from the body to the overturned table and the broken TV set; his face went a shade whiter and he looked visibly shaken.

'What possessed you, Judge?'

'The man was trying to blackmail me.'

'Through Julie?'

'Yes – but it's a long story and we're already late in informing the police.' He handed Barrett a paper slip with the phone number. 'You'd better ring them, but don't tell them who I am or they won't believe you.'

'What do you mean, they won't believe me?'

'I mean, English judges do not commit murder, and the police know that.'

Barrett dialled the number, explaining who he was, and spoke to a detective-sergeant who ordered him to wait there and leave everything untouched until he and his chief arrived.

While they waited, the judge handed Barrett the Criminal Records Office file on Strang, instructing him to put it in his briefcase and say nothing; he then passed him the statement he had written.

'But Judge, this is tantamount to a confession of murder and a plea of guilty,' Barrett said, almost choking on the words.

'It is. I intended it to be a confession of murder since I have indeed committed murder.'

'But this paper will get you twenty years in jail, at least. Even with remission you'll be an old man when you come out.'

'Barrett, I know what I am doing and I am fully aware of the consequences.'

A buzz on the interphone silenced them. A couple of minutes later, two detectives entered. Judge Knox introduced himself, and when the two detectives had verified his identity, they introduced themselves as Chief Superintendent Pritchard and Detective-Sergeant Fay. They kept the judge's Old Bailey security pass. Barrett identified himself with a driving licence.

'Of course you know, Sir Laurence,' Pritchard began, 'you are not obliged to say anything unless you wish to do so, but what you say. . . .'

'. . . will be taken down in writing and may be given in evidence,' the judge said, completing the formula. He handed the man his statement and said, 'Here is what I have said and I do not intend to make any other statement, orally or in writing, at this stage. You have there enough evidence to charge me with murder.'

'Sir Laurence, may I ask you one thing – have you touched anything?'

'I have said all I am going to say at this stage,' the judge replied.

A police car took him and Barrett to West End Central police station, a couple of minutes away. There, the judge was charged with murder, then found a comfortable cell in keeping with a man of his judicial standing.

BOOK II

The Trial

I

At West End Central, they treated him as a privileged guest rather than someone accused of murder. If Judge Knox was often unpopular with the public and the mass-media, the police respected him and way he spurned the soft line adopted by many of his colleagues who courted publicity. A police doctor placed a dozen stitches in his gashed hand and gave him a sedative against the pain. He slept well, better than at any time in the past fortnight.

When Barrett arrived from his hotel at nine o'clock, he was astonished to discover the judge, showered and shaved, eating a good breakfast delivered from the police canteen. He had already done *The Times* crossword and was looking at the *Telegraph* and the *Independent*.

'Not a line in any of them,' Barrett said, 'and I've been through the *Sun, Mail, Express, Mirror*, the lot.'

'Anyway, they would only have been able to give my name and the charge, when I have been charged.'

'Only!' Barrett gasped. 'Just think of the screaming headlines that it *will* make when they bring you up at Bow Street this morning.'

'Have you had breakfast?'

'A small bite at my hotel,' Barrett said. 'But I'll have some coffee and toast if you can spare them.'

'Help yourself.'

Barrett sat down on the unmade bed and attacked the judge's breakfast. He confirmed what the judge had guessed would happen. His statement, and a summary of the evidence gathered at the flat had already gone to the Director of Public Prosecutions. Since it concerned an eminent High Court judge, the DPP had referred everything to the Attorney-General, his head of service, for his perusal.

'And of course, John Spencer-Smith is already licking his lips and will probably insist on the case being prosecuted, if not for its publicity, then just to do me down.'

'He's no friend, then?'

'If we still hanged by the neck he'd come and tie the noose himself.'

'Like that,' Barrett said. 'It goes without saying I shall apply for bail.'

'You can apply, but Spencer-Smith will have the police oppose on the grounds they have other enquiries to make, and I might try to influence witnesses.'

'He wouldn't dare.'

'Wouldn't he just?' Judge Knox layered butter on a piece of toast and spooned marmalade on it. 'Anyway, I don't want bail. Three weeks or a month in peace and quiet to prepare Julie's case and what there will be of my own is what I need. Whereas, if they let me out I shall be badgered and hounded by the press, radio, TV and God knows who else.'

'But where will they keep you?'

'That's their problem, but Brixton is where the hard cases and the Old Bailey cases go.'

'But you're not a hard case and Brixton's a rough jail.' Barrett shook his head. 'Surely they can't put you in among prisoners you might have sent down. They'd lynch you in five minutes.'

'That would solve many of their worries.'

'Another thing, who's going to judge you?'

Judge Knox shrugged as he ate another mouthful of toast and washed it down with coffee. 'I don't know and neither do they. They've got to find somebody a bit higher than a Crown Court judge, and since I know the whole bench of High Court and Appeal Court judges, I wouldn't know whom they'll pick.'

'You'll need somebody with the tongue of Demosthenes to defend you if the Attorney-General is prosecuting.'

'I have my defence lawyer.'

'Oh! May I ask whom?'

'You.'

'Me!' Barrett caught the coffee spraying out of his mouth on his handkerchief.

'Me! But I'm only a junior and Spencer-Smith will gobble me whole then spit me out on the Old Bailey floor.' He shook his head emphatically. 'Anyway, the Bar Council wouldn't agree and, with the evidence you've left in that flat and your statement, it'll take a couple of QCs with two juniors to hold their hands to save you from a life sentence.'

Judge Knox put down his newspaper and coffee-cup and fixed Barrett with that stare which the young barrister knew meant his objections were overruled.

'Barrett, as a former Queen's Counsel of ten years' standing and as a judge with twelve years on the bench, let me enlighten you – a QC is no more than a junior with good connections, a silk gown instead of a stuff one, a blue bag for his briefs instead of a red one and a full-bottomed wig he wears only on ceremonial occasions. In point of intelligence and talent, there is often little or no difference. Another thing, I don't much care for most QCs and it's reciprocal. Now, you're bright and you have enough character to stand up to an attorney-general and a judge as you've proved to me. So, I want you to defend me.'

Barrett got up and walked to the cell window, small, barred and above even his tall head. It was half-open and he filled his lungs with the cool, fresh air from the courtyard. He could imagine himself in the Old Bailey before the world's press, tangling with the country's fore-most lawyer aided by a couple of QCs and half a dozen juniors, and an intransigent, hostile judge.

It would be slaughter. Flyweight against heavyweight. Knock-out in round one. Even the thought filled his mouth with bile mixed with what was left of the taste of coffee, toast and marmalade. His career, maybe his whole life would be put on the line. And for what? A crusty old reprobate who'd get his come-uppance from the law he revered. For nobody, nobody on earth could doubt his guilt. He, Barrett, would be on a hiding to nothing, nothing.

'Well, Barrett, are you willing to help me?'

'Help you?' he repeated, dubiously.

'To take my case as well as Julie's?'

'I don't know.' He shook his head. 'If you think I can. . . .'

'I know you can. Now, what do you say?'

Barrett hesitated for another moment or two. 'All right, Judge,' he said. 'But on one condition.'

'Your condition?'

'That I write and speak my own lines – that I'm not just a dummy reciting your script.'

'You have my word on that. We shall comport ourselves like any good barrister and reasonable client – that is, we shall conjugate our talents and act in concert towards the desired end. Now sit down and finish this excellent toast and coffee.'

'No thanks, Judge.'

Judge Knox looked askance at him, wondering what had happened to that crooked, compulsive mouth to shut it against anything comestible. 'Anything wrong, Barrett?'

'I was thinking of the plea, Judge. We'll have to enter a plea this morning before the Bow Street magistrate. How do we plead?'

'Guilty, of course.'

'But why plead guilty?'

'Because I am guilty and because any jury will find me guilty because I am considered a modern Judge Jeffreys and because my peers will know that any other verdict would provoke the public conclusion that the judges were looking after their own.'

'You sure there isn't another reason?'

'What other reason?'

'Well, a guilty plea means there won't be questions asked about why you killed Strang and what happened in that flat last night.' Barrett again rose and walked to the cell window to suck in air several times before turning to the judge. 'You're pleading guilty to save Julie, aren't you?'

'I'm sorry if it seems that way to you,' the judge replied, a cutting edge to his words.

'Look, Judge, if I'm going to defend you I must know the truth. Strang was blackmailing you on your own admission. What could he be blackmailing you for, except something Julie had done – drug-taking, prostitution, drug-pushing, something like that?'

'Barrett, I will not have my daughter's name dragged into this case or sullied in any way, do you hear?'

Barrett raised an admonitory hand. 'Keep your voice down, Judge. The screws.'

'Screws?'

Barrett thumbed towards the policemen guarding the cells, and the judge dismissed his objection with a wave of his hand. 'Let them listen; their hearsay evidence would never stand up. What were you saying?'

'I was about to say I'm sorry, but you must find someone else to plead for you if you are unwilling to trust me with the facts. If you like, I shall find a solicitor to represent you this morning in court which will give you time to think of appointing others to defend you.'

He picked up his briefcase, snapped it shut and had turned to take his leave when the judge put a hand on his shoulder.

'Sit down, Barrett,' he said, very softly, pushing him into the one chair and sitting on the bed himself. 'You know, when Julie asked me to seek you out and request you to defend her, she pleaded with me not to pull my rank on you, and I'm afraid I've done nothing but that from the outset of this whole affair. If I have upstaged you or behaved towards you with condescension or discourtesy, I humbly beg your forgiveness.'

Judge Knox perceived that he had embarrassed the young lawyer. He rose and soft-footed to the cell door to see if one of the policemen was on duty. Reassured that they were alone, he beckoned Barrett to come and sit beside him on the bed.

There and then, he recounted everything he had kept to himself about his enquiries; what he had drawn out of Katie Gamble and the girl in the Greensward; how, two nights previously, Strang had steered him towards Blackwell and Wilkins and what that pair had divulged about their betrayal of Strang and the whole justice system.

'So it was they who got Strang – or Flint as he's called in the CRO file – his ten years in Pentonville.'

'And, of course, I sentenced him.'

Judge Knox finished by relating everything he could remember about that hour in the Pitt Street flat; how Strang had attempted to blackmail him by showing those revolting pictures of Julie injecting herself with drugs, then prostituting herself, presumably to earn the money to satisfy the heroin craving that the monster had bred in her.

'It was too much for me to watch Joan's daughter, Jeffrey Armitage's daughter and my daughter in those disgusting situations with that man gloating over them.'

Barrett realized that the judge's head had sagged and he was sobbing quietly. Putting an arm round him, the barrister reached into a pocket for a handkerchief which he handed the judge who wiped his eyes and blew into it.

'Judge,' he said, 'I don't want to upset you any further, but what did you do with those video-cassettes?'

'I destroyed them,' the judge said, still sniffing. 'Oh, I realized it was legally and morally wrong to destroy evidence, but nobody, not even Julie herself should see those obscene pictures.'

'Didn't you realize, too, you were throwing away any chance of escaping with an acquittal or a light sentence which we might have obtained by pleading great provocation.'

'Of course I did. And if those cassettes cost me the remainder of my life, I would consider it a bargain.'

Barrett punched his left palm with his fist. 'But we're going to fight, aren't we? You're going to plead not guilty to murder and the manslaughter charge they'll throw at you as well.'

Judge Knox lifted his head and looked at Barrett, then nodded. 'All right, Peter,' he said, using the barrister's given name for the first time. 'But first things first. You must stop thinking of me as a judge. I ceased to consider myself a judge when I bludgeoned that villain to death.

Even if they acquit me, I shall resign from the bench.

'And if they find me guilty, which is more than highly probable, they shall unwig, unfrock, unhouse, unpension, undo me completely before installing me in the high-security wing of their roughest prison. So, I'm just Sir Laurence until they remove the Sir, which you can drop anyway. Call me Laurence. I'd like that in any case.'

'But no talk of resignation until after the verdict?'

'If that is how you wish it.'

'You won't change your mind about bail?'

'No, I'm better off lying low wherever they put me and letting you run the show. That way, as you might put it, we won't tip our hand.'

For a quarter of an hour, the judge dictated how Barrett should set about freeing Julie and interviewing the witnesses in her case, and his. When he had finished, the young barrister looked at him with respect and awe, astonished at the ingenuity of his instructions. He folded his notebook, picked up his briefcase and took his leave, saying he had several things to arrange before the Bow Street hearing which was fixed for eleven o'clock.

A thought turned him at the cell door. 'Judge . . . I mean, Laurence, there's something I must do before the hearing – tell Julie and Aunt Meg. I wouldn't like them to get the news from TV, the radio or the press. Sanderson, the prison trick-cyclist, will break the news to Julie in his own way if I ask him. But what about Aunt Meg? Is there anything you want me to say to her?'

For a moment, the judge reflected, then shook his head. 'No, nothing in particular . . . she'll know better than most people why I acted as I did. But if she cares to visit me in prison, it would give me much pleasure.'

Before the Bow Street magistrate, Barrett entered a plea of not guilty to murder and manslaughter. Even the magistrate seemed surprised that the barrister made no application for bail, so he committed the judge for trial at the Old Bailey and sent him to Brixton to await his trial.

They had even caught the media unawares. When the judge entered the dock under a police escort, he noticed only one reporter at the press bench, presumably from the Press Association.

By the time the news had filtered through to the evening papers, the radio and TV, and had been composed into bludgeoning front-page headlines or breathless radio and TV bulletins, the judge was safely out of reach in the chaplain's room one floor up in Brixton; it had been hastily prepared with a bed, table and chair to keep him out of sight and isolated in that large prison.

II

His first three days as a remand prisoner, the judge spent alone in his small room near the prison library, feeling something of a relief after the stress of the previous three weeks. Solitude had never bothered him, and since he had spent his working life rubbing shoulders at small remove with the criminal classes, he hardly noticed the constraints of prison life. Word had evidently filtered down from the Lord Chancellor's office to treat him as a special case. His meals came from the governor's cook, he had TV and a radio, his own washroom and toilet and visitors whenever they wanted to come.

Barrett, he knew, would be busy searching for the evidence to free Julie. Everything hung on that: her future and his own, for what that was worth. Margaret had written him a note which he received on his second morning in detention, saying she would make the journey with Peter on his next visit. She had signed it, 'with love.' She had also seen Julie, who had taken the news badly but was now determined to get out of prison herself and fight for his freedom.

Those things cheered him and offset the effect of dozens of anonymous letters addressed to him through the prison governor, mostly expressing delight that his own form of justice had caught up with him and it was a pity they had abolished the death penalty, for he should hang by the neck.

He did not doubt that most if not all these letters came from families and friends of prisoners he had sentenced, for a few stated their hope that he would meet some of his victims in Brixton and suffer summary justice there.

Judge Knox had expected some sort of official démarche or at least a reaction from the judicial authorities. Especially the Lord Chancellor's department. It came on the fourth morning. In awed tones, the assistant governor came to announce that Lord Justice Birley was here to visit him. It did not surprise the judge, for they would of course send one of his best friends to sound him out.

'My dear Laurence,' Birley said, his stumpy figure advancing, arms outstretched and his hands grasping and pressing the judge's. His snub nose was visibly curling at the prison stench. His head and that mane of greying hair which had been his most distinguishing feature at the bar, shook as he said, 'There was I, thinking you were lazing under dazzling sunshine and azure skies quaffing the blushful Hippocrene, or climbing your magic mountain in Provence – and here you are in this of all places.' His arm traced an arc embracing the room and the courtyard beyond. 'How are they treating you, my poor friend?'

'No complaints, Ranald, no complaints.'

'Food all right?' His eye ranged rapidly over the pile of letters and the several sheets the judge had covered in his neat, precise hand. He caught the judge's nod. 'Keeping you away from the real villains, are they?' Again a nod. 'Getting your mail all right I see from those fan letters.' He chuckled. 'From the hang 'im, flog 'im fraternity, eh?'

'Some of them are, I'm afraid, rather uncomplimentary about myself and British justice,' the judge murmured. 'However, a few expressed an ardent interest in the subject of my indictment, though a mercenary one.'

At that, he noticed Birley's thick eyebrows clash in the middle of his forehead as he picked up half a dozen typed letters with headings of newspaper and TV organizations. 'Would you believe it, these are unsolicited requests for me to grant them serialization and film rights to my memoirs of which I have not written a line?'

Birley's face had become a study in perplexity and discomfiture as he stuck half-moon glasses on his nose and ran his eyes down the pages.

'I had no idea, Ranald, that they paid upwards of two hundred thousand pounds for serialization and more for film rights.'

'Nor had I.' Birley's breathing was audible. 'Nor had I,' he repeated. 'I'm sorely tempted.'

'No, Laurence. Never. English judges just do not write memoirs, it's against their ethic.'

'Yes, but English judges don't normally murder people and stand trial in their own courthouse, do they?'

'You have something there.' Birley shook his head. 'We live in a free society.' He had no need to add, 'Alas.' It was implied in his tone.

He changed the subject, chatting for a few minutes about mutual friends, changes, promotions in judicial circles; his remarks reminded the judge that, when they had last met in the golf club-house at Hampstead, Birley had whispered that the Lord Chancellor viewed him as his next appointment as a Lord Justice of Appeal. Suddenly, Birley broke across his thoughts with a question.

'How about your defence? Have you chosen a couple of our best QCs whom you can trust? Hambly would like to defend you, and Thornton would agree to work with him. They have a couple of excellent juniors in their chambers. You couldn't do better, Laurence.'

'I've already made my choice.'

'Oh, who? Do I know him?'

'I doubt it. He's the junior counsel who has been defending my daughter on a stolen-car and drugs charge.'

Birley was literally rocked back on his heels. 'You surely don't mean young Barrett from Hervey Longdon's chambers in Oxford?'

'You know him, then?'

'No, but I've read the documents in the case against your daughter.' Birley shook that neckless head, clamped tight on his shoulders. 'Laurence, you can't be serious, you can't possibly do that. A junior! Somebody who has handled nothing more complex and stimulating than car-theft and reckless driving cases. You can't possibly brief a junior in a serious case like yours which will have national and even international repercussions.'

'It's not against the rules.'

'I didn't mean that, but . . . but a junior against Spencer-Smith in a court presided over by the Lord Chief Justice? They'll crucify him, and they'll crucify you.'

'I trust him, and that is important to me.'

'Up to you, Laurence.' Birley finger-combed that thick mane of hair. He paced the small room twice, reached into an inside pocket to produce a silver cigarette-case and lighter. He lit up and the judge knew that the preliminaries, the small talk, were over.

'In any event, he won't have much to do, will he?'

'What do you mean?' the judge asked, though well aware of the answer.

'I mean . . . well, your written statement is pretty damning, isn't it? In the judgement of the DPP and the Attorney-General, it amounts to a complete avowal.'

'Fortunately we still have juries and a minor thing called the presumption of innocence, Ranald.'

Birley waived that notion, his mind obviously on something else. 'Of course, you're aware, Laurence, it complicates things, a plea of not guilty.'

'I know, Ranald.' He gazed at the square, troubled face. 'They didn't suggest you should bring a gun, did they?'

'A gun?'

'I thought Spencer-Smith and one or two others might have the idea that I could be persuaded to blow my brains out and leave things tidier for them, the way Mr Justice McCardie did in 1933 when he got into bother.'

Birley gave a hollow laugh. 'Nooh, nooh, nothing like that.'

'Then what's the problem – finding a judge of the required stature who doesn't know me and can therefore be called impartial?'

'You've hit it exactly.' Birley slipped one of those silk handkerchiefs the size of a small shawl out of his pocket and snorted into it, perhaps as he had so often done in his QC days, to gain that second or two to ponder things; or maybe on this occasion to clear the prison odours out of his nose. 'Who is there?' he said. 'Short of bringing someone down from Scotland, there isn't anybody. We can't draft in some unknown Crown Court judge from London or the sticks for a trial like yours.' He peered through his beetling eyebrows at the judge. 'You've set us a pretty problem, Laurence.'

'Sorry, Ranald,' the judge murmured, conscious of the fact that his personal fate was of no concern to Birley and his colleagues – it was the ritual of the law that worried them.

Birley was talking. 'Hmm, you've probably guessed what we have to do. As an *ex-officio* judge of the Old Bailey, the Lord Chief Justice himself will have to conduct the trial since he doesn't know whom to appoint and, in your case, justice has got to be seen to be done.'

He snorted and pondered for another moment. 'But Lord Slade would, of course, prefer a guilty plea, which might be reduced to not guilty of murder but guilty of manslaughter. That would obviate a long, drawn-out trial and thus limit the damage done to the judiciary. It would then be just a question of sentencing.' He stuffed his huge handkerchief into his pocket and stubbed out his half-smoked cigarette. 'But even the sentencing? Difficult enough, don't you think?'

'Yes, I would find that difficult.'

'The LCJ was thinking it was worth ten years. What would you say?'

'I might have gone to twelve. But ten is fair.'

'But in your case, Laurence, he'd probably fix it at eight years. Which means you'd do five and a half with good conduct, and you'd probably be eligible for a parole at three. There'd be no quarrel about paying your pension if you resign, which you would do anyway. In the circumstances, I'd say a good bargain.'

'And if I retain my plea of not guilty to both counts?'

'Ah! Then the game is transformed and you take everything the Attorney-General can throw at you.' He spread his short arms in a gesture of helplessness, 'It's your dear friend, Spencer-Smith. He's wanted to see your head on the block for twenty years and he'll resort to every trick in the book. He'll demand twenty to put you away for good. He has a way with juries, whether you like him or not. And what do you have? Your Boy David with his sling!'

'Let me sleep on it, Ranald.'

Birley nodded. He put his head round the door and told the prison officer his interview was ended. As he waited for the assistant-governor, he turned to the judge. 'In your case, Laurence, I'd be inclined to take the LCJ's offer. It would give you three years to write your book and sell it for a fortune then fill the rest of your life drinking the Hippocrene, watching your olives and oranges grow on your estate while you brushed up your Provençal and read Mistral in the original.'

He put out both his hairy hands to grasp the judge's in them. 'Of course, you'll treat this as a confidential chat if you decide to plead not guilty. Believe this, Laurence, I fully understand your motives and I am with you. Good luck, my poor old friend.'

Judge Knox watched him stump along the corridor on those short, thick legs.

Eight years reduced to five and a half and again to three with a parole. Well worth thinking about. No explaining to do about Julie. If she escaped with a small, suspended sentence or an acquittal, he would consider three years a small price to pay, albeit with the loss of his career and the brand of murderer on his record, and his conscience.

Even if Barrett combined the flamboyant eloquence of a Marshall Hall with the courage of Edward Carson, the subtle logic of Birkett and the irreverent wit of F.E. Smith, no court in the land would acquit him. Fight, and he risked twenty years, meaning more than thirteen in prison. Set against three, where was the argument? His pension would keep him wherever he wanted to live and he could settle his fortune on Julie.

Which nineteenth-century judge said that when you were on the horns of a dilemma, you had to listen to both horns? All that day, he tossed the two alternatives back and forth in his mind and went to sleep at lights-out no nearer a decision.

When he arrived at the prison the next day, Barrett was so cock-a-hoop about the progress he was making on Julie's case that the judge did not have the heart to tell him about Birley's offer. Having carried out the judge's advice to the letter, Barrett was certain that Julie would emerge with a fine at the most.

'You were right about Redhead, Judge.'

'Laurence.'

'Sorry. Anyway, when I accused him of trafficking in drugs and pornography and faced him with the fact that he had hidden the car for a fortnight after reporting it stolen and I was laying all this evidence before the police, he broke down and swore an affidavit. He will give evidence provided the police drop all the charges against him.'

'Good. Now what about Massey? He's a much cooler customer, but there's no doubt that if he gets an assurance there'll be no prosecution, he'll testify that Strang threatened to kill or cripple him unless he managed to turn Julie into a prostitute by seducing her himself then pimping for her.

'Of course, he knows he risks a long term in prison, having been there twice before,' the judge mused. He thought for a moment, then said, 'I know the chief constable and the whole hierarchy from my circuit days, but they're not much use to me now that I'm here.' Barrett watched him tap his forehead with his middle finger, a mannerism he had when chasing an errant thought. 'Mason, that's him. Frank Mason. He was the inspector who solved what they called the Mill Wheel Murder when I prosecuted at Oxford. He may still be there.'

'He is, Laurence. He's chief-superintendent in charge of detectives now.'

Judge Knox sat down, unsheathed his pen and filled half a sheet of paper with writing, which he stuck in an envelope. This he handed to Barrett. 'Find Mason and give him this. Explain everything that has happened and whisper that, with the right timing, he can break the drug ring centred on the Greensward and pull in Massey.' He shrugged. 'It may be stretching the Judges' Rules, but if he leans hard enough on Massey, he'll testify for Julie now that his boss, Strang, is dead.'

Barrett bunched his fist and gave himself a playful punch on his twisted chin. 'If we can break Massey down, he'll have to come and testify for you as well. Just think what effect that'll have on the jury.'

Judge Knox looked at the craggy face, now alight with fervour and conviction. How could he possibly tell him about Birley's visit and the offer from Lord Slade, the Lord Chief Justice?

Anyway, that would also mean revealing that the LCJ would be conducting the trial himself, and he wondered about Barrett's nerve as well as his talent, faced with the Old Bailey filled to overflowing with the public and the international media. In his own first case there, he had quaked so much he could not hold his notes, had had to speak extempore and had fluffed several cross-examinations.

Even now, he thought he noticed a trace of stage-fright in Barrett as he gathered up his documents and thrust them into his briefcase.

'Anything on your mind, Peter?'

'Er . . . er . . . well, there is, Laurence.'

'Hadn't you better tell me what it is?'

'I don't know . . . but, well I suppose I should tell you even if it's hard to know how to put it . . . it's just that I misjudged you, Laurence. At first, I thought you were a vitriolic, sadistic, sour-tempered, bloodyminded reprobate . . . as a judge, you were harsh, uncompromising, inhuman and had a law-book for a brain . . . not to put too fine a point on it, a real bastard. I have now amended that opinion.'

'Oh, you mean now you're *sure* I'm an old bastard.'

Barrett gazed at him and perceived the faint crease developing round his eyes, then the smile. 'Perhaps I'm putting it badly—'

'Not at all,' interrupted the judge. 'If you are half as abrasively eloquent in the Old Bailey, I don't think we can lose.'

'What I meant to say was this – it was a noble and unselfish thing you did to save Julie. Oh, I know it was murder. But not cold-blooded murder. You murdered a rat or a piece of worse vermin to save her, to save someone you love. However the trial goes and whatever the judicial outcome, I for one shall always think of it as one of the noblest actions I have ever met.'

'Thank you, Peter,' said the judge, blushing at this impassioned speech, and realizing that he could never go back on his not guilty plea except at the risk of betraying this young barrister's trust.

Barrett had only just gone when the duty prison officer knocked again, this time to usher in Margaret Denham. She came over to take the judge's hands in hers. Her hands felt numb and cold and he saw she was nearly in tears. He murmured to her that everything would come out right in the end.

'Peter has explained everything, and nobody could ever blame you for what you did.'

He could feel the tremor going through her hands and arms. 'Sit down, my dear,' he said, pulling her gently over to his one chair.

'What will happen?' she asked, taking a handkerchief out of her bag to dry her eyes.

'Who knows, Margaret?' he said, unwilling to fool her with false optimism. 'I have sat on the bench for more than twelve years and was a barrister for about the same time and I never knew how a jury was going to vote. When I thought I'd influenced them one way, they went another and vice versa.'

Before he replied he had seen worry on her face, and his statement seemed to have deepened it. She enlightened him by saying, 'Peter told me he had been retained to defend you. Shouldn't you look for someone with more experience, more authority and, well, more of a reputation? Peter will be very much the underdog.'

'Juries quite often distrust the high-and-mighty QC and take the side of the underdog. Peter will do brilliantly, you'll see.' He hoped his voice carried more conviction than he felt, uttering that statement. However, it seemed to set her mind at rest.

'Julie took the news badly,' she said. 'You see, she blames herself for everything that has happened to you.'

'Well now, if she does that, she'll have to look after me, won't she?' he said with a smile. 'She can start when Peter secures her release.'

'Do you really think he will? He had doubts at one time.'

'She'll get a suspended sentence or a complete acquittal.'

'It'll be wonderful if she does.'

'*When* she does,' he amended, 'the moment she's out you can get her to bring me one of your cakes.'

'Why, is the food bad?' she asked, concerned.

'No, it's the prison governor's own fare – but don't tell Julie that.'

'I follow you. It'll give her something to think about.'

'Precisely. I'll give her a few chores as well and ask her to help Peter prepare my defence. It'll be good training for her and keep her mind off other things.'

When the prison officer hinted that their time was up, Margaret rose. 'I feel much better now than when I came,' she said.

'So do I, Margaret.'

She smiled at him and took his hand. 'Laurence, did I ever tell you what an extraordinary man you are?'

'You did, and though I refused to believe the import of your affirmation, and still do, I did not for one moment question its sincerity or undervalue the compliment you were paying me.'

Not for the first time did Margaret Denham wonder if nearly everybody was wrong about Mr Justice Knox, the bogeyman of the Old Bailey. Weren't there two Knoxes? One, Sir Laurence, the judge who lived and breathed and applied to the letter the law of England; and another, who disguised his kindly instincts, kept a straight face and a tongue firmly in his cheek and his very private self to himself.

'Well, you are an extraordinary man,' she said.

He inclined his head, pressed her hand and watched her walk along the corridor leading to the stairs and the main gate.

Those six last words rang for a long time in his mind and lifted part of the load from his heart.

III

His whole working life had revolved round the criminal courts, those grim theatres where life and death dramas had been played out by the score in front of him as barrister and judge. Now he was the accused, the pivot round which the whole law machine turned. More than most, he realized how that machine worked, how its intricate mechanism had already enmeshed him and would process his case as though it were stamping out bottle tops or ball bearings.

Yet, in a sense, it was he who was pulling the strings back stage and off stage. Spencer-Smith might imagine he possessed all the facts, and so might old Slade the LCJ. But no. They did not have the video-cassettes that he had destroyed. Probably they knew nothing about them; they were equally ignorant of the part played by Connie Blackwell and Gus Wilkins; they ignored his own error of judgement. He could stage quite a few *coups de théâtre.* English justice, with its adversarial method and Socratic dialectic, did give the defence every chance, if the accused and his counsel were clever enough to take advantage of the system.

For instance, the prosecution had a duty to let the defence have access to documents such as depositions and forensic evidence in the interests of fairness, even if a wily customer like Spencer-Smith would almost certainly try to wrong-foot them. But the defence had no such obligation to show its hand before the trial or at the committal stage.

So, during those monotonous prison days, Judge Knox spent long hours sifting through all the evidence and deciding how to marshal it to his advantage. He and Barrett rehearsed cross-examinations of men like Detective Chief Superintendent Pritchard and Professor Langham, the pathologist.

It intrigued him to be on the other side for once, and even amused him. One morning, the prison governor arrived unannounced and stopped at the door before knocking. Inside, he heard the iron judge, as some prisoners dubbed him, humming the tune of that ditty from Gilbert (the barrister) and Sullivan's Iolanthe:

> The law is the true embodiment
> Of everything that's excellent.
> It has no kind of fault or flaw
> And I, my lords, embody the law.

Only one thing troubled the judge. Julie. How would her trial go? It would start in Judge Dawson's court three weeks before his own trial. Barrett had done his work and Chief Superintendent Mason had struck so much fear into Redhead and Massey that both had agreed, albeit reluctantly, to testify. But even in the smallest trials, things could go wrong.

On the day it took place, he fretted, turning his transistor radio on and off, hoping that one of the local bulletins or Radio Four might mention it. Nothing. He was concluding that once again they had postponed the trial when the governor himself arrived, a paper in his hand. Barrett had just rung with a message which the man solemnly read to the judge. It said: ALL CHARGES DROPPED. SEE YOU TOMORROW.

To the governor's astonishment, Judge Knox, who had been standing, suddenly collapsed on his bed, tears welling in his eyes.

'Anything I can do for you, Sir Laurence?' the governor asked.

'No, no, you've done me a splendid service.' As the governor turned to go, the judge called him back. 'There is something. Phone Barrett and ask him to bring all the newspaper cuttings and the trial transcript. Tell him it's important.'

Next day Barrett arrived with the court transcript and a dozen newspapers, everything from the *Oxford Mail* to the national dailies which had mentioned the trial only because of his involvement and imprisonment. They obviously realized the link between Strang's murder and Julie's arrest on drug charges, but the law of contempt had prevented them from exploiting this.

Sitting down with Barrett in his improvised cell, the judge went through the transcript line by line, indicating how the barrister could use the evidence by Redhead and Massey during his trial. He would have to subpoena these witnesses and explain the penalties if they failed to appear.

'Of course, we keep these witnesses up our sleeves,' he said.

'Of course,' Barrett repeated.

Judge Knox turned to glance quizzically at him. 'You don't seem as bucked as I am with your success, Peter. Anything bothering you? Is the prosecution playing the game and releasing all the evidence they should?'

'Yes . . . and no,' Barrett replied, having feared the question.

'What does that mean?' He banged his fist on the wooden table, shaking everything on it. 'They have to inform you about their investigations up to a point.'

'Laurence, do you know a Crown Court judge called Anthony Mansfield?'

'Tony? Of course, I play golf with him.'

'Well, he buttonholed me at a bar dinner a couple of nights ago in Oxford – he was speaking there – and whispered that Spencer-Smith has discovered half a dozen video-cassettes in Strang's safe. Said to tell you about it.'

'And they've said nothing about them to you?'

'Not a smell,' said Barrett. 'But there's a whisper at Scotland Yard and round the Temple.'

'Does anybody know what they show?'

'Not really, since the prosecution are keeping them under wraps – but the police seemed pretty certain they're copies of the ones you destroyed.' He looked at the judge, screwing up his crooked mouth into a wry expression. 'And they're probably right in believing that a blackmailer would sell you one set but always keep a copy in hand.'

Judge Knox had risen and was pacing the length of the small room, stopping by the window to watch some prisoners in the exercise yard tossing a basket ball around in the drizzling rain. He was drumming his fingers on his temple. Suddenly, he turned.

'Whatever we do, they mustn't know we know they have those cassettes,' he said.

'But isn't that playing into the prosecution's hands?' Barrett came back. 'Those tapes could be vital to our case and Spencer-Smith knows it. Which is why he's hiding them.'

'Well, let him continue to hide them.'

'Look, Laurence, you know the law, and they're your valid motive for murdering Strang, the proof he invited you there to blackmail you. And the proof also of the extreme provocation that armed your hand. You know, too, that without them we haven't much of a case.'

'I know – but I will not have them used, and that is final.'

'So you'd rather do fifteen or twenty years in jail than have the whole truth revealed.'

'Exactly.'

Barrett rose and faced the judge. 'Laurence, you're tying my hands.'

'Your hands!' the judge retorted with bitter irony. 'You have not seen those tapes. I have seen them and I shall never be able to expunge those filthy pictures from my mind as long as I live. And that is why I refused to let anybody and everybody who has a few coins to buy a paper or access to a TV set to share that horrible experience.' He glared at Barrett. 'Now do you see why?'

'All I see is that I'm the bit between the hammer and the anvil.'

'Meaning what?'

'Just that I have to listen to both of you trying to protect each other. Julie was pleading guilty to protect you and you're prepared to rot away slowly in prison, destroying your life and two others besides.'

'Two others.'

'You wouldn't know it, and I wouldn't know why and perhaps I shouldn't tell you, but Aunt Meg just happens to believe you're where the sun rises and sets. And Julie? She'll go round the bend and probably go back on drugs believing she's landed you in gaol for the rest of your natural. Why don't you ask her what she thinks about showing the jury those tapes?'

'If I was put on the rack then hanged, drawn and quartered, I'd never do that.'

'Why. Are you scared she'd say yes?'

'Don't be insolent.' He glared at Barrett as though he might even strike him. 'I refuse to ask her because I refuse to exert emotional pressure amounting to blackmail on my daughter.'

'In that case, you, the man of truth, will live a lie, Judge,' Barrett said, stressing the last word. 'And it'll tell harder on your conscience than if you agreed to have those tapes shown.'

'I can handle my conscience, thank you.'

'But Julie? What about her? Won't she always wonder what Strang did for you to murder him so brutally? Won't she always wonder how much you really know about her?' He paused to let those questions strike home. 'She'll wonder, that is, until she finds out. For find out she will.'

'That is as may be. But Julie shall never hear it now, from me or from you during my trial.'

Barrett laughed, a hollow, derisive laugh. 'That's just how Julie talked to me in prison,' he said.

'Can we forget about Julie's part in the case, and forget about the cassettes? We can win without either.'

Barrett shook his head and tossed the papers he was holding on the desk in resignation.

'There's not a snowball in hell's chance of winning or even getting away with a light sentence, and you know it better than anybody.' He pointed to the papers and spat the words out of the good side of his mouth. 'Now I know why you didn't send for a brace of QCs and half a dozen juniors. Not because they don't like you. No, because they'd all have refused the case on flimsy evidence like this knowing it was a lost cause and would dent their splendid reputation. But me?'

He beat himself on the chest with his clenched fist, the blow echoing in the small room. 'Me? I'd jump at it because it's the Old Bailey and I'm from the sticks with a track record of car cases and the odd breaking-and-entering on good days. It would be my big chance, wouldn't it?' His voice reverberated in the tiny room, loud and bitter with anger and emotion.

'None of that was in my mind,' the judge murmured, embarrassed by the outburst.

'Oh no! Another thing that wasn't in your mind was telling me that as well as Spencer-Smith, the slippery, slimy, venomous Attorney-General, I'd have the Lord Chief Justice himself against me. You must have known that when we last met.'

'Yes, I knew,' the judge admitted. 'I had a visit from Lord Justice Birley and he said the LCJ would probably have to judge the case for want of anyone else. I should have told you.'

'But you didn't want to frighten me off, was that it?'

'I was merely holding my hand until you had finished with Julie's trial and were getting to grips with our trial before informing you.' He looked at the warped face confronting him. In the grey afternoon light, it seemed pained, grief-stricken.

In a sense, Barrett was right. One reason for choosing him was that he could manipulate him in a way that self-respecting QCs might have resisted. Yet, he had also trusted this frank, outspoken young barrister who concealed his talents behind the complexes caused by his broken nose, twisted mouth and a sense of deficiency; he could understand why Julie had placed her trust in him.

But perhaps it was unfair as Margaret had hinted, to thrust such a burden on a young man with something of an inferiority complex and no experience of a big trial, let alone this one, which would cause a sensation for the best part of a week. If it might make his name, the chances were greater that he would fail and this might wreck any career he might have had at the bar.

Barrett's eyes were fixed on him, intently, waiting for the rest of his response. He chose his words carefully, leaving enough room around them.

'Lord Chief Justice Slade is a judge like myself and most of the others,' he said.

'But everybody knows he just happens to have a vitriolic tongue, a brittle temper, a low flash-point, a bloody-minded streak and a heavy hand when it comes to passing sentence.'

'Those are some of his weaknesses, I admit.'

'Only some – I omitted to mention he has a sadistic and perverse streak and takes pleasure in ridiculing and humiliating counsel, especially defence counsel.'

'Peter, if you feel I haven't been honest with you, and if you feel that way about the LCJ and think the case against us is too one-sided and possibly lost already, then of course I shall release you from any obligation to represent me in court. But I shall, personally, be extremely sorry if you drop me.'

Barrett did not reply straight away; he picked up the papers and stared at them as if wondering what to do with them. He replaced them on the table, then grasped his empty briefcase. Watching him, the judge felt that the young barrister had decided to leave the evidence there and say goodbye. Although he made no move, he realized at that instant how much he would miss that crooked face and that perpetual and compulsive need for it to chew on something, anything. But it was Barrett's choice

Suddenly, Barrett turned and looked at him, his expression saying that he, too, might have similar thoughts. He fingered his broken nose and hoisted his shoulders.

'Me? I've been so knocked about that another knock won't show, even if it comes from the LCJ on high and dents my pride as well as counting me out for good.'

'You will keep the case, then?'

'If you still want me to.'

'Of course I do.' His face lit up as he grinned at Barrett. 'Do you think I'd have submitted to such a fierce cross-examination if I hadn't?'

Barrett picked up the papers and thrust them into his briefcase, murmuring that he would have copies made that afternoon and hand them into the governor's office so that the judge could study them at his leisure.

As he turned to go, he halted and looked round.

'Laurence, don't run way with the notion that the LCJ and Spencer-Smith frighten me. Only one thing frightens me and stopped me walking away from the case – how I would face Julie and what I would say to her if I couldn't prevent them from putting you away for the rest of your life?'

IV

Julie seemed transformed. Of course he had not seen her for more than a month, when they were weaning her off heroin with methadone and other substitutes. Now, as she came into his room, he noticed her blue-grey eyes had recovered much of their brightness and her skin had lost that parchment appearance. She looked alert, alive. Catching her gazing anxiously at him, he wondered at the changes she must observe in him after more than three weeks in prison.

Of course, their perspectives had altered, and their mental attitudes to each other.

For him, Julie could never again be the innocent girl he had reared from infancy. Not after he'd seen those pictures and listened to Katie Gamble and Strang. But he did not love her any the less for that.

How did she now see him? No longer the Olympian figure handing down justice like some Greek deity. No, a remand prisoner, a man on a charge of wilful killing. A man who had lost control and murdered someone she had known.

'Papa,' Julie said, coming towards him, then slipping into his arm and burying her head on his chest. 'Papa, I'm sorry, I've ruined my own life and now I've ruined yours as well.'

'No, Julie darling.' He stroked her head. 'You might even have saved me from myself.'

She lifted her head to gaze at him. 'Saved you! I don't understand.'

'Come and sit down,' he said, holding out the one chair for her and seating himself on the bed. 'If you want to smoke, there's no law against it.' He watched her light a Gitane and pull on it several times before continuing.

'How did Peter do in court?'

'Out of this world,' she said, throwing her arms out in a gesture of incredulity. 'I just couldn't believe the way he handled Massey and Katie and Redhead. What happened? It must have been something you did to him.'

'I didn't do a thing – except place my trust in him and give him a bit of self-confidence.'

'But his twitch, his inferiority complex—'

'Just your sick-tricyclist jargon.'

'Oh no. I told you he's sensitive about his face and that's why he has never done as well as he should at the bar. But it's deeper than that. He's changed.'

'We've all changed.'

Julie nodded. She had cupped her face in her left hand, supporting the elbow in her right hand in the way she had done as a child, regarding him working on briefs, her large eyes fascinated by their bright-red seals and scarlet ribbons and the ornate, copperplate calligraphy on their title-pages. She would caress the thick parchment, built to resist centuries of archive air, dust and mites. She had that same wide-eyed look now.

'Papa, you've changed . . . you've changed a lot.'

'Oh, how?'

'In everything, though you might not realize it yourself . . . I can't explain, but you're more relaxed, easy. And another thing, you've started using apostrophes, saying it's and there's and we've and that sort of thing.' She smiled. 'I bet Peter had something to do with that.'

'It's not the only beneficial influence he's had on me,' the judge said with a smile.

'Peter thinks you're something special.' She paused, a frown crossing her face. 'Do you think he can get you off next week on self-defence or some plea like that?'

'I wouldn't bet on it,' he said, shaking his head; then, seeing her crestfallen expression, he added, 'Julie, my dear, not even Patrick Hastings or Marshall Hall on their best days could get me off. I'm afraid all we can do is what Peter would call a damage-limitation exercise.'

At this, Julie screwed the butt of her Gitane into the ashtray on the table, viciously. 'That means you'll go to prison for years and have to resign from the bench, and even when they release you, you'll be miserable.'

'People can make new beginnings, reshape their lives.'

Hardly appearing to listen, Julie was running her yellow fingers through her hair, catching and tugging handfuls of it in her agitation. 'It's all my fault,' she muttered. 'All my fault.'

He took her hand and pressed it. 'Julie, nobody knows how far back the fault lies in both of us, so don't blame yourself.'

'How can I stop when I've ruined your career and your life?'

He pulled her chair nearer him on the bed and spoke softly. 'Who knows, you might have saved me by pulling me up, by making me perceive things in a different way, which is a priceless thing? What would I have done otherwise? Gone on either in the Old Bailey or the appeal court like Birley as a crusty old reprobate or recluse, judging cases or appeals that had ceased to have the slightest significance for me. You might have saved me from withering away on the bench like so many of those old antiques I pleaded before at one time.'

'But in prison. . . .'

'What's wrong with a nice new open prison with books, radio, TV and a bathroom *en suite*?' He grinned. 'And knowing the ropes, I can work a parole sooner rather than later.'

Never before had she heard him talk in this strain; indeed, they had never had a real conversation, except about some legal case that she was studying, one that set a precedent. On those occasions he could become animated, even eloquent. Yet, here he was in Brixton jail opening his mind to her, treating her as someone important to him, more important than his career or even his freedom.

'It's very odd and ironic,' she murmured, 'but it seems we had to meet in two prisons before we could talk to each other like this.'

'Just what I thought myself when I was walking back from your prison the day I brought you Margaret's cake—'

'Which Peter gobbled,' she interjected, and they both smiled at the recollection. Julie's face turned serious and she said, 'You met Dr Sanderson, the psychiatrist, I believe.'

'I did, and I'm afraid I was a bit gruff with him, which I regret.'

Julie was toying with that bright-blue cigarette packet as if deliberating whether to have a second cigarette; she flipped one into her hand, rolled it in her fingers then replaced it in the packet. 'He helped me more than I can say,' she whispered. 'Especially that day he had to tell me you had been charged with murdering Strang.' She fixed her eyes on something beyond the window as though to avoid his gaze. 'I didn't think I would survive that day without something . . . heroin, cocaine . . . methadone . . . anything. . . .'

'But you did.'

'Only because of him,' she said, nodding. 'He sat with me for hours talking me out of it . . . telling me to hang on for a minute, two minutes, ten, twenty, half an hour, an hour.'

Holding up the cigarette packet against the raw light from the window, she gave a wry laugh, 'I must have got through three packets of these that Peter had brought in that very day.' She turned, moist-eyed to look at him. She sniffed. 'You were all I had . . . apart from Peter . . . and he didn't really know me like you . . . you were a sort of lifeline, a way out and up for me again.'

'You should have asked me for help long before all this happened.'

'I would if I'd known that, underneath, there was someone like you are now, but I couldn't when I knew it would ruin your career.'

His career? Julie was right, it had overlaid everything else in his life. It was all he had lived for, even when Joan was alive. Something Sanderson had let drop during that frosty interview echoed in his mind, something about the difficulty of sharing your experience with someone else and he or she with you. He might have lived with Joan and Julie, but he hadn't lived for them and through them. He had lived for himself, identifying himself solely and selfishly with his own experience and his own reputation.

'We really know very little about each other,' he said.

'That's why I came here,' Julie murmured. 'To tell you what really happened, what I couldn't bear to tell you when I thought you might be judging me like someone in the dock, if I can say that.' She paused. 'What I went through was for me like living some nightmare without any hope of waking up and finding it wasn't true. It was only too true.'

Her voice was breaking, and he leaned forward to grip her hand in his. 'Julie, my darling, you don't have to talk about it if you don't want to.'

'But I must, for my own sake as well as yours. I must talk about it to somebody I love.' She sniffed, accepted the handkerchief he offered and blew her nose. 'Anyway, it will all come out at the trial.'

'I suppose so.'

So, he had to listen as she recounted the story, the long pauses, the rise and fall of her voice testifying to the emotion she was reliving with these revelations. It came as a relief to him that she knew nothing of his own enquiries and did not suspect he had already learned a great deal of her story.

It had all begun with a stupid accident, the car he had given her for her birthday colliding with another in an Oxford lane. Exchanging insurance details with the other driver, she discovered she had stupidly let her car policy and road tax lapse.

She should have gone to the police there and then and reported the fact. Instead, she tried to compromise with the other driver. He seized his chance and, although it was technically his fault, accused her of reckless driving and injuring his arm, which was bruised and bleeding. So, she faced prosecution and a fine and was scared. She had confided these fears to Redhead, the bookseller.

'Why Redhead?'

She had bought books from him at favourable prices and he'd gone out of his way to be friendly. Redhead knew friends of the other driver and persuaded him to drop the case, providing she paid for his car repairs. She agreed, then had another shock when the garage estimate was nearly £1,000. Again, Redhead came to her aid by lending her the money without interest.

'But he asked for a service in return, was that it?'

She nodded. It seemed simple. She drove to London in Redhead's car and picked up several packages from Strang's gambling-club in Mayfair and handed them over to the bookseller or Massey.

'They were consignments of drugs like heroin or cocaine,' he prompted.

Yes, but by the time she found out it was too late, they had sucked her into the conspiracy. Her accident, too, had been staged by one of the gang on purpose to involve her. However, she knew nothing of this when she met Strang, who had impressed her with his good looks, his *savoir-faire*, his smooth line of talk, his top-drawer friends and his free spending.

He flattered her, wining and dining her in the best restaurants, putting her up in his Pitt Street apartment when she had to stay overnight. She thought she was in love with him. When she became his mistress, he told her about his drug business and persuaded her to try cocaine and crack. In a few months she would have done anything, committed any crime for the drug. Strang had then dropped her and handed her over to Massey.

'So you became his mistress.'

Here Julie paused, as if her mind had seized up or balked at putting words to the thoughts and images going through it.

'No . . . anybody's. Papa, I couldn't help it, I had to have money to buy heroin, and Massey showed me the only way to get it, with no alternative.' She was crying openly, uncontrollably. 'By prostituting myself . . . by turning myself into a common prostitute.' She gripped his hand as though she meant to crush it. 'God forgive me,' she mumbled through her tears, 'for I'll never forgive myself.'

'Don't cry, Julie,' he said, drawing her into his arms and embracing her tightly. 'All that's in the past and everything will now turn out for the best, you'll see.'

When she had gone, the judge watched some of the prisoners playing soccer in the exercise yard with a rubber ball and goal-posts chalked on the walls. No doubt that crowd of fifty-odd prisoners numbered quite a few whom he had sentenced, and maybe, amid the mounting pile of anonymous hate mail that he had received, were some from relatives of Brixton prisoners like those.

His post-bag had also grown to about thirty letters from newspapers, radio and TV organizations in Britain, America and even France and Holland, asking him to write and sell them his story for a small fortune. One or two evidently thought he might be free to narrate it himself, or act as adviser at an enormous fee to the film or TV serial that they proposed making.

But that assumed a verdict of not guilty, which, at his most sanguine, the judge had never envisaged.

Indeed, any optimism he had about the trial was dashed within a couple of hours of Julie's departure.

At six o'clock that evening when Barrett entered his room, he realized it had taken something serious to bring him at such a late hour.

'We've just lost two of our best witnesses,' Barrett said, while still on his feet. He explained he had gone to run over their evidence with Redhead and Massey only to learn that the prosecution had persuaded them both to give evidence for the Crown.

Both had refused to explain their change of heart, but he understood from Chief Superintendent Mason that the police had threatened to move heaven and earth to incriminate them if they did not become prosecution witnesses. They had obviously been promised freedom from any sort of prosecution if they gave evidence against the judge.

'That's our friend, Spencer-Smith.'

'Yes, he put the police up to it. But why?'

Yes, why? Judge Knox could have answered that question directly for the barrister. Both men were friends and gangland accomplices of Strang, a villain. But Strang was also a murdered man, the victim. And victims, regardless of their villainy, always had the jurors' respect. Respect for the dead counted triple or quadruple or more for the murdered dead.

Therefore, Spencer-Smith would play those two rogues for all they were worth, exacting testimony from them that Sir Laurence Knox had been quizzing them about Strang and was obsessed with the idea of revenging himself on him. Their evidence, unchallenged, would point to premeditated murder with no extenuating circumstances and thus render him liable to the most several penalty, which Slade would not hesitate to apply.

If he had expected some cunning, underhand trick like this from the Attorney-General, it still shocked him.

'Why?' he repeated aloud. 'Because, Peter, they'll lie in their teeth and testify that I threatened what I would to Strang for corrupting Julie and turning her into a drug addict.'

'But in their evidence in the lower court at Oxford,' Barrett objected, 'they said how they obeyed Strang's orders to trap and hook Julie.'

'In the mind of a judge and jury, that does not necessarily conflict with any evidence they may give about me.'

'Then we're lost,' Barrett said, dumping himself on the bed and throwing down his briefcase.

'It's highly damaging,' the judge admitted, 'but we still have Blackwell and Wilkins to rebut some of what they'll say. And it may well be a blessing in disguise.'

'How – a blessing in disguise?'

'I mean, they're hostile witnesses, so you can hammer them in cross-examination, which is where cases are won and lost. Juries only half-listen to prosecution and defence witnesses being taken through their prepared scripts. But when they're under fire from the opposition and have to ad lib and often give things away, the jurors sit up. So trip them up, discredit them, caution them against perjury, rough them up.'

'If only we had those cassettes, Laurence.'

Judge Knox shook his head and was about to say something when a prison officer rapped on the door and handed him his evening meal on a tray. Two plates, one under an aluminium hat which, he knew, would conceal the usual stewed meat, potatoes and cabbage or another vegetable, and the second with rice pudding. A couple of slices of bread, a pot of coffee and a dish with a few lumps of sugar also sat on the tray.

Putting the tray on the table, the judge fixed Barrett with that glare which had struck fear into so many of those he had sentenced.

'Now, what have you said to Julie?'

'Well, I had to answer her questions about how your private quest took you from Redhead to Strang by way of Katie Gamble and Massey.'

'So you told her what happened in Pitt Street?'

'Only so far as I had to.'

'Does she know about the cassettes I destroyed, or those the prosecution has procured?'

'No, neither.' Barrett hesitated and saw, by the lift of his chin, that the judge had noticed and was waiting for the complement of the answer. 'But don't forget, Laurence, Julie's intelligent and has legal training, so she could put two and two together.'

'She must never know about those cassettes, do you hear?'

Barrett returned that steely look as far as he could. 'Laurence, I gave my word and I shall keep it, though you also know my opinion. We should make them produce those cassettes to prove that you acted out of excessive provocation in your own defence and in defence of your daughter. They will show what sort of vermin Strang was and rebut anything Massey and Redhead can say that's good about him.'

Judge Knox shook his head. 'I'd rather plead guilty than allow that.'

Lifting the aluminium cover off his plate, he pushed his chair up to the table to signal their interview had ended.

Barrett had walked downstairs and halfway along the corridor with a prison officer before cursing himself for his *ésprit d'escalier*. Always at the stair-bottom before he remembered his best lines!

That argument about cassettes had driven the most important question out of his head.

Was Judge Knox prepared to risk everything, go into the box himself and tell the court everything, the truth, the whole truth and nothing but the truth?

They had discussed everything but that.

Their trial – yes, theirs, for Barrett felt himself as much on trial as the judge – was listed to start in ten days' time and he had not resolved that vital question.

V

When the two Brixton prison officers brought him up the narrow stairs from the cells below the court and escorted him into the dock, the brighter light dazzled him for several moments before his eyes adapted. Court Four gradually fell into place. For three weeks on one occasion when his own Court One needed some repairs, he had used this court; although they looked the same, he had never liked it. In his own court, he could see the sun and rain on the glass roof, whereas here the glare of the artificial roof-lighting had always disturbed him. As it did now.

Everyone but the judge and jury was already there. From the court well, Barrett nodded; he was nervously shuffling the cards on which the judge had advised him to block in the questions he wished to put to his own witnesses and the prosecution witnesses whom he would cross-examine. Over the previous week, they had spent hours in Brixton jail distilling out the essential elements of both cases, the prosecution and their own.

He noted Spencer-Smith's diamond eyes flicker towards him. Neutral. Impassive. A look signifying that their amity, whatever that had amounted to, was no more. Whereas Barrett had one other junior from his Oxford chambers, the Attorney-General had another QC and two juniors to assist him. Bob wigs normally did nothing to enhance the appearance, but the Attorney-General was an exception to the rule; his wig hid that oily layer of dark hair and lent some character to his hatchet face. So the judge thought.

Not a single seat remained unfilled. In front of the empty jury box, the press was jammed tightly into its bench and a dozen reporters had been forced to grab public seats in the court well; court officers, counsels' clerks, ushers, policemen had taken post; between the bench and the witness box, the shorthand-writer was checking her machine; beside the judge's chair, immobile in black jacket and pin-striped trousers, stood the LCJ's clerk almost beneath the sword suspended over the chair and the legend that read, *Domine Dirige Nos*.

They had done him proud, the media whose output he had skimmed that morning. His was an unprecedented case in the annals of English justice. A judge indicted for murder and tried in his own court! Headlines an inch high proclaimed the fact over texts liberally stippled with superlatives.

Although the law restricted comment, most had plumped for guilty, though a few had hedged their bets on manslaughter. As usual, the popular press had bracketed him with Judge Jeffreys, though the serious broadsheets stressed his impartial though rigorous application of the law.

For most papers, the court battle was a David and Goliath encounter, and nobody gave Barrett with his slingshot a chance against the Attorney-General's heavy artillery. Few journalists saw the one-sided contest lasting more than a day, two at the most; some went as far as speculating where they would jail the judge when he was found guilty.

There came a shout of 'Silence' and the court rose as a door to the left of the bench opened and Lord Chief Justice James Vernon Slade appeared, holding the traditional nosegay of flowers, once carried to ward off jail fever but now, presumably, to neutralize the spent breath and exudations of the crowd packed into that small courtroom.

A small-boned man with a bloodless face, he had a turkey-bald head under his bench wig, and his pale-blue eyes peered over half-moon glasses round the court, then at the judge sitting in the dock. Friendship with the Lord Chancellor and astute lobbying of his peers had hauled him to the top of the judicial pyramid, they said. Judge Knox did not dislike Lord Slade, but had warned Barrett to step warily, for the LCJ was short-fused and inclined to hector and bully counsel.

When the court had settled, the clerk and the judge rose together. The clerk, in level voice, intoned:

'Sir Laurence Knox, you are charged that on 1 September 1998, you did wilfully murder Derek Clifford Strang at Number Eleven, Pitt Street, Mayfair. How do you plead – guilty or not guilty?'

'Not guilty.'

'You are further charged that on the same night and in the same place, you caused the death by manslaughter of the said Derek Clifford Strang. How do you plead – guilty or not guilty?'

'Not guilty.'

As the jury was empanelled, Spencer-Smith nodded each man and woman through, but Barrett questioned every one, much to the annoyance of the Lord Chief Justice, who manifestly wished to begin and end the trial as quickly as possible. Did they, Barrett asked, have a relative or friend who had ever been tried before Mr Justice Knox? Had they themselves ever been charged even with a minor offence? What did they think of the law? To one woman, who had a brother found guilty of car theft, he asked: 'Did it leave a nasty taste in his mouth about the law?'

'It certainly did,' she replied, and he rejected her.

'Counsel,' Lord Slade had a petulant nasal soprano voice, 'we have already dismissed a dozen potential jurors for no very good reason that I can see. Is this time-consuming form of interrogation relevant to the business before us?'

'M'lud, you are trying a judge, and many people do not have the esteem for the law and the court that you and I do.'

Watching this face-off, Judge Knox noted the pink spots on Lord Slade's cheeks, a sure sign that the defence was walking blind in a minefield.

Go on like this and Barrett will throw the case before it begins and I'll get twenty years and he'll never get another brief, damned to eternity by the Lord Chief Justice himself.

But Barrett resolutely continued his cross-examination which took them to quarter to one when Lord Slade adjourned for lunch.

How well Judge Knox knew those hermetic lunches with the twenty Old Bailey judges, wigs and red robes doffed, all meeting for their solitary sherry before slotting themselves along the narrow tables. Everyone embedded in the court and its ritual like Cistercian monks in La Trappe, or flies in amber. Everyone versed in the other's small-talk, tall-talk, shop-talk, table-talk, bar-talk, car-talk – everything but their pillow-talk.

Round and round they went like circus horses, or the under-sheriff's menu of roast beef, roast lamb, roast pork, roast veal, roast chicken, roast turkey with slight variations. A glass of claret to moisten the fare. Nothing to raise the blood pressure or foment bile, nothing to inflame the mind, nothing to make the hand drop the gavel or the head droop on the notepad. In brief, nothing to affect the judgement. Lord Slade did not even touch wine and imbibed his coffee thick and black. A no-lump man.

His own lunch Judge Knox ate in the cells under the court. Barrett had sent in a plate of cold chicken-breast with a green salad, Cheddar cheese, biscuits and an apple, table-water and a pot of coffee. While he ate, he wondered how Spencer-Smith would script his case. As a short, one-act play, perhaps. After all, there were few characters and most were walk-on parts. He and Strang were the hero and villain, or villain and hero, depending on the viewpoint. He fancied S-S might open with a short curtain-raiser, perform several small scenes, then give a long and powerful peroration, the final cutain would drop on the villain, Mr Justice Knox.

Idle speculation. Nobody, not even the Attorney-General, could script a trial.

When the court reassembled and Spencer-Smith got to his feet, it became evident from his opening sentence he meant to play for maximum stakes.

'Members of the jury, you are called to decide a case unique in the annals of English justice, the case of a man who has spent most of his life defending, prosecuting or judging his fellow-beings, a man who as a judge should be above and beyond all reproach in his social and professional conduct.

'And yet, as I will prove to you beyond a peradventure, this man committed the most heinous crime known to the justice he was appointed to uphold. He committed murder. A brutal and savage murder that shocked even case-hardened detectives and an experienced pathologist. Nor does the accused attempt to deny his crime, even though he pleads not guilty.

'Now, it may be that he was provoked. We do not know how he means to justify the murder. But we know one thing: however great the provocation, however deep the hatred for the victim, no man has the right to take another man's life, short of defending his own life. No man can be his own executioner.'

Warming to his theme, Spencer-Smith extolled the impartiality, the integrity, the wisdom of the British judiciary, citing figures to prove how few judges had fallen from grace during the period for which they had records. How few had abused the trust the public placed in them. When a judge erred or committed a crime, it was worse – a thousandfold worse – than when a policeman stepped out of line and used his authority to corrupt the law or wreak vengeance on someone.

Then there were hot-blooded and cold-blooded crimes. By calling certain witnesses and expert opinion, the prosecution would show that, without doubt, this man, Sir Laurence Knox, had murdered in cold blood. There was nothing in this crime that had not been planned and premeditated over a period of at least a month, and perhaps much longer.

Pointing to the judge in the dock, the Attorney-General said that incontrovertible evidence would demonstrate how he had tracked Derek Clifford Strang to his home, somehow gained his confidence to the extent of being invited to his flat. There, he cruelly and brutally bludgeoned Mr Strang to death.

Spencer-Smith's voice droned on and on, and Judge Knox's mind, absorbed only the relevant statements in a welter of rhetoric signifying little. How much did the man understand of the whole business, or want to understand?

Spencer-Smith spoke and acted like a man in a hurry, someone who would go in with fists and feet flailing to win a quick decision. Had he even done his homework? He sounded as though he knew nothing of the Flint case nearly eight years before, nothing about Connie Blackwell and Gus Wilkins. Still, it might be another of the Attorney-General's sly little stratagems to secure the verdict. Was he omitting to call relevant evidence that he knew about because it might prejudice his own case and aid the defence. If so, he was in for a shock.

It was nearly three o'clock when Spencer-Smith wound up his opening statement and called his first witness, Miss Catherine Semple Gamble. In a sober, grey suit and a button-up white blouse, with her hair gathered in a slip-knot and falling elegantly on the nape of her neck, Katie looked the antithesis of the girl who had offered him Egyptian 'grass', cocaine and all of herself for £500.

Yes, of course she knew the man in the dock. He had come to her flat to ask about his stepdaughter, Julie Armitage, and her connection with Mr Massey, manager and a director of the Greensward Club, and Mr Strang, who ran several clubs including the Greensward.

'Miss Gamble, did you know Julie Armitage, the defendant's stepdaughter, well?'

'Yes sir, we lived in the same residence for about a year.' Katie's voice was demure, her accent impeccable. Judge Knox could see she had touched whatever was gallant in Lord Slade.

'Did you know what had happened to her to cause her stepfather to question you about her?'

'She had got into trouble with the police?'

'Objection, m'lud,' Barrett put in.

'On what grounds?' Lord Slade piped.

'The impression is given that my client's stepdaughter had committed a crime, which is not the case.'

'But she was in police hands at that moment, was she not?'

'I suppose so, m'lud.'

'Objection overruled.'

Spencer-Smith stopped staring at a seam in his gown-sleeve and shot a critical glance at Barrett before resuming.

'Why do you think Sir Laurence Knox was interested in Mr Strang?'

'Because he believed Mr Strang turned his stepdaughter into a heroin addict.'

'Did he blame Mr Strang for anything else?'

'Yes, he thought Mr Strang had turned Julie into a prostitute and had used her to peddle drugs.'

'What did you reply to these suggestions?'

Katie thought for a moment. 'That I never knew about her prostitution or drugs and I had never heard of Mr Strang.'

'Do you remember anything else about Sir Laurence's attitude to Mr Strang?'

'I remember he said that if he found him he would like to kill him.'

During Katie Gamble's evidence, Judge Knox was watching the jury, especially its foreman, who was named Charles Harmsworth and was an aeronautical engineer from Ealing. There was also a serious young man with floppy hair and a denim shirt who took copious notes, and a female chartered accountant. In his experience, juries took their time from certain members like those three. And they seemed to believe Katie Gamble's damning evidence.

Barrett was on his feet.

'Miss Gamble, I believe your friends call you Katie, is that right?'

Ah! He's going for the soft, friendly approach, the judge thought. Trying to alter the jurors' impression of the demure creature. He thought Barrett looked nervous.

'Yes,' Katie replied.

'What do you do for a living, Katie?'

'I have a little money of my own.'

'Of independent means, then. You have a flat in an expensive district of Oxford. Do you own the flat?'

'No, it's rented.'

'Mr Barrett.' Lord Slade was leaning over his desk, pen pointed at the barrister. 'Where exactly is all this leading?'

'I hope to a conclusion which will justify my questions, m'lud,' Barrett replied and laughter rippled through the court, quickly stifled by the LCJ's gavel.

'Your flat is rented then. Can you tell us what rent you pay a week, a month, a year?'

That fazed Katie, but she braced herself and said, 'It's about a hundred pounds a week . . . about that.'

'A hundred pounds a week. Cheap for that area.' Barrett took time to study one of his cards and the judge noted that pink flush creep over the LCJ's face. Barrett waited for the fuse to run out. 'Who do you pay this rent to?'

Again, the girl looked uncomfortable. 'I can't remember exactly.'

'And I don't suppose you can remember if your independent means come from investments or wherever.'

'Counsel,' came that high, nasal voice from the bench, 'you make it seem that this witness is on trial and not your client. If you have direct questions then pose them and do not waste the court's time or try its patience.' From the LCJ's scarlet complexion, the judge reflected that if Barrett had not advanced their case, he had at least proved there was some blood in Slade.

'Apologies, m'lud, I was coming to the point.'

'Then make it.'

'Miss Gamble.' Barrett's tone had changed. 'Do you know what perjury is?'

'No.'

'Perjury is when a witness deliberately lies to or misleads the court. It carries a heavy penalty. Now, you are on oath, so answer truthfully. You are what is known as a call-girl, are you not?'

'No, that is not true.'

Barrett passed one of the court ushers a piece of paper to hand her. As she read it, the barrister said, 'These are the names of three of your clients who are willing to swear on oath and in writing how they visited you in your apartment to have sex, how much they paid and so on. If you wish to waste the court's time and suffer the penalty of imprisonment, I shall produce their evidence. It's up to you. I shall ask the question again: Are you what is known as a call-girl?'

Katie Gamble hesitated, her eyes fastened on the papers Barrett was extracting from his file and holding out as though they were further evidence.

'Yes,' she whispered.

'And isn't your landlord the Greensward Club?'

'I don't know.'

Again, Barrett produced several copies of a document, asking the usher to hand them to the LCJ, the jury, the prosecution and Katie Gamble.

'Well, now you have proof,' he said, then turned to indicate the judge, sitting between two warders in the small, panelled oak box. 'How was this man introduced to you?'

'Through a friend,' she said, most of her assurance evaporated.

'Did you know who he was?'

'Not then, but he mentioned Julie.'

'Did he say he was her stepfather?'

'I don't remember.'

'I put it to you that he didn't say who he was but in order to elicit information he said he had a date with Julie. Isn't that the way it was?'

'I can't remember.'

'But you remember his saying he would like to kill a certain Strang, a man you had never heard of before?'

'Yes, he said that.'

'And you still say you did not know who Strang was?'

'Yes.'

Barrett had them all listening now, even the Lord Chief Justice. Harmsworth, the jury foreman, was gripping the moulded panel of the jury box and the press were scribbling the dialogue. For her part, Katie Gamble was eyeing Barrett's hand as it emerged from his thick pile of papers with yet another document.

'You didn't know that Strang owned most of the Greensward Club and was therefore one of your landlords, to whom you paid your flat rent and who levied three-quarters of everything you earned with your body? You still maintain you didn't know that?'

Katie Gamble used the only defence open to her at that moment; she burst into tears. Barrett seized his chance. Reading from his own notes, he said, 'Miss Gamble, you are on record as saying, and I quote, "I remember he said that if he found him he'd like to kill him." Now why, if a man like Sir Laurence Knox knew more about Strang than you admit knowing, did he come to ask you about him, then threaten to kill him?'

'How do I know? I don't remember.' She was sobbing.

'Can I suggest to you why you don't remember much of what went on that evening? Wasn't it because you were "high" on the cocaine you had sniffed into your lungs when my client was with you?'

'Objection.' Spencer-Smith had leapt to his feet, beckoning to Katie Gamble to make no reply. 'My learned friend surely cannot expect the witness to respond to that improper suggestion, or incriminate herself.'

'Sustained,' Lord Slade said, then to Barrett, 'Have you finished brow-beating this witness, counsel?'

'No more questions.'

During these exchanges, Judge Knox sitting in the dock, had the curious sensation of mentally transposing himself on to the bench and weighing all the evidence for and against himself, trying to gauge the effect of the testimony impartially, as it might strike the jurors.

It was just after four. Spencer-Smith was looking at the clock and whispering to his fellow-QC. He addressed the bench. 'With respect, m'lud, I should like to change the order of my witnesses and call Professor George Langham for the forensic evidence since we can probably finish it before the court rises.'

In Judge Knox's interpretation, that meant that the Attorney-General did not wish to risk having Massey or Redhead mauled as Katie Gamble had been.

Professor Langham, a dapper, silver-haired pathologist in his fifties, described the injuries inflicted on Strang. They were consistent with some twenty or more powerful and violent blows from a blunt instrument.

'An instrument like this, Professor?' Spencer-Smith held up the flint-glass lamp, its flex ruptured, dark bloodstains and blond hairs still on the jagged edges.

'Yes.'

He went on to relate how he had analysed the blood and hair from part of the lamp. Most of this tallied with the blood-group of the dead man, but he had also found blood with the same genetic component as that of the accused.

'Is there any doubt in your mind that this is the murder weapon?'

'None whatever.'

Spencer-Smith sat down with that self-satisfied smirk on his face and nodded at Barrett, who rose, went to the table and picked up the lamp.

'A pretty heavy piece of glass, Professor. How much does it weigh, exactly?'

'Exactly I wouldn't know, but I'd say about three kilos.'

'Ah!' Barrett's exclamation filled the courtroom. 'So, you didn't bother to weigh it exactly?'

'Does its exact weight bear on the case, Counsel?' Lord Slade interrupted with a sigh.

'With respect, m'lud, I think so and I had it weighed and it comes out at three kilos, two hundred and twenty-four grams.' He turned to the witness box. 'Twenty-odd blows with something weighing about three-and-a-quarter kilos would require a lot of energy, wouldn't they?'

'A fair amount, yes.'

'Would the accused have needed to expend all that energy?'

'I don't follow the question.'

'Counsel,' Lord Slade called, plaintively, 'please put your questions in such a way that the court and the witness can understand them as well as yourself. Do you mean how many of these blows with that instrument would the accused have required to murder his victim?'

'Precisely, m'lud, thank you.'

'At the most I'd say half a dozen,' Langham replied.

'Professor, you mentioned the accused person's blood on the murder weapon. Did you see the gash on his hand?'

'Only photographs of it.'

'You know it needed a dozen stitchess?'

'Yes, it was a pretty severe gash.'

'Well, what I should like to put to you is this, Professor Langham: Would a man who is alleged to have premeditated and planned a crime for at least a month choose the first thing that came to hand, a crude, clumsy, heavy glass lamp and strike so many tiring and frenzied blows injuring himself badly in the commission of his crime?'

'Mr Barrett,' the LCJ called out, 'you are asking a man to give a personal opinion and not one based on his scientific and medical expertise, and he need not reply unless he so wishes.'

'M'lud, I was asking the sort of question which some or all of the jurors might have asked themselves, but since I have no wish to embarrass the eminent witness, I shall withdraw the question.'

Before they escorted the judge back to Brixton, he and Barrett met in the basement cell. Barrett believed he had won on points that day, but the judge cautioned him. Points didn't count, only what the jurors took on board, plus the LCJ's summing-up and the jury verdict. All right, he had manhandled and annihilated Katie Gamble and had scored points off Professor Langham. But he still had Massey and Redhead to deal with. And the Lord Chief Justice.

'He's not exactly unbiased, is he, old vitriol?'

'No, Vernon Slade has never been able to sit on both sides of the fence at the same time.'

'But all those interruptions and supplementary questions and objections. He accuses me of time-wasting then takes up half our cross-examination time.'

'That's his style.' Judge Knox put a hand on Barrett's shoulder. 'You have to watch Slade. He's as impartial as a football rattle, he's grudge-bearing, he's sitting on Spencer-Smith's side of the fence for this one and he's determined to do us down – both of us. Me, because I'm me, and you because you're not wearing silk and that he'd consider an insult to his dignity if not outright contempt of court.'

'Well, he's in for a few surprises when he hears Connie Blackwell and Gus Wilkins.'

'You've had them served their subpoenas ordering them to appear?'

'A week go.' He tapped his briefcase. 'I've got all the documents.' He grinned. 'I can't wait to see Spencer-Smith's face – and the LCJ's.'

'How are Julie and Margaret?'

'Julie was in the public gallery, but Aunt Meg thought the suspense would be too much for her – both you and me on trial at the same time.'

VI

Before the second day began at 10.30, in his cell below the court, Judge Knox had time to read the half-dozen newspapers he had ordered a duty policeman to buy him. Normally, he blocked in *The Times* crossword, then read the headlines; this morning he could not avoid confronting either his picture or Barrett's on page one of all the papers, even the *The Times* and its antipodean stablemate, the *Sun*, Most of the writers dwelt on the antagonism between the junior defence counsel and the LCJ, one tabloid scribe even suggesting that Barrett, as the accused man's puppet, was settling old scores against the LCJ by proxy.

When the court assembled, Spencer-Smith had manifestly decided to play his hand in gently, calling Chief Superintendent Robert Pritchard, the detective who had answered their summons to Pitt Street and had charged him.

After taking the CID chief through details of finding the dead man, the Attorney-General restricted his questions to the attitude of the judge.

'How did Sir Laurence appear to you, Chief Superintendent?'

'Very cool, calm, in full possession of himself.'

'Not at all like a man who has just lost control and committed a murder?'

'Objection,' Barrett called.

'Oh no, Counsel,' came Lord Slade's high-toned wail. 'On what possible grounds?'

'On two counts – one, my learned friend was leading his witness and two, he was asking him to state not a fact but an opinion.'

'Very well, for once I'll allow it and the question will be struck from the record.'

'Did he say anything?' Spencer-Smith asked, visibly nettled by the interruption.

'Yes, when I cautioned him, he said' – here, the Chief Superintendent read from his notebook – ' "Inspector, I do not intend to make any other statement, orally or in writing, at this stage. You have my statement and enough evidence to charge me with murder.'

'Did he give you the statement?'

'Yes.' Chief Superintendent Pritchard identified the statement which an usher handed him and it was passed round the jury before Spencer-Smith sat down.

No one, including the LCJ and even Judge Knox, expected Barrett to put more than a couple of routine questions to the detective. But the young barrister picked up the glass lamp, still on the table, and showed it to the witness.

'There was another of these lamps in that room, Chief Superintendent. Where did you find it?'

'Yes. In the smashed TV set.'

'Someone had thrown that lamp at the TV set to smash it. Who do you think?'

'I could only think it was Sir Laurence Knox.'

'Why, in your view, would he do that?'

'He didn't like the programme.'

For a moment, the court convulsed with laughter before the LCJ silenced it by banging with his gavel. Barrett waited until everyone had settled.

'So, you verified there was a programme which both the judge and his victim might have been watching?'

'I had a technician look at the set. It had been switched on, for it had blown a thirteen-amp fuse in the box.'

'Could you tell which programme it was on?'

'No.'

'Did you look at the programmes listed, say between nine o'clock and five past ten to see what those two men might have been watching?'

'No.'

'Well, I happened to make a list of everything that particular TV set would receive. Here it is.' He had copies handed round, including one to Lord Slade, who glanced at his and leaned forward to look at Barrett.

'Could Counsel enlighten us with an assurance that this cross-examination is leading somewhere, albeit at snail's pace?'

'It is both relevant and, in my view, important, m'lud.'

'I trust that you're right.'

Barrett turned to Chief Superintendent Pritchard and read from his list: An American police series, a panel game, the Nine O'Clock News and the beginning of the Ten O'Clock News on the other channel. 'Nothing there to evoke such a violent reaction from Sir Laurence, would you agree?'

'Yes, I agree.'

'A TV set with a video-recorder. Did you check that?'

'The video compartment was empty.'

'But had that video-recorder been playing?'

'I don't know.'

'You mean to tell the court you did not check to see if it had been switched over?'

'No, I didn't.'

'So you didn't check the number of the digital record on the video?'

'No.'

'Well, I had it checked and it read three hundred and thirty-five. Which, if the cassette had run from zero would mean that it had been playing for about thirty-five minutes.'

'Mr Barrett, I fail to penetrate the relevance of all this,' Lord Slade called out, his voice showing more and more exasperation.

'So do I, m'lud,' Spencer-Smith put in.

So did Judge Knox at first. What in heaven's name was Barrett doing? In a moment he would be revealing that he, the accused, had destroyed those cassettes, then the jury would want to know why and whether any of the vital cassettes remained.

Then Judge Knox had a flash of intuition. Barrett was doing no more than plant the notion deep in the jurors' minds that this senior policeman, and by extension Spencer-Smith and the Director of Public Prosecutions, had not carried out a thorough investigation of the facts, let alone the motives; they had left too much to chance. As indeed they had.

'Chief Superintendent, you didn't wonder enough about the reason why Sir Laurence threw the lamp at the TV screen to search for the missing cassette that might have explained the mystery?'

'I did not, sir.'

'Oh well, let's leave it a mystery and turn to the murdered man. He is described as a company director and businessman. What sort of company did he run?'

'He had several restaurants and clubs.'

'Three of them night-clubs combined with gambling-clubs, am I right?'

'You are, sir.'

'Had he ever been in trouble with the police?'

'No, sir.'

'You checked with the Criminal Records Office and the Yard computer?'

'Yes. There was nothing against Mr Strang.'

'Not even under his real name, Derek Clifford Flint?'

That question stopped the court in its tracks and sent excitement eddying and buzzing through everyone from the jury to the court officials, the prosecution counsel to the public gallery.

'We have no record of that name,' said Pritchard, by now looking uneasy and apprehensive.

'Hmm, don't let's say, Chief Superintendent, that Scotland Yard is turning slovenly about its detective work. My own investigations show that Derek Clifford Flint changed his name to Strang some two years ago when he emerged from Pentonville prison where he had served six and two-third years of a ten-year sentence for rape imposed on him at Southwark Crown Court.'

That half of the press which was reporting for the evening papers and agencies headed for the phone boxes with this new sensation. And despite the repeated cries of 'Silence . . . Silence in court,' the audience, even counsel, were all discussing the revelation.

It took Lord Slade two long minutes before he could place a word.

'Counsel,' he piped at Barrett, 'I trust you are able to substantiate all these statements.'

'Do you think, m'lud, that I would advance such facts to this court if I couldn't? May I continue with my cross-examination?'

'Very well, but let's get on a bit more quickly with this case.' Lord Slade sniffed into a silk handkerchief and glared at Barrett over his half-moon glasses.

'Superintendent, why do you think there was no trace of Flint alias Strang in your Criminal Record Office?'

'I have no idea.'

'It would never occur to you that he might have bought his criminal record to erase it from your files?'

'No, it wouldn't.'

'Bought his criminal record!' Again, Lord Slade stopped the show, his bloodless face going a grey shade at the thought. 'Bought it! Do you mean to insinuate, Counsel, that this man, Strang, corrupted members of the police force in order to procure and destroy his criminal record?'

'Procure and erase, m'lud – but not destroy.'

'Oh! I confess I find it difficult to accept that police officers in responsible posts can be thus bribed to erase someone's criminal record,' Lord Slade commented, his face a study in disbelief. 'I suppose we can see proof of this, too.'

'Yes, tangible proof.' Barrett produced the original of the CRO files which Strang had flaunted before the judge, and enough copies to go round the various active members of the court. He let them study the document for a few moments before continuing.

'I may add, m'lud, without pre-empting my opening speech for the defence, that I shall also adduce evidence from witnesses to the effect that Strang, alias Flint, was convicted and sentenced in error – and this is really why we are here today.'

'What!' Lord Slade was almost beside himself, jerking upright in his chair and glaring now at Spencer-Smith, who had remained silent throughout the cross-examination and now looked miserable and uncomfortable. 'Is the Attorney-General not aware of all these facts?'

'No, m'lud, but I shall see that appropriate enquiries are made immediately.'

'Well, see that we have all the answers before tomorrow's hearing. This case is rapidly developing into some kind of farce.' He glowered at the press bench and called for silence before turning narrowed eyes on Barrett, as though blaming him for the shortcomings of the police and the Attorney-General.

'Do you have any further questions for this witness, Mr Barrett?'

Barrett suppressed the impulse to pull another card out of his sleeve. He shook his head.

'No more questions, m'lud.'

'Thank God.' Lord Slade sighed and subsided in his chair as though someone had let the air out of him.

Against its high, green-leather back, Slade reminded the judge of Cézanne's famous portrait of his friend and fellow-artist, the dwarf Achille Emperaire. Cézanne had rendered him even smaller and more misshapen by placing him in that high-backed chair. Slade seemed to have shrunk into his scarlet gown, his face pinched under his bench wig.

Barrett had certainly stirred things up and made an impression on everybody by the way he had used an innocuous CID witness to shock Slade, the jurors and the public into doubting the whole prosecution case. It did not alter the fact that he had a long way to go before turning that thread of doubt into the lifeline of certainty that he, Knox, was the wronged party and therefore innocent of murder.

But how he had misjudged Peter Barrett! Was it the crooked mouth and nose? His diffidence? Lack of opportunity? In his years at the bar and on the bench, the judge had seen no more than a handful of juniors capable of such a performance in the face of the Crown's most senior law officer and highest judicial authority, and with scant evidence on his side. Whatever the verdict, Barrett would undoubtedly make his name, if he curbed his impetuosity.

Spencer-Smith put up one more witness before lunch: Herbert Hugh Massey. Described as a casino manager, aged thirty-four, Massey wore a sober, well-cut grey suit and a tie. He looked serious, reliable. He had already given evidence in Julie's trial that he had set the girl up as a prostitute on Strang's orders; he said Strang wanted her to stay on drugs though he, Massey, never discovered why.

Now, with some prompting by Spencer-Smith, he told how Judge Knox had arrived at the Greensward Club looking for Strang, the man who had corrupted and ruined his daughter.

'What was his attitude to Strang?'

'He said he felt like killing him.'

'Can you remember the exact words he used?'

'Yes. He said: "If I ever find that villain, I shall kill him, so help me God." '

'Did you tell him where to find Strang?'

'No, but he already had some idea.'

'What makes you think that?'

'His daughter knew Strang . . . intimately.'

Spencer-Smith inclined his head and sat down, indicating he had finished with the witness.

Barrett did not beat about the bush.

'Mr Massdey, there is a question which must have slipped my learned friend's mind. It is this. Have you ever been in trouble with the law?'

Massey sucked in his cheeks and thought for a moment. 'Yes, I have,' he said.

'How often?'

'Twice.'

'Sure it's only twice?'

'Yes, I'm sure.'

'What were your convictions? And speak up so that m'lud and the jury can hear you.'

'Six months for receiving stolen property and a year for possessing heroin and cannabis.'

Barrett filled his lungs slowly, studying the notes before him and pausing for twenty long seconds before posing his next question, a vital one. Massey ran a gambling-club, but could he play poker? Could he, Barrett, get away with bluff? He had to take the chance.

'It was in Pentonville Prison that you met Strang, was it not?'

'I can't remember.'

'Try harder, Mr Massey. Strang was in cell block D, one floor up on the west side. Weren't you in cell block D as well?'

'I can't remember. . . . Maybe I was.'

'Of course, Strang was called Flint then. Does that refresh your memory, or do I have to get a prison officer to come and testify that

171

you were prison mates.'

'All right, I did meet Flint there.'

Barrett could have shouted his relief at hearing those seven words. Instead, he went on calmly, 'Did Strang – or Flint – ever mention Judge Knox, the judge who sent him down?'

'No.'

'He never mentioned that he had been framed, as they say?'

'No.'

'He never said to you that he would get even with the judge who gave him ten years?'

'No.'

When you get three noes in a row during cross-examination, call a halt, the judge had told him. It was his questions, not the negative answers that counted. But he could see Lord Slade twirling his pen in his hand, fidgeting, poised to make one of his constant interventions. Barrett sat down.

Twenty to one on the clock. No time to call the next witness, Redhead.

A duty policeman who knew the judge found them a table and two chairs, and he and Barrett had lunch in the basement cell to plan the next stage of the trial. Redhead would be the last prosecution witness, which would leave him time to make his opening address but not enough to call both Connie Blackwell and Wilkins. However, he would call Wilkins, the more reticent of the two, and hope to get through most of his evidence by five o'clock.

'What a sensation that'll create,' Barrett said, navigating a hunk of bread and cheese into his mouth and washing it down with lager.

'Both Blackwell and Wilkins in court, are they?'

Barrett nodded. 'Both kitted out in their Sunday best.'

'You haven't paid them anything, I hope?'

'Not a sou – but I might give them a handout for their expenses afterwards.'

'Then cover yourself with an expenses form. And when you go upstairs, tell the duty policeman in the witness room to keep an eye on them.'

'Oh, why?'

'Just a hunch.'

When Barrett went to pour himself another lager, the judge put his hand over the can. 'Sorry Peter, but one's enough. In half an hour you're going to have to make the best speech of your life and you've got Slade breathing fire not only at the points you score but at your casual attitude to the court.'

'I'll watch it,' Barrett murmured, pushing the beer can away and pouring himself some coffee which he sipped thoughtfully. 'What do you think of S-S's performance?' he asked.

'Frankly, it puzzles me,' the judge replied. 'I can only think he considered it an open-and-shut case with no defence to speak of, and he therefore failed to do all his homework.' He reflected for a moment. 'Of course, he knew nothing about Flint, the prison term and the fabricated case against him.'

'It might have been a mistake letting that drop. I mean we should have kept the error of judgment bit up our sleeves until we produced the real evidence.'

'I wondered at the time,' the judge said, taking a small mouthful of the milk that had come with the coffee. Barrett noticed he had hardly touched the cold meat and cheese. 'That information knocked Spencer-Smith off his stride, but he's wily and he'll come back with something.'

A bell went, telling them to return to Court Four before the trial resumed.

VII

Redhead looked assured as he swore the oath. He had trimmed his beard and wore tinted glasses, presumably to conceal his squint. He said Sir Laurence had come into his shop ostensibly to look at law books but in fact to quiz him about Strang.

'How did you meet Strang?'

'He came into my shop with a young lady who I later found out was Sir Laurence Knox's stepdaughter.'

'Did they buy anything?'

'Yes. The young lady was studying law, and Mr Strang presented her with a set of *Blackstone's Commentaries*, a late eighteenth-century copy.'

'That must have cost him a pretty penny,' Spencer-Smith said, then observing the LCJ's raised finger at that leading statement, he amended it quickly. 'How much did those law books cost?'

'If I remember rightly, four hundred and fifty pounds.'

'What impression did that make on you?'

'Objection,' Barrett called. 'He's asking the witness's opinion.'

'Overruled – it's a fair question. Answer the question, Mr Redhead.'

'I thought it meant Mr Strang was very fond of the young lady.'

'And her?'

'She seemed fond of him.'

True or false? Listening to this dialogue, Judge Knox began to wonder seriously if the truth ever really showed a face in courtroom dialectic. No one had come within light years of the truth in this case – at least his truth, the only one he could vouch for, but the one that most closely matched the facts.

Ironic, that on the sole occasion of his whole career when he had inside knowledge of a case, he had heard the facts twisted and bowdlerized in this way. Katie Gamble had lied in her teeth. So had Massey, and now Redhead. Pritchard, the detective who should have garnered most of the facts, had bungled things and obscured the real issues. But could he blame Pritchard when he himself had destroyed vital evidence which might have transformed his trial. He, the protagonist in the case, had tampered with and perverted the truth by that act. Professor Langham's evidence added up to nothing much. And now they were hearing these half-truths from this pervert and pimp of a bookseller.

Had Julie ever been in love with that verminous thug? He, for one, would never believe it. But what could he do? Like every other accused person, he was enmeshed in the law machine, caught up in its intricate cogs and gears and pulleys, forced to contain his frustration and listen dumbly.

'When did you find out that Julie Armitage was Mr Justice Knox's stepdaughter?'

'The accused told me himself when he visited my shop.'

'Was he looking for books, or something else?'

'He was looking for Mr Strang.'

'Did he say why?'

'He was very angry, accusing Mr Strang of having introduced his daughter to drugs and corrupting her.'

'How angry?'

'He threatened to settle scores with Mr Strang.'

Spencer-Smith nodded to Barrett who rose and faced Redhead. He had not intended to waste time on this witness, but the smooth hypocrisy of the man irked him, and especially his suggestion that Julie was in love with Strang.

'You got to know Strang or Flint fairly well, didn't you?'

'Yes.'

'In the Greensward gambling-club, among other places, you met frequently.'

'That is so.'

'Why did Mr Strang scare you so much?'

'Scare me?'

'Yes, scare you so much that at his behest you reported your car stolen when it was in your own bookshop warehouse, according to your testimony in another court three weeks ago.' Barrett peeled off several copies of the court transcript and had them handed round.

'Mr Strang asked me as a favour.'

'Oh, so you were willing to give false witness out of friendship.'

'I didn't know what he wanted.'

'You mean, you didn't know that Strang intended Sir Laurence Knox's daughter to use that so-called stolen car with the drugs he had hidden in it?'

'No, I didn't know that.'

'You didn't know that the police would receive anonymous information indicating where and when to stop your so-called stolen vehicle?'

'No.'

Redhead's assurance had gone; he stood, head cast down, refusing to look at Barrett or anyone else in court.

'Was it worth perjuring yourself for, Mr Redhead?'

'No.'

Barrett had another sheet in his hand which he studied for a moment before continuing. 'What sort of bookshop do you run?'

'Mainly technical, scientific, medical and law books for students.'

'But you sell other types of book. Can you give us some idea about those?'

'Mr Barrett, do these questions really connect with this case – if they do, make them brief.' Barrett nodded his assent to the small, bewigged head peering over the bench desk. 'Your other books, then,' he prompted the witness.

'Travel, biography, sport, games.'

'You haven't mentioned two other categories – sex and drugs. How many books would you say you have in those two categories?'

'A few, maybe a hundred.'

'Not a good guess. When I was there a few days ago, I counted two hundred and sixty-three books on sex and drugs. Do you have a flourishing trade in erotica and books about drugs like *Junkie, Mainline* and the like?'

'I sell a few.'

'Mr Barrett. . . .'

'Just one more question, m'lud. Mr Redhead, how many times a week or a month do some of your student and other customers come and ask you where they can procure not the literature of sex and drugs, but the real thing.?'

'That is an offensive question,' Redhead got out.

Barrett sat down, aware of the fact like everyone else. He might not have convinced the jury that Redhead was a liar and a lackey of Strang, who used his bookshop as a front; he had planted the image of Redhead as something of a pimp for prostitutes and drug-pushers.

Spencer-Smith evidently thought so, for he decided to re-examine Redhead with a long series of questions to limit the effect of Barrett's cross-examination. But the Attorney-General went on and on, irritating Lord Slade who interrupted several times to demand why the prosecutor was ploughing his own furrows twice and three times. Spencer-Smith ignored the LCJ and continued until Barrett realized that he had some other motive for spinning things out. His suspicion deepened when he caught Spencer-Smith glance several times at the clock.

Having finished with Redhead, he called an expert witness to verify that he had identified the judge's fingerprints on both glass lamps: the murder weapon and the other, found in the TV set. 'That closes the prosecution case, m'lud,' he said.

'Mr Barrett, do you see any reason why we should not proceed immediately with the case for the defence – or would you prefer a short adjournment?'

Barrett looked at the clock. The hands were at 3.35. Spencer-Smith had gone on for just under an hour and a half. At the most, his speech would last three quarters of an hour, even allowing for Lord Slade's inevitable sallies; that would allow time to call Wilkins and send the jury home with his evidence in their minds before Spencer-Smith could try to rebut any of it.

'I can go straight on, m'lud,' he replied.

Although he had carefully prepared and rehearsed his speech the previous evening, his mouth had gone dry, his palms moist and his legs a bit wobbly at the thought of holding the attention of the jury and the court for more than half an hour.

However, on Knox's suggestion, he had singled out the juror, whom he would address and try to convince. He was a young man with tortoiseshell-rimmed glasses, floppy hair and an open-necked shirt. He had watched him scribbling, polishing his glasses, fidgeting while Spencer-Smith was handling his witnesses. Convince him and he'd have the lot.

'M'lud, members of the jury, you have now heard the prosecution case which, though based on highly dubious testimony, sought to prove that Sir Laurence Knox killed Derek Clifford Flint alias Strang. That is a fact that neither myself nor the accused disputes. However, what the defence does contest absolutely is that Sir Laurence was guilty of murder or manslaughter in the legal understanding of those terms. No man who is provoked beyond human toleration, no man who resists attempts to corrupt and blackmail him, no man who defends his honour and his self (and I use "his self" as two words) can be guilty of murder or manslaughter.

'My learned friend, the Attorney-General, has been obliged to accept the simplistic view of this case. Why?

'Because with all his authority and the means at his command, he has gathered only a smattering of the facts. Only one man knows all the facts and anything like the whole truth in this case, the man sitting there.' Barrett turned to flourish his papers at Judge Knox in the dock.

'No, members of the jury, I go further and suggest that the Attorney-General has garbled even the account of those facts he possesses, and I mean to correct them as well as complement them with most of the other facts. Indeed, I shall stand the whole prosecution story and its broken-backed logic on its head; I shall prove it was not Judge Knox who was tracking this dual figure called Flint or Strang with the intention of killing him.

'In reality, it was Strang who baited several traps for the judge, Strang who spun a subtle and malevolent plot to lure a High Court judge into his power, using his stepdaughter as the bait. You have met some of Strang's hirelings: Redhead, Massey, Gamble. Strang had his thugs as well. And three of them waylaid Sir Laurence as he came home on foot from the Greensward Club and all but beat him to death then left him lying all night in the garden of an unoccupied house. I know how close he came to death that night. I saw his injuries.'

His juror, he noticed, had stopped finger-combing his floppy locks, his neck twitch had calmed and not once had he fiddled with his ball-point pen, though he had taken several notes. Barrett continued:

'Strang, under the name of Flint, had spent two thousand four hundred and thirty-five days in Pentonville prison and he meant to make Judge Knox pay double for every one of those days. Why? Because Strang had been convicted of rape by a jury of twelve like yourselves – but on false evidence.

'I shall call two witnesses to prove how this was done, and produce the relevant documents. I shall show how Strang had already settled

scores with the people who had, as he put it, set him up. Yes, even with
the jury foreman who pronounced the guilty verdict. It remained only
to make the judge pay. And that was Judge Laurence Knox.

'Here, unfortunately, I am only at liberty to tell you part of the
story. . . .'

'Meaning exactly what, Counsel?' came the shrill voice from the
bench. 'Does that mean you are wittingly withholding information
from this court?'

'In a sense, m'lud. . . .'

'In whatever sense you may view the matter, Counsel, do not forget
this court has the power to order you to divulge all the information
concerning the case before us.'

'Since you raise the matter, m'lud, I was going to say that a barrister has a duty to his client that is equal to, if indeed it does not over-
ride his duty to the court or anyone else. You are trying a serious
crime, and if the accused person has decided to withhold information,
and in this instance, information which might influence the jury in his
favour, then I bow to him with the greatest respect to the court.'

Barrett inclined his wigged head, looked round at Spencer-Smith
and his row of prosecuting counsel, then again at the LCJ. 'But m'lud
might consider putting the same question to my learned friend to
ascertain whether he has laid all his evidence before the court.'

'Counsel, do not presume to tell me what I should and should not
do in my own court, or take the consequences.' Lord Slade was jump-
ing up and down his high-backed chair, furious. 'Now, proceed with
your remarks.'

'Before the interruption, members of the jury, I was saying that
Strang settled scores with everyone whom he connected with his
wrongful conviction, and now he meant to square his account with
the judge at Southwark Crown Court on that occasion, Mr Justice
Knox.

'As I was saying, Sir Laurence has instructed me to leave one part of
the story untold, but those who know him will not doubt his integrity
or his purpose in withholding that information. However, what I lay
before you will, I am convinced, persuade you that he is neither guilty
of murder nor manslaughter. You will see that he was acting in self-

defence in the strictest sense of that word.'

Barrett went on to describe how the judge had been manoeuvered into the trap by having to cancel his annual holiday and go to aid his stepdaughter, Julie Armitage, who had been arrested in a stolen car with drugs planted in it.

'Against his daughter's will and contrary to her decision to plead guilty, he placed her defence in my hands, and I was able to secure a complete acquittal on the charges of car-theft and possession of drugs.'

Barrett paused for a second to sip some water, then went on: 'But the judge wondered why his daughter had gone astray. Perhaps he made an error of judgement in not informing the police, but he decided to act alone. And the trail, sowed by Strang, took him first to Redhead through the so-called stolen car, then to Miss Gamble, the call-girl, from there to Massey, the Greensward Club and a mugging which nearly killed him.

'Yet, he was making progress, gradually uncovering the truth. Still another part of the puzzle unravelled when Strang steered him towards Miss Constance Blackwell and Augustus Wilkins. They will come and testify how they and a policeman plotted to have Strang, or Flint as he then was, convicted of a rape he never committed.

Finally, Sir Laurence was contacted by the man who had spun this Machiavellian web around him, Derek Clifford Strang. That call led to the confrontation in Pitt Street, a blackmail attempt by Strang to corrupt the judge and the consequences which we are dealing with here.'

Barrett signalled that he had finished. Only then did he notice the young juror move. When he thought about it, even the LCJ had forgotten to interrupt. And, as the barrister sat down, the court cleared its throat and gave a long sigh that sounded like a breaking wave.

Barrett gave himself a minute to get back his composure, then rose again. 'M'lud, I shall call my first witness – Augustus Wilkins.'

Silence.

Both ushers left the court to return with the policeman in charge of witnesses. He approached Barrett to whisper that neither Wilkins nor Blackwell was in the building; they had not come back from lunch. He had waited, thinking they were late and would report. He had informed the City police who had issued warrants for their arrest.

Barrett addressed the court, explaining that his witnesses, although subpoenaed, were not available. Arrest warrants had been issued against them. He glanced a the clock. Ten past four.

`But, Counsel, you have other witnesses?' Lord Slade said.

'One other, m'lud, but I wished to call him after the evidence from Wilkins and Blackwell. Would the court and your lordship be indulgent and grant an adjournment for the remainder of the day to enable us to find these witnesses, who are vital to the defence.'

'Oh very well,' Lord Slade said, grudgingly. 'But be in court at ten-thirty tomorrow and let us try to finish this case.' As he shuffled out the court rose. Judge Knox was led downstairs and Barrett followed him when he had stopped in the hall to have a word with Julie, whom he told to wait for him there.

Judge Knox shrugged. 'You can try, but you'll never find them. They've scarpered, in their parlance. Who can blame them? They've weighed the penalty for failing to answer a subpoena and give evidence against the penalty for perjuring themselves nearly eight years ago, and they've decided in their own interests to disappear until this trial is over.'

'Then why accept the subpoena and why turn up this morning?'

'Good question. Why don't you ask Spencer-Smith?'

'You mean. . . .'

'Exactly what I mean. Did you watch him spinning out his re-examination of Redhead with all those inane questions?'

'To give him and his police friends time to put the scare into Blackwell and Wilkins. I wondered why he was playing the clock. He kept on his feet until he had the signal from Pritchard that he had warned our witnesses they'd get five years for perjury.'

'That's why we can't blame them for bolting.'

'No, but it lands us in it up to the neck.' Barrett thought for a moment. 'I could recall Pritchard and put him through the hoops.'

'That might backfire on us and ruffle the LCJ's wig even more than you've already ruffled it.'

'It'll be ruffled even more tomorrow.'

'How will that benefit us?'

'It's just part of my overall strategy,' Barrett said but did not elaborate. He produced his cigarette-case, asked the judge's permission to smoke and went outside to offer the two Brixton prison officers cigarettes and tell them he would be no more than a few minutes with their prisoner.

Back in the cell, he took a deep breath and said as casually as he could, 'Julie's upstairs. She wanted to come down and see you, but I thought it would only upset her after what happened with the witnesses.'

'You did the right thing.'

'She wanted something else, Laurence,' Barrett said in a whisper. 'She wanted to give evidence herself to make up for the missing witnesses.'

'No, never.' Judge Knox's shout echoed along the tiled corridors, alerting the warders who looked round but resumed their march when Barrett waved a reassuring hand.

'Barrett, you cannot and must not do that,' the judge said. 'Spencer-Smith would jump at the chance to crucify her and she would never hold her head up again.'

'You don't know Julie,' Barrett said. 'She would never admit this to you, but she wants somehow to purge her own guilt and her guilt at ruining your career and the rest of your life. That's how she sees it – the witness box as a sort of confessional.'

'She's wrong and you're wrong. I don't see things your way, and I'm the accused man after all.' He was pacing back and forth in the small cell, visibly shaken. 'You would be giving Spencer-Smith the chance he's been waiting for. Not only to humiliate her but me as well.'

'Judge, are you sure that's not what is really worrying you – that he'd crucify you?'

For a moment, Barrett thought the judge was going to strike him as he saw his clenched hands and the angry set of his face. He had expected as much and tensed, waiting for the blow, intending to roll with it, hit the ground and lie there without retaliating.

But Judge Knox stayed his hand. Instead, he said in that voice which so many criminals had heard, depriving them of their freedom:

'It you dare call my daughter, I shall never speak to you again.'

'Then you will never speak to me again, judge – for I mean to call her.'

Julie stood directly beneath the dome of the Old Bailey topped by the goddess of Justice holding a sword in one hand and scales in the other. Barrett did not mention either his discussion or his row with her stepfather, confining himself to saying that Knox seemed cheerful and was still optimistic.

'It's more than I am,' she said. 'Can we find the two witnesses?'

'I mean to have a go, now.'

'Mind if I come with you?'

'No, I'd be glad to have you along.' He took her hand and led her through the court building, past the check-point and into the street where they hailed a cab, Barrett commenting that in multiracial, polyglot Brixton his new Rover would last ten minutes.

At Connie Blackwell's flat no one answered their knock, but a buxom, gap-toothed black woman put her head round the door of her flat. 'Ain't home the party lives there,' she said. She had seen Blackwell that morning at nine, but nobody since.

'No policemen?' Barrett asked.

'Naw, I'd've seen them, specially if they'd been coppers.'

Nobody had seen Wilkins in the pub that day, or at his sordid lodgings in Truscott Street. As they walked to the tube station at seven o'clock, Barrett turned to Julie. 'Well, it proves one thing – neither Spencer-Smith nor Superintendent Pritchard is taking any risks that Blackwell and Wilkins will be found, arrested and brought to Court Four.'

'You mean, they've hidden them somewhere?' Barrett nodded.

'But surely that's against the law,' she said.

'They are the law,' Barrett retorted. 'And who's to prove they're guilty of taking every step to arrest them, short of actually doing anything.'

'We're as good as lost,' Julie whispered. 'The trial will be over tomorrow and nobody will ever know the truth.'

'No, we have a chance, a small chance.'

'You really think so?'

Barrett stopped in the middle of the crowd in Brixton Road and took her hand and squeezed it. 'Julie, are you strong enough to go into the box tomorrow?'

'I don't know,' she said, hesitantly. 'Is that our only chance?'

'In a way, yes.'

'But if I do, Papa will never speak to us again.'

'So he's just told me – but I'm his lawyer and I'm asking you if you'll do it just the same.'

'If it'll help to save him.'

'It might . . . it just might.'

They picked up his car at the Old Bailey. He drove her to Paddington and saw her on to the Oxford train. 'I'd like to have taken you and bought your dinner somewhere in town and perhaps taken in a theatre, but I don't think we're in the mood.' She gave a nod of assent, and he went on, 'Anyway, I've got to get back to my hotel and go over my performance for tomorrow – and I have a lot of word-counting to do.'

Julie did not ask why. She wanted to thank him for what he had already done. She wanted to kiss him on his crooked mouth, or at least on his cheek. But perhaps it was too early for that after everything that had happened to her, to her father, to him. She pressed his hand and promised to be in court at 10.15 to give him time to brief her before the case resumed.

From the window she watched him, waving her hand to answer his wave until he shrank and finally disappeared.

Barrett walked through the station to the buffet bar where he bought himself a beer and a sandwich and sat down with them to reflect about the next day. He did not like himself, or the thought of deceiving Julie and the judge. But if he had learned anything recently, and especially in past two days, it was that the Old Bailey was more of a theatre of war than a courtroom, and that, despite Ecclesiastes, the race and the battle were to the swift, the strong, the cunning.

Tomorrow would be more like a knock-down street brawl where he would have to fight with everything he had, bare knuckles, his head, his feet and anything else that came to hand.

It cut his thirst and appetite thinking about it.

VIII

As Barrett squeezed through the security barrier the next morning and deposited his briefcase on the conveyor belt for X-ray scrutiny, he wondered whether the papers he had placed there were explosive enough to blow the case against Judge Knox to smithereens; or would they go off under Spencer-Smith like a wet match?

He felt he had prepared the defence ground well; but in any trial there were always the imponderables, the unexpected, the unforeseeable; a verdict might be tilted one way or the other by one seemingly innocuous piece of evidence, or by breaking just one or two of the threads in the web that the prosecution had spun round the accused person.

As he marched along the corridor towards the older part of the court, he felt sure of one thing: today would make or break him as well as Judge Knox.

Julie was standing outside Number Four court. To his surprise, he saw that Aunt Meg had come with her. 'I'm just here to hold her hand,' she said, kissing Barrett on the cheek. 'She's petrified, poor thing.'

'Not because of me, I hope.'

'No . . . the opposition.'

He took Julie aside and reassured her without explaining what he meant to do. He then found the policeman who was in charge of the witnesses, to confirm that neither Blackwell nor Wilkins had shown face. 'Have you seen Chief Superintendent Pritchard this morning?' he asked and the man replied that the detective had gone across the road for a cup of tea. 'Well, go and tell him I may have to call him first thing and he'll have to be in court from the word go.'

For the first time since the trial had begun, Barrett did not visit Judge Knox in his basement cell, knowing the sort of reception he would get. He hoped Laurence would keep control of himself when he saw Julie in the box. It would spoil things if he lost his temper.

In the robing-room, Spencer-Smith was standing with his three prosecution colleagues; he had just cracked some joke, for they were laughing. Barrett's entrance quashed both their grins and the laughter. Spencer-Smith muttered a good-morning, the others took their cue and did the same.

But they seemed embarrassed. Even in the adversarial atmosphere of English justice, certain things were not considered fair play, such as putting pressure on the other side's witnesses, or knocking them out altogether.

Well, two could play, Barrett thought as he pushed his arms into the sleeves of his stuff gown and adjusted his bands in the mirror. His hands shook slightly. His broken nose and twisted mouth stared back at him. Reproachfully, he imagined. Judas was as handsome as an angel, they said – but him, he was as ugly as sin.

How would the judge and Julie both feel when they realized he had duped and betrayed them? Even if he had done it by a subterfuge that displaced some of the blame from himself to a witness and perhaps to the LCJ himself? Hadn't Knox told him that old Slade was a mental magpie? Anything bright and shiny and he'd go for it, however tinselly.

Judge Knox was shrewd and would probably see through the whole ploy, but forgive him in the interests of justice, if not in his own interest. After all, Barrett had only promised not to demand those cassettes from the prosecution; but if a witness let drop that they existed, what could he do about it?

Julie worried him even more. How would she survive if those pictures came to light? That question caused him more concern than the fact that she might never forgive him or see or speak to him again. During his visits to the Oxford prison and her trial, they had come together again, had begun to pick up their old relationship.

He thought he had lost her completely when she walked away from him two years before, just after her car accident when they had quarrelled about her keeping company with Katie Gamble and the set that orbited round the Greensward Club.

That had really dented his ego and increased his insecurity and his compulsive appetite. Now that she was coming back, he did not care if her legal trouble and her crisis over drugs had caused her change of heart. It was enough for him that she was there.

When he took his seat a few minutes before 10.30 the court had already filled up; he was relieved to see Chief Superintendent Pritchard sitting near the policeman on the door. Beside him, the prosecution pew came alive, the jury filed in, Judge Knox materialized in the dock. Finally, the LCJ appeared.

Barrett remained on his feet. He apologized for the fact that his two witnesses had still not answered their subpoenas and this had compelled him to add another witness to his list.

'I call Miss Julie Armitage,' he said, and the court vibrated with this announcement which Barrett noted also raised eyebrows on the prosecution benches.

Julie stepped into the witness-box; she had left her coat behind and was wearing a patterned summer frock with an open collar over which she had knotted a silk foulard; her blond hair tumbled to shoulder length. How pretty she is, he thought – though he noticed she was pursing and moistening her lips nervously; she fumbled when the usher handed her the Bible and she came to the words, 'I swear to tell the truth, the whole truth and nothing but the truth.'

Barrett saw Chief Supenntendent Pritchard was watching Julie intently as the clerk took her through the ritual identification.

'Your name and address?' he asked.

'Julie Armitage of Middle Temple Lane.'

'Age?'

'Twenty-two.'

'Occupation?'

'Law student.'

As the clerk resumed his seat, Barrett stood up and turned to the LCJ. 'I'm humbly sorry, m'lud, but I don't intend to examine my witness and I therefore request her to stand down.'

Lord Slade beckoned to Julie to stay where she was. 'Counsel, this is most unusual. May I ask why you have suddenly decided to stand this witness down?'

'In the interest of my client, m'lud.'

'Then why did you call this witness in the first place?' Anger had etched two bright-pink patches on Lord Slade's cheeks.

'It was a mistake, m'lud and I apologize for it.'

Spencer-Smith had leapt to his feet. 'May I speak, m'lud?' When the LCJ nodded, he went on, 'I think it is in the court's interest to hear this witness since she has been cited several times in evidence as the accused man's stepdaughter.'

'What does Counsel for the defence say to that?'

'I object most strongly. There can be no cross-examination of my witness since I have asked no questions and have no intention of examining her.'

'Then why call her in the first place?' Lord Slade shrilled. 'If Counsel for the defence is deliberately wasting this court's time, I shall have no other remedy than to report him to the Bar Council.'

'I have apologized to you and the court,' Barrett said. 'There was no question of time-wasting. If the court wishes to know, I had to call Miss Armitage as a matter of identification and court record. However, since you, m'lud, have raised the question of time-wasting, we should have been much further advanced in this case had there been fewer interventions from the bench.'

A deep hush fell over the court and the dozen-odd officials glanced at each other, astonished that a junior counsel should take the Lord Chief Justice himself to task. They waited for the storm to break.

'Counsel.' The voice was almost a shriek and accompanied by a bang with the LCJ's gavel. 'You are being impertinent.'

'With every respect to the court, m'lud, and at the risk of being considered impertinent again, I have to tell your Lordship that in at least one instance, this case is likely to go to appeal in the highest court in the land. . . .'

'What are you implying, Mr Barrett?' But now the tone had subsided.

'I am implying, m'lud, that an appeal might have to have recourse to the House of Lords since, your lordship empanels the appeal court yourself.'

'On what possible grounds?'

'On the grounds that the defence counsel can hardly ask two questions without some intervention or interruption from the bench, and this interferes with the fairness and impartiality which is my client's right in this or any other court.'

In utter silence, Barrett reached into his file to produce a paper. 'It may interest the court to note that a study of the two previous days' transcripts reveals that you, m'lud, asked one hundred and fifteen questions, eighty-three of those during cross-examination by the defence and the defence counsel's speech. My learned friend and myself asked only thirty questions more in our examination and cross-examination.

'If we count the words, you m'lud used two thousand and twenty-seven words while the totality of our questions amounted to three thousand three hundred and two words. There are sufficient grounds for believing this could amount to excessive intervention and impeding counsel in the exercise of his brief.'

'Well, we'll see,' said Lord Slade. But he raised no objection, nor did Spencer-Smith when Barrett dismissed Julie from the box.

That spat had cleared the press benches again as reporters went to ring their news rooms with yet another sensation from the Knox trial. An attack by a junior on the country's highest judicial officer in the middle of a murder case. Unprecedented. Even the Old Bailey policemen and ushers, who had seen and heard everything, sat up and took notice. While the LCJ had to silence a faint ripple of applause from the public gallery.

Those who were watching closely might have caught the look exchanged between the young barrister and Judge Knox in the dock. That slight twitch of Judge Knox's head carried more meaning for Barrett than the reams of paper in his file. No one else in court could have understood his purpose in calling Julie except the accused man.

He seemed also to realize why Barrett had provoked that joust with the LCJ. Now, he could no longer be the butt of Lord Slade, for even an LCJ had to watch his step.

When the court had again settled, Barrett looked at the LCJ. 'M'lud, I intimated to my learned friend my wish to recall Chief

Superintendent Pritchard if you have no objection.'

'No objection.'

'Chief Superintendent, you were in court a few minutes ago when Miss Armitage took the stand and identified herself, were you not?'

'I was.'

'Did you know of her involvement in this case that concerns us now?'

'Of course?'

'Did you view her as an important element in this case, or only as a minor one?'

'A minor one.'

'So, in your view, the motive for this murder doesn't much matter.'

Pritchard drew a deep breath. 'I didn't say that, sir.'

'Then what other inference do we draw? Julie Armitage is at the centre of Sir Laurence Knox's quest for the truth, you learn from the prosecution's version of the affair that he means to kill Strang for ruining his stepdaughter, yet you don't consider her of much account.' He paused, looked at the table, then again at Pritchard. 'Is she important for you – or not?'

'I suppose she is important.'

'Good so far. Now was this morning the first time you had seen Miss Armitage?'

'Yes.'

'You mean, of course, in the flesh.'

'Yes.'

'But you had seen pictures of her before.'

'I saw photographs of her in the press and on TV.'

'And would you, as an officer highly trained in recognizing people, have been able to identify the Miss Armitage you saw this morning from those pictures?'

'Yes, I think so.'

Barrett made a show of reading a document from his file before lifting his head to fix his gaze on Pritchard. 'But you have seen quite a few other pictures of her, Chief Superintendent, isn't that so?'

'Other photographs, sir?'

'Pictures, I said. Video pictures. Have you or have you not seen video pictures of Miss Armitage?'

'I have, sir.'

'Where did those come from?'

'Five cassettes were found in a safe when we investigated the dead man's apartment.'

'Interesting,' Barrett murmured. 'Any other interesting items in his safe, were there?' When Pritchard hesitated for a few seconds, the barrister said, 'You're still on oath Chief Superintendent, and you must tell us what else you found.'

'Heroin, sir.'

That caused the court to stir, and Spencer-Smith.

'How much heroin?'

'Just under ten kilos.'

'And its street value – roughly?'

'About half a million pounds.'

A murmur ran round the public gallery and Barrett noted the jurors looking at each other with astonished faces.

'Let's return to the five cassettes. Did you view them on a TV screen?'

'I did.'

'Could you speak up a little, Chief Superintendent so that m'lud and the jury can hear you,' Barrett said, adding slowly and spacing each word: 'What effect did those video pictures have on you?'

'I was disgusted.'

'Why?'

'They were films of a girl injecting herself and being injected with drugs and films of people having sex.'

'You said "people having sex" – did you mean different men and women.'

'No sir, it seemed the same woman with different men.'

'And the sex they were practising – how did that strike you?'

'It was . . . well degrading, perverted.'

'Did you recognize the woman?'

'No, sir.'

'Even though you have just testified to having seen pictures of her which allowed you to identify her in this court. You did not realize from those close-ups that it was Miss Armitage?'

'No, sir.' His voice had dropped again and Barrett had to remind him to raise it.

'And you did not connect those pictures and that face with the smashed TV set and the murder committed by Miss Armitage's step-father, Sir Laurence Knox?'

Behind him and to his right, Barrett could almost sense the discomfiture of Spencer-Smith and his colleagues. For once, Lord Slade had kept completely quiet, and in the court no one coughed and shuffled or stirred.

'Would you consider that an error of perception on your part, Chief Superintendent?'

'I'm afraid so, sir.'

'A grave error.'

'Yes, sir.'

'For of course, you submitted those pictures to the Director of Public Prosecutions with the rest of your evidence?'

'That is so, sir.'

'Did you hear what the DPP and counsel for the prosecution thought of them?'

'No, sir.'

'You mean to say, they also failed to connect those disgusting, obscene pictures with Miss Armitage who, in you own admission, played an important part in this case?'

'I don't know, sir.'

'Well, perhaps when he broaches the subject, my learned friend will enlighten us about his reasons as to why the defence was not made aware of the existence of such vital evidence when it applied for discovery of documents.'

Barrett turned again to Pritchard. 'I have only two more questions for you, Chief Superintendent. You are a married man with two sons and a daughter in her teens. Am I right?' Pritchard nodded. 'I realize I am asking you to give an opinion rather than state facts, but since you are one of the few people who have seen these disgusting and obscene pictures, I hope m'lud will allow the question and answer. My question is this: As a father, how would you have reacted if the girl in those pictures had not been Miss Armitage but your own daughter?'

'May I answer, m'lud?'

Lord Slade glanced at him over his glasses. 'Yes, Chief Superintendent, you may answer.'

'I would have found it hard to control myself.'

'Would you even have gone to the length of committing an assault on any man showing you such pictures?'

Pritchard hesitated for a moment, then said in a low voice, 'Yes, I might.'

Barrett sat down. Pritchard stood nervously in the box, aware he had opened the coffer door. On the bench, Lord Slade was peering at the Attorney-General, who was having a whispered conference with his fellow-QC and the junior in attendance. Everyone was watching them, intrigued by the indirect way Barrett had uncovered the hitherto concealed evidence and waiting for the sequel. At last Spencer-Smith got to his feet and addressed the LCJ.

'M'lud, may I request a short adjournment to see your lordship in chambers with the defence counsel if he is willing?'

Lord Slade looked at Barrett, who nodded.

'Accorded,' said the LCJ.

Barrett followed the two QCs into the judges' chambers behind the court. Lord Slade had thrown off his scarlet gown. To his surprise, Barrett noticed that underneath he wore nothing but a cashmere pullover, white shirt without a tie and light flannel trousers. His bench wig sat on the kneehole desk in front of him, and the downy tufts of hair behind his ears and his bald head shone against the window light.

Even as bald as a bald eagle and as bloodless as a veal scallop, the homunculus looks almost human, Barrett thought. Amazing, the power and influence of judicial props like robes and wigs and jabots and the ritual that went with them, he reflected. Even the move from the court into these austere chambers seemed to drain away some of the law's majesty. They took seats facing the Lord Chief Justice.

Lord Slade proved that he was human. Without giving Spencer-Smith the chance to say his piece, he rounded on him, his pale face flushing with temper.

'If I felt for a single instant that you had attempted to deceive this court by withholding vital evidence I would quash the charges here and now and report you to the Bar Council and your political superiors. I am listening.'

Spencer-Smith grovelled; he admitted he had made a gross error of judgement in assuming that the cassettes Chief Superintendent Pritchard had passed him just represented one of Strang's perversions; although he had viewed the pictures, neither he nor his colleagues had suspected that the girl videoed was Miss Armitage, Mr Justice Knox's stepdaughter.

Had they realized this, they would, of course, have given the defence every opportunity to produce those pictures to support its case. Now that they had proof that the videos were of Miss Armitage, they would unhesitatingly release them and allow the defence to use them as it deemed fit.

While he was talking, the LCJ's clerk entered with two pots of coffee, milk, biscuits and four cups and saucers. When the clerk had poured the coffee and gone, the LCJ turned to Barrett. Did he wish to introduce these videos into his evidence and have the court see their contents?

'In my view,' Barrett replied, 'the jury should see those pictures – but my client has given me strict instructions not to have them shown.'

'He knows of their existence, then?'

'Yes, m'lud. In fact, he destroyed the ones that Strang had shown him, even though knowing that they would have helped his case. I assume those in the prosecution's hands are copies of the destroyed videos.'

'Hmm! Hmm!' The LCJ sipped his coffee and nibbled a biscuit. He looked at Spencer-Smith. 'Now, apart from these videos, what is your submission?'

'I should like to suggest that we drop the charge of murder against Sir Laurence Knox, but sustain the charge of manslaughter, providing the defence will plead guilty to that charge.'

'What do you say to that, Barrett?'

'It would be entirely up to my client to accept or refuse such an arrangement, and I would have to consult him and receive his instructions.'

'Would half an hour give you time enough to do that?'

Barrett nodded. As Spencer-Smith rose to go, Barrett raised a hand to stop him. 'There is a point I would like to raise while I have your lordship's ear and that of the prosecution concerning my witnesses who disappeared yesterday afternoon. When I sought them last night at their homes and work-places, I was surprised to find the police seemed not to have attempted to find and arrest them.'

'What point are you trying to make?' Lord Slade asked.

'Just this, m'lud. When these witnesses are eventually arrested and brought before a court, their evidence may still have a bearing on the final outcome of this case – especially if it be proved that they were in any way influenced by the police to avoid bearing witness.'

'Your point is taken.'

Barrett walked down the steps to the cell block where Judge Knox was waiting for him.

'Well, you fooled me – and everybody else – with Julie,' said Knox. 'But why the verbal assault on the LCJ.'

'Well, I figured that he's going to have to hand out some sentence, and if he thinks we'll appeal he'll make it so light that we'll think twice about risking having it stiffened by the appeal court.'

'You might have something there,' Knox murmured, glancing admiringly at Barrett.

Barrett went on to explain what had happened in chambers, repeating what he could remember of the LCJ's tirade against the prosecution and his implied threat to quash the case. What did Laurence want to do? Plead guilty to manslaughter with a probable five-year sentence or take a chance on being found guilty of murder or manslaughter or, more improbably, acquitted?

For several minutes, Judge Knox sat quite silent and immobile. Then he rose and walked to the window, gazing upwards at it as though seeking the answer there. At last he turned and smiled at Barrett.

'You know, Peter, I remember once reading a suspense story that had engrossed me, and then I found that the last half-dozen pages had been torn out. It bothered me for months wondering how it had ended.' He smiled and shrugged his shoulders. 'If we plead guilty to manslaughter, I'll forever wonder how the story would have ended if we'd gone on. Another thing – I've always upheld the jury system and pleading guilty under this plea bargain would run counter to everything I've ever stood for as a judge.'

'So we go on defending both murder and manslaughter?' Judge Knox nodded, and Barrett seized the cue he had offered. 'Laurence, it's not only you who wonders how the story goes on,' he said. 'We have kept not only the LCJ and the jury guessing but the media and the whole country.' He looked at the judge's blue eyes. 'Are you willing to fill in the holes for them, too?'

'You mean, you want me to go into the witness-box?'

'Since you alone have the missing bits – yes, I do.'

Back in court, he called Judge Knox who exchanged the dock for the witness-box and took the oath. Hardly an inch of space was vacant and reporters were crowding round the doors and standing in the aisles to take notes; many of them were household names on TV and the press.

Apart from the dialogue, the only sound was the dry click of the shorthand machine as Barrett prompted and gave Knox his head to describe in his own words the quest he undertook to find out why his daughter had become a drug-addict and prostitute; how this led him to check garages, to visit Redhead's bookshop, Gamble's flat, the Greensward Club and the sordid area where Connie Blackwell and Gus Wilkins lived.

'Tell us about your meeting with Constance Blackwell and Gus Wilkins, Sir Laurence,' Barrett prompted.

Then with great skill, he steered the judge through what he could tell of his encounter with Connie Blackwell and Gus Wilkins. Judge Knox described his meeting with the pair but knew that anything they had told him about their part in the false accusations about Derek Clifford Strang or Flint would be ruled inadmissible by the LCJ on the grounds of hearsay.

But Barrett also produced the trial transcript from Southwark Crown Court and cuttings from the loacl and national newspapers to prove that Flint had been convicted and sentenced by Sir Laurence

Knox, very largely through the testimony of Blackwell and Wilkins. In those accounts they claimed that Flint had raped Blackwell at knife-point in front of her boyfriend, Wilkins.

Although Barrett tried to get the judge to recount Strang's revenge on them, Spencer-Smith and the LCJ balked them and reproached them with hearsay.

Only when the judge came to describe the hour he spent with Strang did his voice falter and Barrett had to prime him with questions.

'What were Strang's motives for turning your daughter into a drug-addict and prostitute?'

'On his own admission, to get his revenge on me for having sentenced him wrongly to ten years in jail.'

'And he meant to get his revenge how?'

'By blackmailing me for money and by humiliating me in the way he had done with others, only much more subtly, much more cruelly.'

'Could you explain?'

'He showed me video-cassettes taken of my daughter debasing herself in the most revolting manner by taking heroin and other drugs and by prostituting herself with the vilest men of every colour and in the crudest, most perverse way.

'Strang offered to sell me these videos one by one, the first for two hundred thousand pounds. I knew if I acceded to his blackmail demands I was finished, as good as dead. It was plain he would force me to administer his justice in my court and not my own justice, true justice.'

'Did you resist the blackmail demand?'

'Of course, or I wouldn't be here.'

'Were the video-cassettes his only blackmail weapon?'

'By no means. Strang also threatened that unless I did his bidding, he would ensure that my daughter stayed a drug-addict – even if he had to force the drugs on her.'

'How did you feel, Sir Laurence, when he showed these video-cassettes of your stepdaughter drugging and prostituting herself?'

'Sick at heart. Revolted to the point of crying out for him to stop torturing me. I felt he was sticking a knife through my chest and twisting it round.'

'Was that the moment you attacked him?'

'I cannot remember attacking him. I remember picking up the glass lamp and hurling it at the TV screen which shattered with a bang. I don't remember picking up the second lamp ... I must have completely lost control.'

'When you came to your senses what did you see and how did you feel?'

'Strang was lying on the couch, dead. I had smashed his head and face in.' Judge Knox paused, shook his head, then said, slowly. 'How did I feel? Had I had a gun at that moment, I believe I would have shot myself.'

Barrett paused to let that thought strike home. Not a sound came from the court or the public gallery. Nobody moved or coughed; everybody hung on the judge's testimony. Not even the agency reporters wanted to miss a word.

'What did you do then?' Barrett asked.

'I collected all the cassettes, including the one in the TV set and went down to Bond Street and placed them in a rubbish bin. When I returned to the flat, I wrote a statement for the police admitting I had murdered Derek Clifford Strang.'

'Do you regret causing Strang's death?'

'I shall regret it to the end of my days.'

Barrett sat down and Spencer-Smith rose to cross-examine.

'Sir Laurence, you have told us how you killed Derek Clifford Strang, and we have your statement confessing to the murder. As a judge and an eminent jurist, do you see any possible reason why you should not be convicted of that murder?'

'That is neither up to me, nor to you, nor to m'lud, nor to anyone else in this court – except the jury. If the jury feel on the evidence they have heard that I am guilty then they must condemn me.'

'I didn't ask for a speech,' Spencer-Smith snapped. 'Just a plain yes or no. Do you see any reason why should not be convicted of murder?'

'Yes – all those reasons I have just given.'

'No more questions.'

As Judge Knox went to leave the box, the LCJ stopped him. 'Just a moment, Sir Laurence. I have a question about the videos you mentioned. Don't you consider that, in the interests of justice, this court should see the sort of film you felt you must destroy? They can be seen in my chambers by the jury, both counsel and myself. You need not be present unless you so wish. Now, reflect for a moment and tell me if you have any objection.'

'I have no need to reflect, m'lud. I have no objections but must exclude myself from your in-camera proceedings.'

Lord Slade glanced at the clock which registered five minutes to one, then at Spencer-Smith. 'When we resume at two o'clock, can you arrange to have those videos here? I shall ask the court administrator to install a TV set with a video-recorder.'

Margaret and Julie were going to a Holborn pub for lunch and suggested Barrett come with them. He declined, saying he would have a sandwich in the refectory in case he was needed. In fact, he wanted to put the finishing touches to his closing speech for the defence. For after the showing of the video and the Attorney-General's closing address, he would have to wind up.

It scared him, for this was his most difficult hour, gathering all the threads of the defence case into a concise, trenchant and yet eloquent plea. Like a knee-length, see-through frock, it had to cover the subject without obscuring it yet be short enough to engage the eye, the mind and the heart.

At the end of the hour and three sandwiches and half a gallon of coffee, he was reasonably satisfied.

He had just time to make his way to the LCJ's chambers where they had placed a score of seats and a TV set on a table high enough for everyone to see. As he took his seat in the front row, someone drew the curtains and the screen came alive.

That morning, they had all seen Julie in the witness-box, looking attractive in her patterned frock and silky foulard and, though nervous, in full possession of herself. Now, they were seeing her in a slip, wrapping a rubber cuff round her arm and injecting herself with heroin. And she looked expert, with that trick of holding one end of the cuff with her teeth and the other under the armpit while she searched for a vein. Shots showed her with several men before the cassette ran out and Pritchard changed it.

This time, Barrett was sure from the judge's description that

Pritchard had chosen the duplicate of the cassette Strang had shown to Knox on the night of the murder. Julie with one, two, three men at a time. It was revolting. He doubted if this jury, composed mainly of family men and women, had witnessed anything like the crude, obscene and often violent sexual play in that video. They watched and listened in dead silence to the moaning and whimpering of the actors in that pornographic play, unaware of the camera recording their actions. One sequence showed two men having oral sex with Julie and the following one had three men having straight sex, oral sex and sodomizing her.

Sitting no more than three yards from the set, Barrett shut his eyes, unable to watch any more of this horror film. But this was a girl he had loved and still loved. How could he stop the images he had seen from flickering through his mind? He felt he was going to suffocate in that small, darkened room; he sensed his neck swell until his collar and the white bands he wore were choking him; his heart was pounding rapidly and a pulse was hammering in his temples.

In a minute, he would either faint or vomit rings round himself. And if he didn't, he could do what the judge had done. Pick up something, anything. A chair, the LCJ's gavel lying on the desk. Anything. Bust that TV set with anything. Smash it even with his fist.

Julie . . . Julie . . . Julie . . . what have those sadistic brutes done to you? Killing was too good for that bastard. He should have been hung, drawn and quartered, then burned, head and all.

Sweat was bursting from every pore, streaming down his face on to his bands and gown. He fumbled for a handkerchief to mop his face. Water. That was what he needed to sluice it. Air to fill his lung and void them of the contamination of this atmosphere with its filthy pictures. Light to erase those pictures from his mind.

He jumped up. 'Sorry, m'lud,' he croaked to the LCJ, who was sitting beside him. 'It's too much . . . too much.' Groping blindly through the room, colliding with legs and chairs, he barged outside then ran through the main hall to the toilets where he was sick, voiding his stomach contents into a hand-basin.

He filled another basin with cold water and plunged his face into it several times until it stopped burning, then ran the water from the cold tap over his neck, wrists and hands to cool himself down.

When he felt composed enough to return to the court, he found that half the jury were back in their box. A few minutes later, the others came through the door from the LCJ's chambers.

Those who did not look completely shocked at what they had witnessed had a strange expression. As though something had altered their whole perspective after viewing the pictures. He felt that way, too. But Spencer-Smith seemed to have taken the whole thing in his stride. Had he seen those cassettes several times before, Barrett wondered?

He glanced at the court clock. Quarter to four. Just over an hour left. Hardly time for Spencer-Smith's closing address. Unless he kept it brief. No, he'd reel it out until stopping-time, to send the jury home with his imperishable oratory in their minds. And so that they'd have a long night to efface those sickening, grisly images from their consciousness.

He had guessed right. For the Attorney-General took it slowly, deliberately, picking up every small point. Everybody knew that House of Commons intonation – its gravelly Oxford resonance, its lift and fall, its broken rhythms, its stagy pauses. And the style. Florid, rhetorical, with pointed finger, clenched fist, flapping arms.

Feeling the breeze where he sat from those flapping gown-sleeves, Barrett feared Spencer-Smith might take off like some giant bat and continue his oration hanging upside down from the ceiling. Yet, he had to admit that his populist approach and playing the tribune impressed the jury. Even the floppy-haired youth had stopped twitching.

For Spencer-Smith no argument, no dialectic. An open and shut case which should not trouble the jury for more than half an hour. After all, what was it but the age-old, primitive story of vengeance.

Sir Laurence Knox discovers his daughter has been charged with car theft and drug possession. To his consternation, he find she is also an inveterate drug addict. But he does not blame his stepdaughter. Or himself. Oh no, the blame lies with someone else, the man who supplied the drugs. This man he believes to be Derek Clifford Strang, once his stepdaughter's lover.

So, Sir Laurence decides to hand out his own justice to Strang and goes in search of him to settle scores. They all knew where that quest took him: to Redhead, Gamble, Massey and finally to Strang himself.

Jury members should not forget that no one had produced hard evidence that Strang had anything to do with corrupting Miss Armitage by supplying her with the drugs she craved, with turning her into the crudest and most common form of prostitute to satisfy that craving.

The defence counsel had offered no witnesses of his own, save the accused; he had merely attempted to impugn the integrity of prosecution witnesses in order to cast doubt on the damning evidence they provided; his learned colleague even tried to blacken the name of the victim, the one man who could really say what took place during that hour in Pitt Street. But he was a man who had been silenced for ever.

All that had taken the Attorney-General nearly three-quarters of an hour and the court clock now said twenty-five past four. Not enough time for the LCJ to call the defence to make its closing speech.

'Of course we have to deal with the question of the drug found in Mr Strang's safe,' Spencer-Smith went on. 'Is it not quite conceivable that, as an old boyfriend of Miss Armitage, he kept a stock of drugs for her use? I put it to you as a probability.'

Strang, he continued, had nothing that anyone could reproach him with. If he had served more than six years of a ten-year jail sentence for rape, the jury must take account of Sir Laurence Knox's own admission that he was falsely accused, convicted and sentenced and therefore could be said, honestly, to have had no criminal record.

And although the defence had concentrated on tarnishing the reputation of Mr Strang and trying to prove that it was he who was bent on destroying Sir Laurence, nothing in the evidence pointed to such a situation. Indeed, Strang was a very wealthy man, highly regarded in his social circle and had little to gain by reliving a past injustice done him, by carrying out the sort of vendetta the defence alleges.

'Then there are the videos found in Mr Strang's safe. Horrible sequences of revolting practices, from drug-parties to sexual obscenities, the images of which are still alive in your minds. Now, the defence alleges that we have just seen copies of the videos that Strang showed

Sir Laurence Knox just before he was murdered. But who can prove this?

'We have only the accused man's testimony that he saw such films and destroyed half a dozen cassettes, just as we have only his testimony that Strang was using these videos to blackmail him. What proof have we of either allegation? We have good evidence that Strang was fond of Julie Armitage. Who's to say he was not offered these videos? Oh, not for his personal delectation or perversion or whatever. No, no. To keep them out of circulation. To preserve what reputation his girlfriend had left. Is that not equally compatible with the account given by Sir Laurence?

'If the defence placed so much store on them as proof of blackmail and provocation to murder, then why did a High Court judge, with all his legal experience in a criminal court, destroy them. Why? To save his stepdaughter's reputation, he has told us. But the defence had already admitted that she was a drug-addict and prostitute. Who is lying, you may ask yourselves.'

Spencer-Smith stopped his finger-pointing and arm-flapping for a moment to sip some water and look at his notes.

'No, members of the jury, the plea of provocation and blackmail won't hold water. No more than the plea of manslaughter. Where are the grounds? Did Strang lure Sir Laurence into his apartment to threaten him with physical violence or kill him? Where was Strang's weapon? We took the flat apart and found none. No gun, no knife, no blunt instrument. Nothing.

'Strang was not looking for violence that night. He might only have wanted to discuss what was happening to Sir Laurence's stepdaughter, still under suspicion of car-theft and drug-possession. Who is to know? We have only the testimony of a biased witness, the man who sits there before you' – he flapped his gown-sleeve and pointed a finger at Judge Knox – 'the man accused of Strang's murder. Can you really believe him?

'Nothing' – he drew a large zero in the air before him – 'nothing justifies murder, except where the murderer's own life has been threatened. And that is not the case here. Far from it.

'Members of the jury, I have said it before and I make no apology for repeating the legal axiom: No man can be both judge and executioner without paying the penalty the law exacts. The verdict must be murder, the penalty, I trust, a long prison sentence. I rely on your judgment to bring in such a verdict in this case.'

He sat down. It was ten to five and the LCJ quickly brought the proceedings to an end. The court rose after the third day of the trial, a day that those who were judging and those observing would not forget in a hurry.

Barrett had meant to run downstairs to get the judge's impressions of the day and in particular what he thought of Spencer-Smith's performance; but the clerk of the court detained him to query a part of the first day's transcript and when he arrived at the basement, the prison van had already departed for Brixton with the judge and his escort.

He mounted the stairs, thinking the Attorney-General had turned in a performance which would be hard to fault; he had planted the right doubt in the jury's minds. It left him with a feeling of apprehension, of inadequacy, faced with his task the next day. How would he rebut those insinuations, how would he erase those doubts about who was tracking and menacing whom?

He took a roundabout course to the robing-room, where he put away his gown, wig and bands; he deliberately avoided the main hall where Margaret and Julie might be waiting. He had no wish to see them, especially Julie. He felt guilty about those devious little stratagems that he had used that day.

Also, he needed time to think; he needed to put time between himself and what he had seen of those pictures. Time to blunt the synapses of his vision and hearing and erode and efface the mental pathways of those images. Time to block in the interstices of his brain which held those pictures and render them amnesiac.

He felt footloose. He should go back to the hotel and work over his closing speech, the most vital that he would ever make. Instead, he strolled down past the Old Bailey and up Ludgate Hill to a small restaurant in the shadow of St Paul's Cathedral. There, he had two pots of tea and several cakes. Just the act of eating seemed to tranquillize him, as it so often did, and he was able to concentrate for half an hour on his speech, making small but significant changes to his notes in the light of Spencer-Smith's closing address.

When the first diner arrived, he should have caught a cab back to his hotel in Bloomsbury, had dinner and an early night. But still foot-loose, he wandered downhill then up Fleet Street and into the Temple enclave.

Up there, on the third floor, was Judge Knox's flat. Unless he fired himself up and put on the performance of his life before the jury and the LCJ, the judge would lose that flat. And almost everything else: his position as a judge, which would be untenable anyway; his profession, which he could no longer practise. Perhaps his pension. And certainly his freedom. He would also lose his good name, and that mattered more than anything else to Laurence Knox.

All that sent a *frisson* of doubt and fear through him.

Back in Fleet Street, his feet led him towards El Vino's wine bar when he stopped them. There he would certainly meet other lawyers, who would wonder at his presence, and refugee journalists marooned by the Fleet Street exodus, who would bite his ear. And he would get sozzled. For that was really what he felt like doing this evening. He craved the anesthetic, analgesic, amnesiac balm of alcohol.

A cab took him back to his hotel where he ordered a pile of smoked-salmon sandwiches to be sent to his room with two bottles of their best champagne on ice. In glorious isolation, he gobbled the sandwiches, gulped down the first bottle, had a breather then started on the second bottle which he took more slowly.

Things began to look brighter and the liquor drew a haze over his doubts and anxiety before the numbing phase set in. He fumbled out of his clothes, burping excess gas from his stomach. He had the surrealistic impression that millions of tiny champagne bubbles were colliding with each other or exploding like coloured ball-bearings or incendiary shot in his brain.

But the champagne had done in his synapses, it had obliterated those abhorrent pictures of Julie, whom he had loved, and still loved. And soon, it brought the curtain down on everything as he rolled into bed and was asleep before his head touched the pillow.

IX

Barrett arrived late next day with only ten minutes to spare before the court reassembled, too late to slip down and visit the judge with whom he had wanted to discuss a detail of his closing address. Too late as well, to run into Julie, who normally waited for him in the great hall outside the court. As he slipped into his seat by the advocates' table under the wary eye of the LCJ's clerk, he chided himself for his moral weakness and that eating and drinking binge the previous night which had caused him to sleep through his alarm clock and left him with a three-aspirin hangover.

Thank God his head had started to clear a little as he watched the jury file into the box; he prayed he would neither dry up before it or utter something outlandish. When they conjured Judge Knox from his cell into the dock, all he could give him was a perfunctory head twitch and even that sent a stab of pain down his neck. He hardly heard the ritual shout or saw the LCJ slot himself into his high chair.

'*Domine Dirige Nos,*' he murmured to himself, as though the words were a mantra.

'Mr Barrett,' the LCJ prompted.

His feet seemed an inch off the floor. Everything was slightly blurred, unfocused around him. Faces, furniture, the shorthand-writer, the pile of Bibles and other books, even the mnemonic paper in his hand. Woozy-headed, he fixed on the floppy-haired youth on the jury bench and began.

'Members of the jury, for three long days you have sat listening to both sides of this complex and tragic story, and I do not intend to keep you any longer than necessary by repeating evidence you have already weighed in your own minds. If you still have doubts, I am sure his lordship will dispel them in his summing-up.'

None the less, Barrett took them through the salient points of the case, dwelling on the false testimony by Redhead, Massey and

Gamble, stressing the failure of the prosecution to produce the videos which they had found and the police to carry out a thorough investigation at the murder scene.

'However, I wish to concentrate on the two leading players of this drama: the man who was provoked beyond his and beyond human control, and his victim.

'Let us take the victim first. My learned colleague, the Attorney-General, has painted us a glowing portrait of Derek Clifford Flint alias Strang; it reveals him as a thoroughly good chap, the sort of fine fellow you might run into at a vicarage tea-parry or rub shoulders with at a Buckingham Palace garden-party. Irreproachable, he said. Highly thought of in his social circle, he said. High-minded and generous, he said. Fond of Julie Armitage, he said.

'It was all too good to be true. Look at his social circle. Some circle, which included perjurers like Redhead, criminals like Massey and high-priced call-girls like Katie Gamble, common prostitutes like Connie Blackwell and con men like Gus Wilkins.

'This irreproachable and social and generous Strang runs several gambling clubs which have more than a faint whiff of cocaine and heroin hanging over them, Indeed, he keeps about ten kilos of heroin at home in his personal safe. Half a million pounds' worth! But there is nothing sinister about that fortune in a hard, addictive drug, the Attorney-General assures us. Like the generous chap he is, Strang keeps it merely to indulge Miss Julie Armitage's drug craving.

'Now if we believe this eulogy of Strang we'll happily swallow anything from the flat-earth theory to a dinner with the Borgias.'

That provoked a titter from the public gallery and a bang from the bench gavel.

Barrett went on: 'And those video sequences that we all had to sit through yesterday afternoon. What about them? Again, it seems to the Attorney-General that the wealthy, kind-hearted and philanthropic Mr Strang had bought them to take them out of circulation and save Miss Armitage's reputation. But, presumably having paid some blackmailer good money for them, Mr Strang illogically decides to keep them in his personal safe, where he keeps his heroin, rather than destroy them.'

Barrett shook his head in disbelief 'All this passes my understanding – and I hope yours as well, members of the jury.' To ease his dry throat, he took a sip of water and went on:

'They were grisly and gruesome, those videos. As well as being obscene and crude. They will live in my mind for as long as it functions, and no doubt you, too, will remember them for a long time. Who but a pervert could have ordered them to be taken? Who but a pervert would keep them? But I am not, members of the jury, concerned here with the perversions of Mr Strang, who might have added them to his private blue cinema. What does concern us is the other, much more sinister motive for his having two copies of such cassettes in his safe.

'Those pornographic pictures were the means by which Strang intended to avenge himself on Mr Justice Knox, the judge who had sentenced him to ten years for rape. And every part of this drama relates to Strang's desire – no, not desire, obsession – to settle his score with Mr Justice Knox. He had already made Blackwell and Wilkins squirm; he had instigated attacks on the jury foreman which left that man crippled for life.

'There remained only Sir Laurence Knox.

'This Machiavellian man, Strang, set out deliberately to corrupt the judge's stepdaughter and turn her into an addict dependent on him. And having achieved that by a form of blackmail, he had those revolting pictures taken to pay the judge out for an error of judgement which he could not have foreseen or forestalled.'

Barrett had to pause again to sip water from the carafe and tumbler on the table. His throat was still parched and he felt light-headed; but he had been over the story so many times on paper and in his mind that if he dried up, he reckoned his reflexes might take him through it.

'So, members of the jury, all Mr Strang had to do was have the judge's stepdaughter charged with some minor offence such as car theft. But there would be drugs in the stolen car to aggravate the first offence – and this would bring Mr Justice Knox, his real prey, into the affair. Strang fixed everything – stolen car, police tip-off, the drugs, the clues that led the judge back to him and his filthy pictures.

'Strang had studied everything about his intended victim. He knew everything about him that he might use: how much he earned; how much compensation he had received for his wife's accidental death; how much he had in the bank; how little he spent. A fairly rich man, the judge. A man he could bleed white with his threat to publish those pictures. But for Strang, the money was a bonus. His real aim was to manipulate this High Court judge like a puppet for his own ends.

'Just think what that would have meant – an eminent judge taking orders from a villain like Strang.

'However, Strang did not reckon with one thing – the character of Sir Laurence Knox.

'Let me now tell you something about Mr Justice Knox. Of course you've all heard of him as a judge because of his rigorous application of the law. But search newspaper libraries from top to bottom and you will find nothing about the private man. Nothing. As my learned friend would put it' – he drew a large zero in the air.

'All his life, Sir Laurence Knox has lived and breathed the law which to him is a priestly vocation; this has meant denying himself pleasures like driving a car, going to dinner parties, to the theatre, to the local cinema, having a drink in his local pub. Things like drinking, driving, betting, partying might disqualify him from applying the law as he interpreted it. Not legally, mind you. Morally. For him, a judge must be as uncompromising with himself as with the offenders he tries.

'This is the man who learned of his stepdaughter's plight, discovered her drug-addiction and asked himself: "Where did I go wrong, how did I let Julie down?" He tries to find the answer to these questions. But mark this well, members of the jury, he knows nothing of a man named Strang. Julie never mentioned him, or anything else to help her stepfather's quest. She felt too ashamed, too fearful that she would ruin his career which, she knew, was his life.

'And so, making his own enquiries, the judge finds himself in the bizarre world of a call-girl's flat, a gambling- and night-club where he received an almost fatal mugging, and finally in a squalid area of Brixton.

'Brixton was the most harrowing part of his odyssey. For there he met Connie Blackwell and Augustus Wilkins, who confessed that they had accused their associate, Flint alias Strang, of raping Blackwell.

That story you know. But can you imagine Sir Laurence's shock and consternation when he learned he had sentenced an innocent man through perjured evidence?

'He would have redressed that wrong – but he didn't have time. That evening, he received the message from Strang, which you listened to in evidence, inviting him to Pitt Street. We have already pieced together what happened that night between nine and ten when the uncompromising moralist met the paranoiac, heartless blackmailer.

'Strang, who had thought of everything else, never for one moment imagined he would encounter a man prepared to spend the rest of his life in prison rather than dishonour himself, his principles and his life's work. A man who, when he had been driven beyond the bounds of sane conduct, cracked mentally and killed. But a man who still wrote and signed an admission of his action and handed it to the police whom he had called to the scene.'

Here, Barrett had to pause to give himself a breather and allow the jury to absorb and analyse what he had just said. He turned to the bench. 'Excuse me, m'lud, I have a slight malaise. Could I ask the usher to fetch another glass?'

'Of course, Counsel.' Leaning forward, the LCJ murmured, 'If you would like to adjourn for, say, quarter of an hour?'

'No, no, m'lud.'

His head was still throbbing with the hangover from the previous evening which whitened the lie somewhat. While they waited for the glass, he reflected that this sombre court with its English-oak panelling, green-leather benches, its dramatis personae all illuminated in the fluorescent glare, was not unlike the old Elizabethan theatre with all the action in its centre. Now, he was making a short curtain drop between scenes.

His glass arrived and, conscious that every eye was on him, he dropped two effervescent aspirin tablets into it with some water which he poured back and forth between the two glasses until the tablets had dissolved and he could drink them.

'Feel better, Counsel?'

'Thank you, m'lud, yes.'

He had reached the trickiest part of his speech, the argument which would probably decide which way the jury would tilt. Laurence had committed murder. No other name for it. He had signed a confession. Was the murder justified? – that was the question he had to answer. He took it very slowly.

'Members of the jury, we have two main questions to ask ourselves. Did Sir Laurence Knox intend to kill Derek Clifford Strang? Was he justified in killing Derek Clifford Strang?

'We have already torn apart the prosecution case, that Judge Knox knew who Strang was and was bent on murdering him. When he answered Strang's invitation that evening, he had no inkling of what was going to happen. Did he prepare himself for a fight, or a crime? No. He carried no weapon. No gun, no knife, not even a pocket-knife. Nothing to strangle him with.

'Had Sir Laurence premeditated murder, surely he would have provided himself not only with the means but also with an alibi. He would hardly have chosen Strang's flat to commit the crime; but if he had, he would hardly have phoned the police and waited for them with a signed confession. No, Sir Laurence had not the slightest intention of harming Strang. Quite the opposite. He intended to right the wrong he had himself unwittingly committed in gaoling him.

'So, when he was provoked beyond all reason by those obscene pictures of his stepdaughter, he was at first shocked out of his mind before he lost control. And when he struck Strang, it was with the first thing that came to hand – the primitive glass lamp on the table before him. And you will remember him saying that he had no recollection of attacking Strang, let alone murdering him.

'So much for intention.

'Now, was Sir Laurence justified in picking up that lamp and hitting Strang with it so hard and so often that he killed him?

'This whole question turns on the mind-numbing horror and obscenity of those pictures. I don't know how many of your jury members felt during yesterday's viewing, but for myself, I had to get up and run, I was so sickened and revolted by them. You'll recall they disgusted Chief Superintendent Pritchard, who has investigated all sorts of brutal crimes, to the point where he would have found it difficult to control himself and might have attacked anyone who had shown him such pictures of his own daughter.

'We mustn't lost sight of the fact that Strang confronted the judge with his blue cinema not only to horrify him, but to intimidate him, to humiliate him, to set him up for blackmail. And above all, to usurp his authority as a judge.'

Before continuing, Barrett had to pause again to sip more water and also to glance at the cards he had written as an *aide-memoire*.

'Now we come to the vital moment when Sir Laurence is looking at those obscenities on the TV screen. I'd like to recall for you the words he used in his evidence yesterday. He said he was, and I quote: "Sick at heart. Revolted to the point of crying out for him to stop. I felt he was sticking a knife through my chest and twisting it round."

'Remember that?' He fell silent for a second or two. 'Those are the words of a man under assault, driven against the wall.' Barrett pointed to the judge in the dock. 'Now, I am not suggesting that Sir Laurence was being physically assaulted by Strang. That is not the point. But Sir Laurence felt that this man with his blackmail threats and his horror films was destroying him and everything he stood for, destroying his very being. Assault is not necessarily physical. Mental assault and mental torture is much worse than physical torture, as any trapped spy or resistance hero will confirm. Destruction of a person's sense of self is as bad as, if not worse than, destroying him physically.

'And this was the form of assault Strang was using on his victim. And as we know, Sir Laurence resisted until he could resist no longer, until his mind lost control and he struck at his torturer with the first thing at hand.

'This is the hub and the heart of our case. Sir Laurence Knox was provoked by Strang beyond endurance, to the point where his control snapped and he acted as he has described. And where a reasonable man suffers such provocation as did my client, then no charge of murder can be sustained.

'As Sir Laurence himself has told you, he will regret his action to the end of his days just as he will forever carry those terrible images of his stepdaughter in his mind. For a man of his moral rigour, that is surely punishment enough. I am sure you will see it as I do and acquit Sir

Laurence of both the charge of murder and of manslaughter.'

Barrett sat down, his mind void. A long sigh came from the body of the court and the public gallery. People coughed, sniffed, shuffled their feet then rose when the LCJ announced he was adjourning until after lunch. Astonished, Barrett glanced at the clock. Had he really been on his feet for just over two hours? Now, he could hardly remember more than a line or two from his speech.

How had it sounded? One of Spencer-Smith's juniors did something to ease his mind. 'Good speech, Mr Barrett,' he whispered.

As Barrett gathered up his papers, several people came to congratulate him and wish him and his client good luck. A journalist crossed the court to quiz him about Judge Knox's reasons for choosing him, a junior, for his defence; a TV celebrity wished to do a profile of him after the trial, come what might.

Barrett was glancing round, looking for Julie, wanting to escape without having to meet her face to face after the ordeal he had caused her to suffer. He saw his Aunt Meg by the door and pushed through the crowd towards her to say he could not have lunch with her and Julie today, he had too much to do before the court resumed.

'Where is Julie?'

'She's gone down to see Laurence and cheer him up.'

'Why?' He must have sounded worried, for she glanced keenly at him. 'Did she think my speech was no good?'

Margaret laughed. 'No, on the contrary, she thought it was brilliant, and so did everybody else including that acid drop on the bench and the folk in the gods.' She punched him playfully on the shoulder. 'Peter, I thought you'd got over thinking you only came up to other people's knees.'

'How's Julie feeling, anyway?' he asked as casually as he knew how.

'Bearing up – but you know, even from where she's sitting, she feels she's really the one on trial.'

'Oh, why is that?' Again, he caught her looking had at him, as though she had dissected his nervousness in that response. Aunt Meg always knew when he'd had his hand in the jam-pot, even after he had washed.

'You must know what she feels – that it all started with her.'

'I thought it was the pictures that upset her most.'

'Pictures?' Those intelligent eyes inched over his face, the skin round them crinkling with amusement.

'You mean, the blue film show you all sat through in camera – much to the disappointment and annoyance of the public gallery.'

'What else?'

Margaret shook her head in disbelief. 'Peter, you may be a dab hand at cross-examinations and closing speeches, but you don't know much about women. Julie knew about those films, since Strang had also used them to blackmail her and shut her mouth. And she even had an idea of what he meant to do with them. That's why she was pleading guilty.'

For a moment, Barrett could hardly credit his ears. 'She knew about them. . . .' he breathed.

'She had seen some of them herself.'

'No wonder she felt she had to plead guilty,' he murmured. 'And no wonder she would say nothing to Laurence. She must have known and she must have been scared of what would happen if they ever met, Laurence and Strang.' It was his turn to shake his head incredulously. 'So, she didn't mind the pictures being shown to the jury?'

'Quite the opposite,' Margaret said. 'She knew how important they were to the defence and she'd have felt more guilty if they hadn't been shown and Laurence was convicted of murder and given a long prison term.' Her face clouded over. 'Do you think they will – I mean, find him guilty of murder and give him a long sentence?'

'Who knows? It depends on *homunculus sapiens* on the bench, how he sums up. And how the jury sees it. And nobody, but nobody can predict on which side of the fence the jury will fall.'

'They must acquit him.'

'I hope so,' Barrett paused for a moment.

She noted the pained face and that nervous quirk he had of fingering his broken nose and clenching his crooked mouth and knew what was coming.

'Aunt Meg . . .' he blurted out. 'Aunt Meg, I wish to God I had never seen them.'

She looked at him, her expression serious; she put out both her

214

hands to grasp his. 'Peter darling, the girl you saw in those pictures was not Julie. Not the Julie you and I know. It was somebody else. Somebody who was going through hell. Somebody who might have died or given up wanting to live. But also somebody who had the will to survive and come back and make a fresh start. We have to give her a chance.'

'Yes, we have to, Aunt Meg.'

She kissed him on the cheek and watched him hurry through the foyer, his gown flapping in its own breeze.

Barrett still could not face lunch. He felt a bit queasy, but managed to eat a sandwich and drink a cup of weak coffee which helped. He wandered upstairs into the library of the new building where he asked the librarian to nudge him just before two o'clock if he fell asleep. His half-hour nap refreshed him and he was back in court just before the LCJ made his entrance.

Lord Slade wasted no time on preliminaries. In that shrill soprano which should have decayed and died long before reaching the public gallery, but somehow got there, he outlined the case in a few minutes. It was, he said, ostensibly a simple case of murder admitted by the perpetrator in a statement written and signed by his hand. But, as in all like cases, there were two conflicting sides of the story; the version proposed by the prosecution; the reading given by the defence.

There was no doubt that Sir Laurence Knox murdered Derek Clifford Strang or Flint in his flat at Pitt Street, Mayfair, and the defence counsel did not dispute his client's statement of admission or the main facts.

Where doubt crept in was when the court heard the story from the prosecution witnesses, their accounts being contested and often amended by the defence counsel. The jury should recollect that three witnesses, Gamble, Redhead and Massey, all told of how the accused was hunting for Strang to have it out with him. To kill him, according to two of these witnesses. The jury must ask itself if these witnesses were credible, or was their version coloured by their association with the victim.

Members of the jury might also remember how the defence counsel with skill, subtlety and much tenacity, challenged the credibility of

215

these witnesses and refuted several of their statements. It was pointed out that one of them, Redhead, had already uttered misleading statements in a lower court.

Reading from longhand notes, the LCJ said: 'Then we have the testimony of the accused, the only man who can truly say what happened in that Pitt Street flat on the night of the murder. Sir Laurence Knox is an honourable man with a long and distinguished career at the bar and on the bench. His account diverges widely from that of the prosecution on a very important point. Sir Laurence affirmed he knew nothing of Strang's part in corrupting his stepdaughter until he met Miss Blackwell and Mr Wilkins, the two errant witnesses. If this is true, it considerably weakens the prosecution case for murder with premeditation. You must ask yourselves if you can place reliance on this part of Sir Laurence's testimony. It may help you if you remember the prosecution did not attempt to rebut Sir Laurence's statements.'

At this point, Lord Slade commented on the evidence of Professor Langham, the pathologist, then went on in some detail to recapitulate Chief Superintendent Pritchard's evidence. How, for instance, it was left to the defence to reveal that Strang had changed his name from Flint and had a criminal record which did not appear in Scotland Yard files or on their computer. Again, the defence elicited the facts known only to the prosecution: that Strang had two kilos of heroin and five video-cassettes in his safe.

'These famous videos.' Lord Slade permitted himself a wintry smile. 'We have all seen them and I may say that in my view they are the key to this case. Did Strang actually show them to Sir Laurence that night? We have the word of the accused that he did. We also have his word that he dumped the cassettes in a rubbish-bin.

'Now, if you believe Sir Laurence, you must ask how such a man would react to seeing his stepdaughter performing such explicit and obscene sexual acts as well as resorting to drugs. He would be provoked. But provoked to what point? To the point of losing his self-control?

'Members of the jury, these are key questions. For the defence has set up a plea of extreme provocation, a plea accepted in English law where the charge is murder. You must think deeply about this, remembering you have heard Cheif Superintendent Pritchard express his disgust at viewing such scenes and the possibility that he himself might have lost control in a similar situation.

'In your case, you have to make up your minds that the things done or said that night were provocative enough to cause a reasonable man like Sir Laurence to lose his self-control. You must also decide whether his reaction in picking up that glass lamp and striking and killing Strang was justified.'

Lord Slade closed his notebook.

'Ladies and gentlemen of the jury, you will now retire and consider your verdict.'

It seemed to Barrett that somebody had switched off the heating in the basement and he shivered as he walked towards the judge's cell. In his bones, he felt that he jury would bring in a guilty verdict.

No one knew how long they would stay out, but he hoped they would decide quickly for his nerves were now on a knife-edge. He had no intention of standing around the hall under the great dome gossiping with barristers and newspapermen; the trial had taken enough out of him without that.

Judge Knox was sitting, unconcerned, reading the law report in *The Times* as a clergyman might read his breviary. Good simile, Barrett thought. One had faith in Divine Providence, the other in Divine Justice. Looking at the judge, he knew that whether the verdict meant he went through the front door a free man this afternoon, or through the back door to Brixton Gaol, the judge would utter no reproach about Justice.

They had not met since the afternoon the judge gave evidence and agreed to the showing of the video film; on that occasion Barrett thought he had detected a certain reticence in the judge's attitude at the roundabout way he had brought the film into the open.

As he entered the cell, the judge looked up. 'Are you feeling all right, Peter?' he asked.

'Almost,' he said, slipping out of his gown and tossing it on the bed. 'Does it show that much?'

'I thought you were going to faint at the beginning and halfway through your closing speech.'

'It struck me that way, too.'

'Well, sit down or lie down.' Judge Knox pointed to the iron bed which, with one chair, furnished the small cell. Barrett sat down with relief. Going to the cell door, the judge called one of the duty policemen and asked him to fetch some black coffee. It arrived in a few minutes and the judge looked at the barrister with a wry smile. 'You see, I still have a certain amount of influence here.'

'Laurence, I don't know how badly I performed . . . did nerves . . . and my hangover from last night show in my speech?'

'No.' He poured two cups of coffee, dropping one lump into his and two into Barrett's and handing him the cup and saucer. He sipped his own for a moment or two, reflecting, as though undecided whether to go on.

'Maybe I shouldn't tell you this, Peter, in case it poisons your ego, but I shall say it anyway.' He spoke slowly as though delivering one of his judgments. 'You once said you had misjudged me. Well, we misjudged each other, for I was very wrong about you. What I would like to say is this: In my twenty-nine years at the bar and on the bench, I have never seen a poor case handled so brilliantly, and I am including our best QCs in that assessment. Some of it was nothing less than inspired and it will read just as well on the record as it was acted out in court.'

He smiled. 'You had them all guessing, sitting on tenterhooks – Spencer-Smith and his whole platoon, the jury, the public, the Lord Chief Justice. Yes, and even myself at times. And God knows, I knew the story better than anybody.'

'But the verdict. . . .'

Judge Knox scythed that thought way with a gesture. 'The verdict doesn't matter. It is the manner that counts. The profession and the public will remember your cross-examinations, the way you manhandled the LCJ and your closing speech. It was masterly, the whole performance.'

'But you may still get life for murder.'

'Haven't you thought of that as well?'

Barrett looked at him and managed a grin through his hangover. 'Well, I admit I hedged my bets and thought that if your old gang

turned round and savaged you, we'd go to appeal for excessive intervention, nobbling of witnesses and the withholding of vital evidence
by the prosecution. And Spencer-Smith and the LCJ both know that
from what I let drop in chambers.'

'You'd have to get my blessing, wouldn't you?'

'But Laurence, you'd appeal, wouldn't you?' Barrett stared at him in
disbelief. 'You don't mean you'd go down for ten, twenty years without a fight?'

Judge Knox shrugged noncommittally, then as an afterthought,
murmured, 'I never liked being appealed against as a judge.'

'But this is different,' Barrett protested, almost spilling his coffee in
his agitation. 'Do you think I'd let them get away with a conviction for
murder after all we've been through.' He halted abruptly, catching the
judge glance quizzically at him for using the phrase *we've been through*.

After a moment, he went on, 'Listen Laurence, I saw those pictures
not even as you saw them. I saw them without Strang, without blackmail, and I couldn't take it. Had it been me in your place, I'd have done
the same. Only I would have battered that piece of vermin into pulp.
Doing that to Julie, and you!' He got up and began to pace back and
forth across the length of the small cell. 'Those pictures,' he muttered.
'I wish to God I'd never seen them.'

He stopped and turned to the judge. 'Laurence, we must never
believe those pictures were Julie. They weren't. They looked like her.
But they were of a zombie with her face and body but nothing else.
They were of somebody whose mind and senses had been numbed,
then stolen with drugs. I know Julie and it wasn't her. . . .'

Judge Knox stopped him and put both hands on his shoulders and
gazed at him as though he had never really seen him before.

'You loved Julie, didn't you, Peter?'

'Yes, even after she walked away from me, I loved her.'

'She'll come back to you if you want her.'

He went to the bed and picked up the leather wallet in which he
kept his papers. Out of it, he drew an envelope which he handed to
Barrett, who saw it was addressed personally to the Lord Chancellor.

'If the verdict goes against me, I would like you to hand this to the
Lord Chancellor in person.'

'Your resignation?'

'It's an offer to resign on certain conditions, one of them that they guarantee my pension for my years on the bench. It'll be about half my salary.'

'He can refuse, of course.'

'If he does, then they'll have to fire me.' Judge Knox gave a wry grin. 'You know what that means – they have to petition both Houses of Parliament for my removal and they'll do anything but that. You can explain that to his Lordship.'

'And if you're acquitted. . . .'

'In that case, the game is exactly the same and I resign. Only, I'll be able to play the hand myself with stronger cards.' He tossed the wallet back on to the bed and busied himself putting their cups and saucers on the tray and placing it outside the cell as if to occupy his hands and mind. 'I couldn't possibly continue on the bench even if I were acquitted since I would have Strang's blood still on my head and conscience. And I'm disqualified from going back to the bar.'

'But you're still a young man, Laurence. What would you do?'

'Travel a bit . . . scribble a bit. . . .' That triggered a thought, and he delved into the wallet to surface with a couple of dozen letters which he handed to Barrett. 'Read these and let me have your advice about whom I should sell my memoirs to,' he said.

Barrett ran a quick eye over them. They were from newspapers, even the serious ones, TV and radio stations, and half a dozen from publishers. All offered to publish the judge's story for six-figure sums, going up in one case to three-quarters of a million pounds.

'Tell me what you think, Peter.'

Barrett had no time to comment. At that moment, one of the duty policemen clattered downstairs to announce that the jury was returning; both prison officers arrived to escort the judge up the narrow steps into the dock.

Before he went, he came and grasped Barrett's hands then, impulsively, put his arms round him and hugged him. 'Whatever happens, I shall always be in your debt for what you've done for me – and I don't mean only in this trial.'

Barrett watched him disappear then grabbed his gown and thrust his arms through the sleeves as he took the stairs two at a time to get back into court before the LCJ's entrance.

Even before the LCJ appeared, Barrett sensed that his first hunch was right, and that the jury had come back with a guilty verdict. His floppy-haired juror was glancing furtively at Knox in dock, and the foreman was peering at a note he had made and concealed in the palm of his hand.

When Lord Slade had settled in his chair, the clerk of the court rose and intoned:

'Members of the jury, are you agreed on your verdict?'

'We are.'

'How say you then – is the accused, Sir Laurence Knox, guilty of the murder of Derek Clifford Strang?'

'Not guilty.'

Barrett breathed again. Some reporters from evening papers were pushing through the people standing in the aisle to the door, with that verdict.

Unperturbed, the clerk continued:

'Is the accused, Sir Laurence Knox, guilty of the manslaughter of Derek Clifford Strang?'

'Guilty.'

'Is that the verdict of you all?'

'Yes.'

For a moment, the foreman hesitated then addressed himself to the Lord Chief Justice. 'My Lord, can the jury make a recommendation in this case?'

'Yes, of course. What is your recommendation?'

Reading from his note, the foreman said, 'The jury recommend that, in view of the severe provocation suffered by Sir Laurence Knox, the court should treat him as leniently as possible.'

Lord Slade had evidently expected some such verdict with its rider, for as soon as the clerk had asked the prisoner to stand, he said:

'Sir Laurence Knox, you have been found guilty of the manslaughter of Derek Clifford Strang. Taking into consideration the recommendation of the jury to leniency, I hereby sentence you to two years in prison.'

They led Judge Knox downstairs, the LCJ shuffled out, the press stampeded for the court entrance.

And Barrett? He sat for a moment or two wondering whether he had won or lost.

X

Julie was crying and Margaret was trying to comfort her when Barrett met them outside the courtroom. He dried Julie's tears, then led them downstairs to the cells where he persuaded the two Brixton warders to allow them half an hour with their prisoner before they drove him to the jail. Judge Knox seemed the least perturbed of all.

'I'm sorry, Laurence,' Barrett murmured.

'Sorry for what?' the judge asked. 'What's two years when it could have been a murder conviction.' He looked at Barrett and the two women through his eyebrows. 'Can you guess what I'd have given myself for manslaughter if I'd been on the bench?'

'Five,' Barrett proposed.

'No, probably eight.' Only when he had uttered the figure did he recall it was the one Birley had come to offer him in prison.

'Do we appeal?'

'No.' Judge Knox shook his head. 'Slade pared the sentence down as far as he could reasonably go to block any appeal.' His face relaxed into a grin. 'I have another reason for not appealing. The appeal court or the House of Lords might just hearken to you, quash the sentence and my resolve might weaken and I might just go back on the bench.'

When he realized that they were all staring at him, wondering how to take his remarks, he said, 'I'm deadly serious. To prove it, Peter already has my resignation letter and knows what to do with it.'

'But your career, Papa!' Julie wailed.

'What career?' He shook his head. 'The one that kept us apart, kept us from knowing each other and nearly ruined your life, the one that

222

took two errors of judgement to make me realize it was a long tunnel bricked up at the far end, a sort of live burial.'

'He's right, Julie,' Margaret put in.

'But what'll you do?' Julie insisted.

'Oh, I'm not going to retire. From his leather wallet, he pulled a sheaf of papers. 'I've already started on my writing career with a memoir entitled *Error of Judgment* in which all of you figure prominently. In the next year or two, I'll have peace and quiet to finish it and think about my future, our future. Her Majesty's prison service will have to find me a pleasant room out west or up north, far enough from here to render me incognito to the other inmates.'

'Not so far away, Laurence, that Julie and I cannot come and visit you every week, I hope?' Margaret said.

'No, I still have enough pull to fix that,' he said. 'And if you don't show up, I'll break out and head for the Penn Lodge Hotel even if it costs me my good-conduct remission.'

Margaret and Julie laughed with relief at his light-hearted mood. 'How long do you think they'll keep you in prison?' Margaret asked.

'If I behave myself, they can't keep me longer than sixteen months.'

'But Laurence, I can get you a parole within a year at the most,' Barrett said.

Judge Knox turned to him. 'Peter, I'm leaving Julie in your hands. You'll look after her, won't you?'

'We'll both do that,' Margaret said.

'I've already arranged to go back to Somerville and finish my law degree,' Julie said.

Judge Knox nodded his approbation then pointed at Barrett. 'You couldn't have a better model there,' he said. 'You know, after this case he'll never look back, providing he stops stuffing himself with his aunt's cakes, concentrates on his legal practice and takes silk.'

Barrett noted the twinkle in the judge's eye and waited for the amending clause. 'How can he go wrong? The public will remember him as the barrister who put a bloody-minded high court judge behind bars, the junior who had the neck to win a slanging-match with the Lord Chief Justice. And the legal *cognoscenti* and the bar mafia will realize how superbly he conducted my defence and hung, drew and quartered the Attorney-General and he'll be snowed under with well-paid briefs.'

When the prison officers finally called time and came to fetch the judge, Barrett and the two women linked arms with him and accompanied him to the prison van in the back courtyard.

He kissed Julie, then Margaret. He embraced Barrett. He looked round the courtyard, then up at the window of his old courtroom, probably for the last time, before the van door closed on him and he was gone.